MADE MARIAN MIXTAPE

A MADE MARIAN COLLECTION

LUCY LENNOX

Cover Art by: AngstyG at www.AngstyG.com

Editing by: Sandra at www.OneLoveEditing.com

Beta Reading by: Leslie Copeland at www.LesCourtAuthorServices.com

CONTENTS

KEEP IN TOUCH WITH LUCY!

Join Lucy's Lair
Get Lucy's New Release Alerts
Like Lucy on Facebook
Follow Lucy on BookBub
Follow Lucy on Amazon
Follow Lucy on Instagram
Follow Lucy on Pinterest

Other books by Lucy:
Made Marian Series
Forever Wilde Series
Aster Valley Series
Twist of Fate Series with Sloane Kennedy
After Oscar Series with Molly Maddox
Licking Thicket Series with May Archer
Virgin Flyer
Say You'll Be Nine

Visit Lucy's website at www.LucyLennox.com for a comprehensive list of titles, audio samples, freebies, suggested reading order, and more!

AUTHOR'S NOTES:

At the end of the book you'll find a Marian family list as well as a suggested reading order that attempts to place these stories into the larger series timeline. Within this collection, they are placed in chronological order.

Special thanks, as always, to the people who help me present the most polished version of my work possible:

Leslie for thorough beta feedback and general moral support.

May for early feedback and frequent laughter.

AngstyG for endless patience and cover brilliance.

Sandra for excellent, fast editing.

Chad for consistency checks and series knowledge.

Victoria and several ARC volunteers for enthusiastic proofing.

You! For loving the Marians enough to read more of their stories.

THE MARIAN FAMILY

Thomas and **Rebecca** Marian

Their children (oldest to youngest):

Pete, married to **Ginger**

Jamie (meets **Teddy** in *Taming Teddy*)

Blue (meets **Tristan** in *Borrowing Blue*)

Thad (dating Tristan's cousin **Sarah**)

Jude (meets **Derek** in *Jumping Jude*)

Simone (dating **Joel Healy**)

Maverick (meets **Beau** in *Moving Maverick*)

Griff (meets **Sam** in *Grounding Griffin*)

Dante (meets **AJ** in *Delivering Dante*)

Ammon (gets rescued in *Delivering Dante*)

Aunt Tilly - Thomas Marian's aunt

Non-Marians:

Granny - Tristan's grandmother

Irene - Granny's wife

Harold Cannon - Tilly's boyfriend (first appears in *Delivering Dante*)

Noah (appears with **Luke** in *A Very Marian Christmas*)

Ben (Griff's biological brother, meets **Reese** in *Made Mine*)

Gideon (Ammon's biological brother)

LOVE SHACK

True Confessions from Lucy: *I originally wrote the following short story about Jude and Derek's wedding, completely forgetting that they eloped in Hawaii as mentioned in* Grounding Griffin. *So, when you read this, imagine that the Marians insisted on a big family wedding shortly after the pair returned from Hawaii, and the traditional event brought up all the standard feelings a big wedding sometimes does, especially after two of the groom's siblings were recently left at the altar...*

1

DEREK

"The pugs aren't participating in the wedding," I insisted. It was a sentence I could have gone my whole life without saying.

Jude stood in the doorway to our bedroom giving me a pouty look. His melty brown eyes made my stomach turn to goo, but I stayed strong.

"No. No pugs."

"But wook at dem," he said with a wink, holding one pup under each arm. "They would look so good in little tuxedos. Just think of the photos in *People* magazine."

I pointed an index finger at him. "Don't test me, Bluebell."

He simpered apologies to our two fur babies and leaned over to set them down. Springsteen chased Patsy Cline down the hallway toward the kitchen where I could hear Ollie fixing something for lunch. Knowing her, she'd slather some peanut butter in Kong toys for both dogs. It was how I suspected she retained their undying devotion despite the hours I spent walking them.

Jude closed the door and came closer. His hair was down around his shoulders which always made me hot. Hell, the man could be shaved bald, and I'd still get hard for him every time I saw him.

"C'mere," I grunted, reaching for the front of his shirt and yanking him against me. "Need some Jude love."

Jude's arms came around my neck, and he hopped up, wrapping his legs around me and leaning in for a kiss as my hands reached to support his ass.

After we kissed for a few minutes, Jude pulled back with a serious look on his face. "You know I was kidding about the dogs, right?"

I kissed his forehead and lowered him to the ground. "I do. I remember what you said about Carrie Underwood doing it."

"All a dog does is take away from the bride. But I'm hardly a bride." Jude climbed up onto our big bed and sat cross-legged. "Are you okay with all of the plans? I mean... we don't have to have a big flashy wedding or anything. I just... I really just want to make sure my family is there. That's all."

I sat on the edge of the bed and yanked him into my lap until he was straddling me. The feeling of his small, tight body against my larger one was as familiar as the scent of our laundry. "I'm happy with our plans. Don't worry about me. All I care about is you being there in the love shack with the words 'I do' ready on your tongue."

Jude smiled, his cheeks pinking up a little. "We've been over this. It's not a love shack. It's kind of like a gazebo. Made of flowers. But also... I do. I do. I doooo."

I leaned in to see how the words tasted in my mouth. Little bit like heaven.

"Good, then we're all set," I assured him. "Besides, there's going to be prime rib there. And lots of it. That's all I need."

Jude swatted my chest. "Animal. Savage. When our children can't breathe anymore because beef cows farted us off this planet, you'll be sorry."

My heart beat double time. "You want a family, Bluebell? Kids, I mean?"

He looked up at me through his lashes as if nervous about my reaction.

"I mean... yeah. Kind of. But... it's also fine if you don—"

I squeezed him so hard, the air squeaked out of him. "Me too," I blurted into his hair while trying to loosen my grip to keep him alive. "So much, me too. I want a family with you so badly. I want to do it better than my parents did, Jude. I want to give our kids everything."

He looked at me with watery eyes. "Can we use a surrogate? Maybe have little baby Wolves?"

I ran my fingers through his thick locks. "Little baby Judes."

Jude curled into me and laid his head on my chest. "We're going to have an amazing life, Derek. Aren't we?"

It was rare for him to call me by my first name. I ran my hand over the back of his hair and down his back. "I never imagined in a million years I'd get this lucky," I admitted softly. "When I met you..." I sighed. "It was like... god. I still remember that moment."

His chuckle tickled the hairs on my chest where my shirt was open in the front. "You had nothing but a tiny towel on. I wanted to lick every inch of your skin."

I continued running my hands up and down his back. "I'd never seen someone more beautiful. You had scrapes on your face, and I remember thinking what I would do to the men who'd mugged you if I ever found them. Hell, I was a mix between hopeful and terrified. Hopeful you were going to let me watch over you, and terrified I wouldn't be able to do my job with someone as sexy as you distracting me."

Jude uncurled and brought his hands up to grasp the sides of my face, sitting up on his knees so he could reach my mouth. He pressed his lips lightly to mine when he spoke. "What if we'd never crashed into each other in the middle of the night? What if I'd never come out to you and you'd never kissed me?"

I pulled him in closer until we were kissing for real. I didn't want to imagine it. It was unthinkable.

The sound of our bedroom door opening snapped us out of the makeup session. Ollie stood there with her hand over her eyes.

"Stop whatever nasty shit you're doing and save it for the wedding night. I'm here to take the bride to the—"

"Asshole!" Jude cried, shoving me down to grab a pillow he could fling at his best friend. "I'm not the bride."

Ollie pulled her hand down to bat the pillow away. Smart woman.

"Well, whatever you are, it's time to git. No seeing the groom until the wedding. I'm taking you to your parents' house for a slumber party."

Jude hesitated a beat before turning back to me, a flash of fear in his eyes. "You're okay with everything? Not gonna... change your mind or anything?"

I brushed a strand of hair back and tucked it behind his ear. "You must know by now that if I could literally tattoo you to my body, I would."

Ollie faked a dramatic sniffle from the doorway. "Awwwww. I need a beefy bodyguard all to my own self."

We both turned to her at the same time. "You have one," we reminded her.

She flapped her hand at us. "Pfft. Kevin's not the same. He's a pussycat."

Jude grinned. "And you think Derek's not?"

I smacked his ass. "Hey."

Jude lunged at me, squeezing me one last time, almost as hard as I'd squeezed him earlier. "I love you. Don't change your mind," he blurted.

I pulled his head back and kissed him on the lips, then the forehead before gently nudging him off my lap. "I love you more than the dogs love Ollie. And I'll meet you under that flower thingy tomorrow. I'll be the one wearing a gigantic smile and looking smug."

After watching him gather his things and leave the bedroom, I heard him coo his love to the dogs and close the kitchen door behind them.

I was alone on the night before my wedding.

As I lay back on the bed and threw my arms out wide, I daydreamed about how Jude would look in his tux tomorrow. How in the world was I supposed to make it through the next twelve hours without losing my mind?

The doorbell rang.

I pushed myself up and wandered to the front door. There, on the thick, wide welcome mat, stood a ready-made party.

"Grab your best jockstrap, Stud Muffin," Tilly commanded. "We're taking you out."

I laughed and gestured for them to come inside. "Where are we going? I thought you'd be at Thomas and Rebecca's giving Jude some kind of last-minute sex talk."

Granny scoffed. "As if. Irene scored half-off coupons for drag night at the Inside Out. We can't get in without a real gay."

I glanced between the two lesbians and raised my eyebrows.

"Chicks don't count," she said, flapping her hand. "We need dick. It's like a magic wand or something. Let's go. And grab all your singles 'cause we're gonna need lots of tips."

Well, if there was a better way to spend my last night as a single gay man than going to a drag show with three horny old ladies, I didn't know what it was.

2

JUDE

I couldn't ever remember being this scared. My entire body felt like it had been shaking since around two in the morning when I woke up for the millionth time and ran to the bathroom expecting to be sick and failing.

My mom met me there. Apparently mothers had some kind of sixth sense about their children even decades after they'd moved out.

"Cold feet before your wedding day is normal, sweetheart," she said, rubbing my back as I leaned over the toilet.

"I don't have cold feet," I said through chattering teeth. "I'm scared to death he's not going to show up. What if he doesn't show up?"

My dad came around the corner and frowned, squatting down to push my hair out of my face. "Oh honey," he said. "That man worships the ground you walk on. He'd do anything for you."

Mom shot a worried glance at him before looking back at me. "Did he say something? Did the two of you get into a disagreement?"

I shook my head and sat back against the cool tile. "No, it's just..." I let out a breath.

"Is it because of what happened to Jamie? Before he met Teddy?"

Mom suggested softly, sending my dad some kind of look that made him stand up and move out of the bathroom.

I shrugged. The tears weren't far off. "Maybe. But I think it's more... I mean... marrying me is a lot, you know? All the media and the... the expectations. I just..." My breathing got more shallow. "I just don't want him to regret it. What... what if..."

The sobs came for real finally, and I cried on my mother's shoulders like I was a child. Part of me was mortified for breaking down like that at my age, but another part of me desperately hoped the heavy cry would release the pressure of all this worry. Leave me empty of fear and ready to approach my wedding day in peace.

Derek deserved a happy day. We'd been through so much to get there. The breakup, my coming out interview on television, the stabbing at the football game. And the worst part was the continued negativity from his family. They'd decided against coming to the wedding, and maybe that was what I was ultimately upset about.

How could I expect him to give up his family for me?

Fresh tears came and my mother sat quietly through it the whole time, handing me tissues when I needed them. I was a snotty, wet-faced mess. At least I wore a pair of pajama pants and one of Derek's old T-shirts or else I would have been a snotty mess in front of my mom in my underwear.

"C'mon, sweetie. It's time to get some sleep before your big day. Maybe after a good cry you'll be able to sleep better."

She helped me up and led me back to my old bedroom. I stopped outside the door and leaned in to kiss her cheek. "Thanks, Mom. I love you."

"I love you too, sweetheart. Your dad and I couldn't be any prouder than we are of you. I hope you know that. And we're thrilled to be growing our family tomorrow by welcoming such a good man in Derek."

I hugged her and sniffled some more, trying to smile through the nervous thrum in my chest. "He's such a good man. The best," I whispered. "G'night."

I turned around and pushed my way into the dark bedroom,

closing the door behind me and letting out a shaky breath. "Please," I whispered into the darkness, not even knowing what I was wishing for. For Derek to show up. For him to stay away and find someone better. For the earth to open up and swallow me whole so I didn't have to worry about it anymore.

I crawled onto my bed and fell against a giant warm body.

"Eep!" I cried. "Fuckfuckfuck."

Derek's familiar chuckle vibrated the whole bed. "You sound like an elf," he slurred. "Dirty elf. *My* elf. And tomorrow I get to keep you forever, hee hee."

The scent of alcohol hit my nose, and I felt a laugh bubble up. "Are you drunk?" I flicked on a light and looked at him. His eyes were glassy, and his nose was red. "Holy shit. Did you drive over here drunk?"

"Noooooo," he said in a comical, drawn-out slur. "Carl brought me. Us. Me. Us."

"Who's us?"

His forehead crinkled in confusion. "Huh?" Derek seemed to notice my face and sat up quickly, reaching for me with one giant hand and cupping my cheek as gently as he'd handle cut glass. "Bluebell, what happened? Why are you crying?"

The tears came again like little, traitorous assholes.

"Never mind," I cried. "It doesn't matter. It's stupid."

"Oh, honey. Your dad called and said you needed me. That's why they brought me here." He pulled me close and leaned across me to turn out the lamp. When he settled back down, he pulled me across his chest in my usual sleeping position. "Tell me. You having second thoughts? We can wait if you—"

"For the love of god, no!" I barked. For some reason, my shout tickled my own funny bone and I found it hysterical. My laughter filled the room until I could barely breathe. Through it all, Derek just held me close and didn't say a word. When I finally calmed down, I was half-asleep.

"Soooo," he said. "Meet you under that flower thingy tomorrow?"

I drew a lazy heart in the center of his furry chest. "Why me?" I breathed. "You could have had anyone. Anyone at all. Why pick me?"

Laughter rumbled through him again. "You have no idea, do you? None whatsoever."

He didn't say anything else, and a few minutes later we were both asleep.

THE FOLLOWING day burned bright and warm. I woke up with my face stuck to Wolfe's hairy chest with a combination of drool and, most likely, snot. It was a common state of affairs for me. But it wasn't common for a wedding day.

"Holy shit," I said in a groggy voice.

"Is your head hurting too or just me?" he mumbled.

"We're getting married today."

"So, just me, then?"

I lifted my head up and glanced at him. "Did you seriously drink yourself into a solo stupor last night?"

He squinched his face together in confusion. "What? No. God, no. It was those women. Those horrible, horrible women."

My bedroom door slammed open and those horrible women came barging in, dressed in a horrid combination of floral house dresses and plastic curlers. They looked like they'd just walked off an ancient sitcom set.

"Get up," Granny barked. "Irene left some of her teeth at the club, and you need to come with us to get them."

The two of us blinked at them.

"What is happening?" I finally asked under my breath.

Tilly threw up her hands in disgust. "They're not even naked, what's the point?" And then she turned around and left.

Irene gave us a gummy smile.

"I'm not nervous anymore," I observed out loud before turning to Derek. "This is just my life now, and you have to stay in it or I probably won't make it through."

His fingers automatically combed through my hair. "Sounds fair," he said with a grin.

Simone bustled into the room and tossed two balled-up T-shirts at us. "Get dressed. Breakfast is ready. And someone needs to drink with me. Derek, that means you. Let's go. Granny, Thad is going to drive you to the club."

Granny turned and muttered something about Thad not owning a gay card. Irene followed obediently behind her.

I unrolled the shirt and held it out to see what it said.

Made for Marryin'.

I looked over at Derek's.

Made for Marian.

We locked eyes and I thought I'd never seen such a big smile on Derek's face.

"Let's do this, Bluebell," he said with a puffed-up chest. "I'm ready to start a new chapter. With you."

Later that day we met each other in my parents' big backyard under the love shack flower thingy and promised to love each other forever. There wasn't a single tear on my face because they were already being used up by everyone else, including Derek.

I stood there completely at peace in the knowledge we were both exactly where we were meant to be.

With each other.

WEDDING MARCH

"Stop," I told Blue for the millionth time. "You're not a hairstylist."

My brother pouted and tossed the brush onto the vanity before crossing his arms and I swear to fucking god, stomping his foot.

"I could have been," he claimed. "And I would have been able to do a bridal up-do with the best of them."

I reached for my phone to see if there was a text from Silvio, who was supposed to be the one dealing with my hair. No luck.

"Not sure Mom and Dad would have paid for cosmetology school since you once shaved off Pete's eyebrows in middle school," I pointed out, tapping a quick text to find out what was keeping Silvio.

Blue huffed and started nosing through my cosmetics bag. "I would have been better at makeup anyway," he muttered. "You should see how gorgeous Tristan is in drag."

The unwanted mental image made me fumble my phone. "So help me god, if you whip out pictures of that, I'm kicking you out of here."

He glanced at me before setting down a pair of eyebrow pencils and leaning his butt against the vanity. This was Blue Marian getting into Dad mode.

I narrowed my eyes at him. "Whatever you're thinking of saying, d—"

"What's wrong?" he asked with a serious face.

"Nothing," I snapped. "And thank god you changed your major away from psychology, too."

His eyes widened in comprehension. "You're scared to death."

"Not." I reached for a concealer stick to start working on covering the sunspots on my chest. I'd only been thirty for a few months, but I already felt every day of it. It was any wonder why Joel wanted to shackle himself to me.

Blue grasped my shoulders through the thin cotton robe. "You are. You're terrified. Holy shit."

I wrestled out of his grip with a huff. "Leave me alone. This is hardly the time for an emotional... whatever it is you're doing." I focused back on the concealer stick. This was critical work. My dress had a lovely neckline, and Aunt Tilly had given me a delicate string of pearls that looked perfect with it.

Blue squatted down next to my stool and removed the concealer before taking both of my hands in his. The look on his face was so damned tender, I thought I might puke. "I'm gonna hork," I warned him.

"You're not. Morning sickness passed months ago. You're strong as an ox now."

I stared at him. "This is not what loving family members are supposed to do on a woman's wedding day. Calling me an ox is just..." I looked down at my giant baby belly. "Cruel."

Blue's hand smoothed over the big tight ball hidden under the layers of the robe. "This is Joel Healy's son," he said in a soft voice. "He's bound to be strong as an ox too."

My brother's sweetness was always my kryptonite, and mentioning my carrying Joel's son was always enough to trigger the waterworks. "Stop," I croaked. "You're going to make me lose it."

Blue brushed the first traitorous tear from my face and grinned up at me. "It's okay to be scared," he murmured.

"What if he's not who I think he is?" I choked out. "What if he leaves?"

He stood and pulled me up into an awkward, tight hug. The familiar scent of his cologne mingled with the dry-cleaning scent of his suit coat. Blue's voice sounded light and happy. "Ah, sister. But what if he stays?"

That only made my delightful, feminine sniffling turn into horrific, heaving sobs. I heard the door open and someone mutter, "Oh shit, she's ugly crying," before slamming it again.

I pulled back from Blue's embrace and reached for some tissues on the table nearby. "Fuck you for doing this to me today."

He reached for the brush again and turned his nose up at me. "If you'd let me work on your hair, none of this would have happened."

Snorting wasn't ever elegant, but it especially wasn't pretty when you were half-covered in tears and snot. Blue muttered, "Gross," before handing me a fresh wad of tissues. "You girls and your emotional outbursts. This is why I'm gay."

I snorted again. Blue was the most likely of all of us to boo-hoo at the drop of a hat. We'd all learned years ago never to let him watch Super Bowl ads. I shoved him. "Not because you like sucking dick?"

He did a melodramatic gasp, fluttering a hand up to his necktie. "Who told you that? No one was supposed to know."

Suddenly, the door slammed open, bouncing against the wall behind it and damned-near beaning the person storming through the door.

"Where is she?" the familiar voice boomed. "And who the fuck made her cry?"

And that's all it took for my heart to calm and a sense of rightness to wash over me. Blue made a squeaking sound and bolted past Joel, slamming the poor door again.

Then it was just the two of us.

"Hi," I said with a smile. Joel Healy was the most beautiful man I'd ever met. Despite spending most of his days behind a desk now, he still had the body of a soldier, stacked muscles and sun-kissed skin.

His blond hair was still thick and shiny despite his being on the other side of forty.

He rushed over and sank to his knees in front of me. "Baby, what is it? We don't have to do this if you don't want to. I already told you, if a formal ceremony is too much—"

I put my fingers over his lips. "That's not it."

Joel's hand came up to caress my cheek, and I let my eyes close for a beat to enjoy it.

His voice was calm and soothing. "I remember the night you tried setting me up with Noah. I'd seen you before, of course, but you were dating Dylan then. That night with Noah..." He chuckled. "I finally thought I had my chance with you, and it turned out to be a setup with a dude."

"My brothers are assholes," I muttered.

"True story. Anyway, I remember the look on your face when you first heard I'd been married before."

I straightened up and looked at him, realizing some of my earlier nerves were exactly because of this. "Are you thinking of Lena today? It's understandable."

His eyes crinkled with a smile. "Of course. It's impossible not to. But all I can think about is how lucky I am to have been struck by lightning twice. I loved Lena. You know that. We grew up together and started our lives together. But she died so young, before we had a chance to get to know each other as adults. Before we faced any challenges. Our love was easy because it was untested. It's so different with you."

I took in a shaky breath, more nervous about what he might say than I cared to admit. "How?"

He squeezed my hands. "Well, for one, we had to deal with an unexpected pregnancy right after we started dating," he said, moving his hands to my big belly. "I was terrified you wouldn't want the baby. Or me."

I ran my fingers through his hair. "I've wanted you both for as long as I can remember," I admitted.

Joel leaned in to kiss my stomach, pulling the robe apart until it revealed bare belly skin over the white satin and lace panties I wore. His lips tickled the tight skin and made goose bumps form all over.

"Then you were taken from us when Ben and Reese…" he said with a crack in his voice. "And I thought… I thought I might never—"

I reached for his face and pulled him in for a kiss, stopping the words before they had a chance to break either one of us. "But you found me," I reminded him.

"Always," he said in a voice roughened by emotion. He cleared his throat. "So you see, this love is very different. It's grown-up love, tested and true. We've been through more in our short time together than most couples ever have to go through. Don't ever doubt my love and commitment to you. I will choose you again and again and again no matter what happens."

I knew he spoke the truth because every action he'd taken in our ten months together had sent the same message. He wanted me. He wanted this child of ours. And he wanted to put down the same family roots I'd daydreamed about my whole life.

He wasn't John, the man who'd made a fool of me in front of my entire family on our wedding day. Joel was steadfast and loyal. His heart was a compass, and I was his true north.

I crawled down into his lap, forcing him to land on his ass and hold on tightly to keep from tipping over onto his back in his nice suit.

Joel's arms held me tightly. "Princess, I will be brave enough for both of us today. I will carry any burden I can for you. There is nothing that will ever keep me from fulfilling my promise to you and our little family." His hand moved to rub possessively over my stomach. The baby shifted in response to his touch. "Is it bad I want to rip these clothes off you and consummate our marriage right here? What are these? Bridal undies?"

His finger plucked at the delicate lace over my hip. I squeezed my legs together to keep from melting into a puddle of mush. "It's bad luck to see the bride, you know."

Joel's hand moved down to my inner thigh. "Fuck that. Nothing sexier than my beautiful bride on our wedding day. No sane person would expect me to be able to stay away this long. You're lucky I made it to four o'clock."

A shriek split the air. "Unhand her, you *monster!*"

We turned to see Silvio flapping his hands in a "shoo" motion. "Out! Out! This is no place for the groom today! Have you no shame?"

As he began muttering and unpacking the giant rolling suitcase he'd trailed behind him into the room, Joel lifted me back into my chair, pulling the robe closed after one more kiss of my belly. His large hands cupped my face. "I will be waiting for you out there whether you show up in ten minutes, ten hours, ten days, or ten years. Do you understand?"

I let out a breath and smiled up at him.

"I do."

2

JOEL

Watching Simone walk down the aisle to me had triggered the water-works in a big way. I knew without even looking that all of my men from On Your Six were watching me cry like a child, but I also knew that they understood why.

After losing Lena, I'd thought I would never again find someone to love, someone to share my life with, make a family with, grow old with.

And then I'd met a fiery little ball of sass who'd turned my life upside down. I was absolutely head over heels in love with Simone Marian. She was everything I'd always wanted in a life partner. Smart, driven, successful, funny, strong, empathetic, kind, generous, and gorgeous. Beautiful on the inside and out.

The other morning I'd walked in on her lecturing our two cats about table manners. Simone's dark curly hair had floated around her head in a tangled nest, and the body-hugging tank top she'd worn with a pair of my boxers might as well have been the most exotic lingerie imaginable. It was the most beautiful I'd ever seen her. I'd wanted her, even as she'd told the cats to fuck off and stop horking up hairballs while she was trying to enjoy her coffee.

But now she stood with me in front of all of our friends and families in an elegant white dress with a satin sash above her baby bump, and I thought I'd been wrong earlier. *This* was the most beautiful I'd ever seen her. And I knew without a shadow of a doubt I'd feel that way about her again and again and again throughout our life together. She was always beautiful to me.

But now she was mine—my partner for life. The mother of my children and the keeper of my heart.

And everyone sitting on that stone terrace knew how lucky I felt.

When it was time for Simone to say her vows, she finally let down the mask of serenity and calm she'd been trying so hard to keep plastered on.

"Joel." She took a breath and met my eyes. The tears hadn't overflowed yet, but they made her eyes bright and clear. "For a long time, I didn't think I'd ever trust anyone with my heart again. I thought maybe there was something wrong with me or I was somehow unworthy. Instead of hoping for love, I decided love wasn't a worthwhile thing. It was toxic and foolish. It was a hoax."

She swallowed, and I heard a few sniffs coming from the general direction of her parents. Tears freely slid down my own face, so I was sure Rebecca and Thomas Marian were probably even further gone.

Simone flashed a toothy smile. "But then I met this really great gay guy."

Everyone in the audience laughed, remembering the time she'd fixed me up with her friend Noah. Simone's brothers had convinced her I was gay. Needless to say, I was grateful she eventually realized I wasn't.

"And he literally swept me off my feet when I twisted my ankle on our first date."

The tears had spilled over when she smiled, so I let go of one of her hands long enough to thumb them away.

She took a shaky breath and continued. "And you've been carrying me ever since. Joel, I've never felt more safe and loved than I do in your arms. You let me be myself. You give me comfort when life is rough. You always seem to know when to hold me and when to give me space. With you, I feel respected and understood. I feel powerful, capable, and cherished."

My knees were going to buckle if she didn't stop crushing my heart.

"How lucky I am to be making this vow to you today. I will love and cherish you for the rest of my life."

Thank you, I mouthed. *I love you.*

The rest of it was fuzzy until I heard the words I'd been waiting for. Kiss time.

I leaned in and pressed my lips against hers, breathing her in. The unfamiliar tang of Silvio's hair spray, the faint scent of the flowers she held, and the familiar spicy perfume she wore. Her baby belly pushed against the front of my suit coat, reminding me Simone wasn't the only person in our new little family. I knelt and pressed a kiss to the front of her silky dress, caressing the moving orb with both hands before standing up to kiss her again.

"About fucking time," Aunt Tilly muttered loudly enough for everyone to hear. "If they'd waited any longer, the poor minister would have had to double up with a baptism. Now, where's the booze?"

Simone's lips curved up against mine. "I apologize in advance for the gift of my family."

I slid my hands carefully over her rosy cheeks to cup her face. "I only married you for business reasons. Your family gets into enough trouble to keep On Your Six profitable for twenty lifetimes."

Her laughter went straight to my heart and made me giddy. I would spend the rest of my life trying to pull that sound out of her again and again.

After walking back down the aisle and into the hotel ballroom for the reception, Blue was the first to grab Simone in a giant hug. "You're almost beautiful enough to turn a gay man straight. Oh wait, you did."

"Har, har," she said, tightening her arms around his waist. "And also, ew."

"Our beautiful baby girl," Rebecca said with a sniff. Simone let go of Blue to hug her mother while Thomas reached out a hand to shake mine.

I pulled him into a hug instead. "Thank you for raising her into the amazing human she is," I said roughly.

Thomas's arms tightened for a beat. "Thank you for not charging me too much to take her off our hands," he said with a straight face.

"Dad!" Simone gasped before laughing. "I can't believe you just said that."

As soon as Thomas turned to her, his face softened until tears appeared. "I'm so proud of you," he said in a whisper. "Joel is right. You've become an amazing human. Not because of anything we did, but because of your own strength, curiosity, and kindness. You deserve all the joy in the world, and I couldn't be happier to welcome Joel into the family as your partner."

"Dammit, Dad. Now I need to find Silvio again to fix my makeup."

Blue sniffed and wiped under his eyes. "I saw him arguing with one of Joel's guys in the back hallway by the men's room."

I looked over at him just as the first notes of music started from the direction of the quartet who'd been hired to play during dinner. "Do you know who it was? Or why?"

Blue shrugged. "Tall guy who looks like he could have played professional basketball. I could be wrong, but it sounded like they were arguing about... teeth?"

I rolled my eyes. "Yeah, that sounds right. Anton is an odd duck." I paused. "And so is Silvio for that matter. Maybe I should go check on them."

Simone reached for my hand. "No way. I've waited a long time to dance with my husband, and I'm not letting you out of my sight until it happens."

Her face was radiant. Gone was all the stress from before, and in its place was a kind of peaceful excitement. She was ready to have fun celebrating our marriage, and I couldn't wait to join her.

I lifted her small hand to my lips and pressed a kiss onto it. "Mrs. Healy, may I have this dance?"

The large group of people around us suddenly went quiet until it seemed you could hear a pin drop. Even the band had stopped playing.

"Oh lord," Granny muttered from somewhere nearby. "Didn't anyone tell him?"

I looked around at all the faces of my friends and family. Mischief danced in Blue's eyes while Simone's expression was somewhere between contemplative and preparing to school me on something.

It was AJ who finally took mercy on me.

"Pretty sure it's the other way around, boss man."

I turned to him and noticed Derek chuckling into Jude's neck. "What do you mean?" I asked.

"You're a Marian, dumbass," Tilly blurted.

I glanced down at Simone, whose shit-eating grin was unmistakable. "You heard what they said. You're a Marian, dumbass."

My son shifted under the front of her dress, automatically drawing my hand to feel the movement. Simone's face softened. "I mean... if you want."

I pulled her into my arms and kissed her cheek, her ear, the warm curve of her neck.

"I do," I said.

And I did.

~

(To find out what happens between Silvio and Anton, sign up for Lucy's newsletter for a bonus scene.)

CLUB MIX

1

TRISTAN

I dropped the jam-covered knife into the sink with a clatter and turned to look at my husband. "You want to go where?"

Blue didn't even look up. He was too busy making exaggerated silly faces at our youngest child, whose cheeks were covered in more jam than the knife had been. "A club. Downtown. We haven't been in ages."

"We haven't been to a club in ages because we live in Napa and have young children," I reminded him. "We're an old married couple. People like us are banned from clubs."

"I want to dance with my sexy husband," he said, bordering on whining. "Please?"

I was capable of many things, but saying no to Blue Marian wasn't one of them. "Fine. I'll call Griff and see if he and Sam want to stay with the kids this weekend."

Blue finally looked up, his strawberry-blond hair still sticking up every which way from sleep. The man was the most beautiful thing on the planet, even sleep-rumpled and dressed in one of my old T-shirts and pajama pants. "I already arranged it. We're going to the city tonight and staying at a hotel. Dinner reservations are booked at that vegan place you like."

I blinked at him. "Vegan?"

His dimple popped, and I wasn't the only one who noticed. Mattie stuck her fat finger in it and giggled. "Kidding. We're going to Birdsong so you can get your pine needle game hens or whatever the hell fancy shit they have that you like so much. I would have picked Mexican food, but I have plans for you later that do not mix well with refried beans."

"This conversation is why married people aren't allowed in clubs," I pointed out.

Blue snorted. "Hey, that's not fair. Even young single guys want to keep things clean on club night."

I turned back to the sink to rinse out my coffee mug. "I wouldn't know. I was straight during those years, remember?"

He stood up, dropping a kiss on Mattie's head before coming over to slide his arms around my waist. His warm body pressed against my back, and his lips grazed my neck just under my hairline, making me shiver.

"Thank fuck you're not straight anymore," he whispered in a low voice just behind my ear. His fingers snuck down the front of my running shorts and cupped my balls.

I sucked in a breath as all the blood in my body rushed south to meet his hand. "Never really was," I breathed. "Just waiting for you to show me the error of my ways."

"Daddy, Papa, why are you hugging with dirty cups?" a familiar little voice called from behind us.

I felt the rumble of Blue's laughter against my back seconds before he thrust his hardening dick in the cleft of my ass. "To be continued."

When he stepped away to greet Ella, I felt the absence of him and decided a night out dancing with his hot body was a burden I was willing to carry.

WE CHECKED into the hotel after a herculean effort to leave the house. The kids were cranky and unsupportive of the plan, but thankfully Sam had a magic way of distracting them. Maybe not magic so much as a giant tin of homemade cookies, but the result was the same. Suddenly, the kids were happy to see the back of us.

"We should nap first," I suggested, eyeing the big king-sized bed in all of its perfect white glory.

Blue lifted an eyebrow at me. "Listen. I know you're a million years old, but you're going to have to rally. We're not napping."

He was so good-looking, only now he was also familiar in a way that sometimes made my heart thump erratically and damned near squeeze out of my chest. "I love you. So fucking much."

His face softened. "I love you too, but we're still not napping."

I reached for his wrist and pulled him close, wrapping my arms around him and leaning down to kiss him. He made a faint whimper noise that jacked up my heart rate even more. No matter how many times I tasted his lips, I still got a thrill from kissing him.

Blue's body melted against mine, and his fingers clutched the front of my shirt so I couldn't pull away.

As if I'd ever pull away.

We kissed for several long minutes, lazy teasing kisses in no rush to turn into anything else. Blue smelled like our laundry soap and the kids' baby shampoo all mixed together overtop of his body's own masculine allure. It was the scent of home, of safety. Of love.

I lowered to my knees, intent on sucking him off before we got ready for dinner, but he grabbed my chin. "Nope. Save it for later."

"There can be more later," I promised. "Just let me—"

Blue pulled away from me, reaching to adjust himself with a little shimmy of his hips. "No. I want you horny and hungry for me all night."

I shook my head in disbelief. "Dude, I will be. I *am*."

"Good, stay that way. I plan on flirting with my boyfriend first over dinner and then over loud music and sweaty bodies."

"Does he know you're bringing your husband?" I teased, standing back up and ignoring the cracking in my knees that accompanied the motion.

On his way to the bathroom for a shower, Blue undid his pants and said over his shoulder, "I'm not bringing my husband to the club. I'm going by myself in hopes of finding some hot dude to bang me in the back room."

The bathroom door closed with a snick while I stood there blinking at it.

And then I remembered.

2

BLUE

I clicked the lock button on the bathroom door so he couldn't join me in the shower. I hadn't been kidding when I'd said I wanted him horny as fuck later, and I knew that if he came in here and got naked with me under the water, I'd beg him to fuck me against the tile walls about two seconds after turning the water on.

Instead, I luxuriated under the hot spray by myself and thought back to the night of Dante and AJ's wedding when we'd gotten shit-faced and wandered out into the snow to look up at the stars. The wedding had taken place near AJ's parents' place in Aster Valley. The ski town was adorable, and the reception hall was perched halfway up the mountain with amazing views.

"I can haz blowie?" I said, turning my head to look at Tristan in his sexy as hell tuxedo. I'd been eyeing him all night and envisioning every second of peeling that fancy shit off him.

"That depends, beautiful. Can you haz boner for blowie?" He looked at me the way he always did, with absolute jaw-dropping affection.

I looked down at my pitiful lack of bone.

"Fuck." I looked back up at the stars. "Guess we're doing this, then."

"Stargazing is romantic," Tristan insisted.

"So is a blowjob," I said with a sniff. "Especially when your kids are a mile down the mountain in their hotel room. But whatever."

Tristan's arm wrapped around my shoulders to pull me close. The warmth from his body seeped over to me immediately. I could smell the intoxicating blend of Hugo Boss cologne and smoky bourbon. It was the smell of my husband on date night, and I inhaled that shit like oxygen.

After a few beats of comfortable silence, Tristan's deep voice cut through the silence. "I've always fantasized about fucking you in public, but I'm not sure I intended to do it in these temperatures. Maybe it's a good thing we're too drunk."

I did a double take before staring a hole in my husband. Tristan Alexander Marian was one of the most modest, put-together men I knew. He was poised, professional, and... for lack of a better term, grown-up. He wanted to fuck me in public?

"Um, what?" I asked. "What?"

He pressed a kiss to my temple. "I said it's cold as balls out here. And I don't want my own balls to get any more frozen than they already are."

"No. Back up. The sex in public thing. Expand on that."

His grin did things to my chest and stomach. And would have done all kinds of things to my dick if it wasn't inverted up inside my body at the moment.

"I mean, you hear all those stories about hookups in the clubs. I feel like I missed out. I never had that. It's hot."

"You've been to clubs with me before," I reminded him.

His eyes bore into mine. "I've never fucked you in one."

I gulped, suddenly missing all trace of saliva in my mouth and throat. "Oh. Ah. No. No, you haven't. I didn't... I didn't know that was something you..."

Tristan shrugged. "Kind of a silly bucket list item, but there it is."

Yes. There it was.

∼

AND THERE IT had stayed until it had built up in my head so big I couldn't stop fantasizing about it.

You will not rub one out in the shower. You will not rub one out in the shower.

I wanted to rub one out in the shower.

"Blue Marian, get your ass out of the bathroom," Tristan called through the door in his commanding voice. I loved his commanding voice. "And you'd better not be masturbating in there." I shuddered. The man had an uncanny ability to read my mind from any location at any time.

I shut off the water and reached for a towel before unlocking the door. "I wasn't. I swear. I'm not even turned on."

Tristan yanked the towel out of my hands, revealing the lie. He lifted his eyebrow at me.

I began stammering. "That's... that's just because..."

"Get dressed before I shove you to your knees," he growled.

I swallowed. God he was sexy as fuck. Why didn't I just forget the whole dinner and club plan and let the man use me for sex however he wanted right here in our hotel room? It wasn't like his threat had been an actual threat. More of a promise, really.

I remembered the last time I'd attempted to take him to a club for sex.

"I THOUGHT *we were going out dancing," Tristan said, turning back from the sliding door to the hotel room balcony where the lights of the city twinkled with promise.*

"We are," I insisted.

"Then why are you lying on the bed playing with your dick?" He squinted between my bent legs. "Is that... is that a plug?"

"C'mere. We can go to the club later."

I CLEARED MY THROAT. We never did make it to the club that time. "I'm getting dressed now," I promised. "But you need to get dressed in the bathroom with the door closed."

He looked back from where he'd hung his clothes up in the closet. "Why?"

"Because I said so, dammit. And hurry. We're leaving in ten minutes."

3

TRISTAN

I didn't even know he owned jeans like that. They made his ass look incredible, and I couldn't take my eyes off those two globes of gotta-have-it.

"Eyes up here, buddy," Blue teased as I held out his chair for him at the restaurant.

"When did you buy those jeans?"

The waiter snickered before handing us the menus and explaining the specials. I took a few minutes to pick out an especially good bottle of chardonnay. While the server was noticeably impressed with my selection, I, on the other hand, was noticeably impressed with Blue's ability *not* to mention we owned a winery. Usually, he was the first to brag to a perfect stranger about me. It was kind of adorable even if it made me uncomfortable.

"Ooooh, fancy choice. What's the occasion?" Blue asked.

I winked at him which made his neck pink and blotchy just like I liked it. "Celebrating a night out with the sexiest man in the entire Bay Area."

"Just the Bay Area? Mpfh."

I reached across the small table and grabbed his hand, lacing my fingers between his. "All the bay areas, baby. Hudson Bay, Chesapeake Bay, Prudhoe Bay, Galveston B—"

"Stop," he said, chuckling into his menu. When the server returned for our orders, he got the full Blue grin. "I think I'm going to go all out and get the game hen. But hold the pine needles please."

With a completely straight face, the guy replied, "We only serve pine needles for dessert, sir," before looking over at me.

I made a quick selection and handed him the menu before turning back to Blue. Before I could ask him how his latest sculpture pitch had gone, he leaned in and whispered, "I'm wearing a plug."

I blinked at him.

He reached for his glass of wine. "Just thought you should know."

Did this restaurant have a coat closet? Or... or a private bathroom? Or maybe—

Two attractive men I'd never seen before approached our table with big smiles. "Blue Marian, look at you. Long time no see!"

Blue clearly recognized them and stood up to give each man a hug. I was long past the jealousy stage with my husband of five years, but I still felt a little squirrelly seeing one of the men drop a lingering kiss on Blue's cheek. Did the guy's eyes just flutter closed, or was that my imagination?

I stood up and cleared my throat.

Blue gestured to me. "Guys, this is my husband, Tristan Marian. Tristan, this is Nate and Kristo. We used to do yoga together in the park every Saturday when I lived in the city."

Jesus. Younger, better-looking, and bendy. "Nice to meet you," I said, holding my hand out for a shake.

The flirtier man, Kristo, looked me up and down like I was a prized steer at auction. "Mm-hm. He'll do."

Blue chuckled and agreed, wrapping his arm around my waist and squeezing me close. They chatted for a couple of minutes before Nate finally pulled his friend away so we could sit back down and enjoy our evening.

Alone.

Blue chuckled. "You're so predictable."

"I liked that guy, Nate," I said, putting the cloth napkin back in my lap.

"You're a possessive ass." Thankfully, he was smiling affectionately when he said it.

"Am not."

He placed his foot between my legs under the table and curled the toe of his shoe behind one of my ankles, a move he'd done a million times over the years.

"You are, but it turns me the fuck on," he said in a low voice. "Maybe I have a caveman complex."

I looked up at him in surprise. "Really?"

The look on his face was teasing. "Only if the caveman is swinging a big, thick club."

Of course that was the moment the waiter stopped by with our salads, but maybe it was for the best that I didn't get a chance to reply about dragging him off to my cave or something equally predictable. Blue was better with words than I was anyway.

When the food arrived, we ended up talking about the kids, the new expansion to the vineyard's bottling capacity, Blue's parents' upcoming wedding anniversary party, and the sculpture project he'd volunteered to do for the local school. All the while we were enjoying each other's company, I made sure both of our glasses stayed full. And when I wasn't on top of it, our server was.

By the time we left the restaurant, we were pleasantly buzzed and Blue's mouth was running a mile a minute.

"So I told him it was totally up to them on whether or not to have another baby, you know? I mean, just because we want like... a thousand kids, doesn't mean Jude and Derek do, right? But then Teddy piped up and said—"

I cut him off, pulling us to a stop on the sidewalk and grasping his chin with my finger and thumb. "Baby, hold up. What? How many kids?"

Blue's glassy eyes and freckle-covered pink cheeks were adorable. "Huh? Oh. I think Derek wants—"

I cut him off with a kiss. The taste of the white wine was tart and warm on his tongue. "Us. Not them. Us," I murmured against his mouth. "Are you saying you want another child?"

He melted into me and tried chasing my mouth with his lips for more kisses. When I pulled back, he blinked up at me. "Huh?"

On second thought, now was not the time to plan the future of our family. "Let's go dance. I want to feel you up to overly loud music while a bunch of half-naked strangers fantasize about getting into your pants."

4

BLUE

All I heard was Tristan saying something about wanting to get into my pants. Which was good, because that was exactly my plan. As soon as we got to the club, Tristan clutched my hand in a death grip and pulled me toward the bar.

"Two Jack and Cokes. Oh, and two redheaded sluts please," he called to the bartender when he caught the man's eye. The sound of his order reminded me of the night we met.

"You tryna get me drunk, mister?"

Tristan pulled me in closer and wrapped one arm around my waist before nuzzling his nose under my ear. "Absolutely, gorgeous. Hoping I'll get lucky later."

"You will," I promised with a little whimper of need. It had been a while since we'd done more than quickie blowjobs in the shower or a furtive frot first thing in the morning. I wanted to feel him inside me. I wanted it hard and hot with absolutely no chance of toddlers walking in and being scarred for life. "You really, really will."

Once we threw back the shots, we took our drinks to a high-top table already half-full of young guys decked out in their club gear. I looked down at my slim button-down shirt. Yeah, it was a nice brand and all, but...

"You're the sexiest man in this room," Tristan said into my ear. I caught a whiff of the cinnamon and whiskey combination on his breath and wanted to taste it. He smelled so fucking good.

"You're a liar or drunk or both," I told him.

I caught one of the boys at our table checking him out, so I shot him with my death glare which Tristan must have noticed because I felt the rumble of his laughter against my arm, and a few seconds later, I felt his hand on my dick.

Oh, hello.

My eyes slid closed, and I enjoyed the combination of the bass beat in my ears and my husband's possessive hand on me. I could tell from the shifting next to me that he was making sure to block anyone's view of him feeling me up. As if there weren't at least ten other guys getting felt up within a ten-foot radius of us.

"Feels good," I admitted in a lazy voice.

Tristan kissed the side of my cheek, the corner of my mouth, under my chin... my throat.

"Mm-hmm."

My dick was making me regret the selection of tight pants. I wasn't actually wearing a plug like I'd told Tristan, but I had spent some time prepping myself in the men's room at the restaurant so I'd be ready for him. "Wanna do it?" I slurred. It was so loud in there, I wasn't sure he heard me.

His lips latched onto my collarbone and sucked. If I hadn't already been leaning so heavily against him, I might have slithered to the floor in a heap.

"I want to dance," he said, taking a sharp nip of my skin before pulling away and reaching for my hand. "Come on, gorgeous."

As we made our way through the crowd to the dance floor, I thought about all the times he called me "gorgeous" or "beautiful" as a term of endearment. Like the night Ella had spent four straight hours puking on me with a horrible bug and Tristan had finally gotten home from a business trip. He'd taken one step into her vomit-covered bedroom and frozen for a beat before his face had softened. *"Off to bed, beautiful. Papa's turn now."*

And the time I'd fallen face-first into a pile of mud, shit, and hay just as he'd brought a winery tour group past the stables. They'd all stood and stared while Tristan had reached out a hand to help me up. *"Hiya, gorgeous. If you'll give me a few minutes to finish up this tour, I'll help scrub you off in the barn shower."*

I loved him so much, my heart overflowed with it. Life with Tristan was amazing. He was such a good man, and he never hesitated to help others and show our children how to be generous and hardworking. But he also made it fun. He was adventurous and energetic. One of Tristan's biggest fears was being too old and boring for our children, so he went to great lengths to make sure he stayed in shape and didn't pass up opportunities to try new things.

"You're looking at me like I have something on my face," Tristan said on the dance floor. His hands squeezed my hips, and one of his long legs pressed between mine, nudging up against my cock.

"I'm in love with you," I admitted. "That's all."

He narrowed his eyes. "Just how much have you had to drink?"

Instead of answering him, I plastered the front of my body against the front of his and held on tight, feeling the music thrum through us both as we moved in time to the club beat. Tristan's lips blazed a hot trail down the side of my neck and back up again until his teeth nipped my earlobe.

We danced like that for a long time, full-on body contact and hands and mouths everywhere. When other men came around to dance up against us, it was fine, but our eyes and lips and hands were only for each other. At one point I turned my back against Tristan's front and ground my ass into his crotch. His hands snaked down my chest and stomach to cup and stroke my dick until it was hard and bent funny in my jeans.

"Want you," I gasped, leaning my head back onto his shoulder and turning so he could hear me over the insanely loud dance music.

He turned me around until I was facing him, and then one of his hands snaked down into the back of my pants, encountering the waistband of a jock and then bare butt below.

Tristan froze. "What... what do we have here, Bartholemew?"

"Call me that again and I'm going to lose my boner," I warned.

"Are you wearing a jockstrap?" he asked in a seductively low voice. His long, warm fingers slid into my crease. "Blue Marian, are you trying to get lucky tonight?"

I sucked in a breath when his fingertip barely grazed my hole. "Oh god," I whispered. "Uh-huh. More."

He continued to tease me with light touches, never committing to actually entering me.

Asshole.

"Want you to fuck me," I said. "Please."

He pulled back enough to meet my eyes. "You ready to go back to the hotel?"

I shook my head. "Here. Want you to fuck me here. In the club."

Tristan's eyes widened in surprise and then burned so hot I felt my breathing kick up in response.

"Men's room. *Now*," he growled.

Hot damn.

TRISTAN

I kept a tight hold on Blue's hand as I dragged him toward the back of the club toward the hallway that led to the bathrooms. We were both tipsy enough not to pay much attention to the sticky floors and the couple making out in the hallway, but when we entered the men's room and came face-to-face with a massive domestic dispute, we had to admit defeat.

"Boner-killer," Blue muttered before turning back around to leave the crowded space.

I followed him through the club to the front door without asking any questions, and when we made it out onto the much-cooler sidewalk, I realized how disappointed he was. But he was still adorably drunk, so he was muttering.

"I don't even know what a sous vide is, but it must be important if they were arguing about it that violently. I mean, come on. Brown hair should have told blond hair they could just share it. Unless it's like... a hygiene item? In which case—"

I leaned over and kissed his cheek. "It's a cooking tool, and you're the cutest thing I've ever seen."

"A cooking tool? Like a Crock-Pot? Those two dudes were in a dance club going at it over a Crock-Pot?" He started to giggle. "And I thought *we* were the biggest losers in the place."

I turned him toward me and cupped his face, meeting his glassy eyes and reveling in his familiar, freckled face. "You were the hottest man in that club. And I still want to fuck you right this minute. We're going back to the hotel."

As we walked, Blue chatted a mile a minute, telling me everything he saw and thought while we were in the club. He commented on outfits, attitudes, people who'd looked like friends of ours, speculation on the hidden sexuality of actual friends of ours, and suggested matchmaking ideas for both the random strangers he'd noticed in the club and the friends of ours who were allegedly secretly gay and/or bisexual.

"Don't you think?" he asked at one point.

"Often," I replied.

He blinked at me. "Ha, ha. You're not even listening."

I squeezed his hand before opening the door to our hotel for him. "Not true at all. Sequined top guy seems like a dream come true for Lila at the Shop and Save, with the teensy caveat that I believe sequined top guy is gay since his hand was on gray T-shirt guy's dick the whole time we were there. I could be wrong. He could be bi. As for the bartender with the green shirt? You're right. He would probably adore your friend Landon, and I'm not even going to comment on the fact that the only reason you think that is because Landon's favorite color is green. I'm sure it's the basis for a strong, lifelong connection."

Blue huffed. "You're no fun."

We entered the stairwell since we'd long ago made an agreement to avoid elevators for our health. Before the door to the dim stairwell even finished closing, I turned him face-first against the cool cement wall and pressed my entire body against his, whispering in his ear, "Wrong. I am fun."

After reaching around to fumble his pants open, I pulled them down just enough to expose his gorgeous fucking ass in that jock. It took two seconds to get my own pants open and press the tip of my cock against his hole.

"Fuck," Blue gasped. "There... there are probably cameras..."

"Mm-hm," I rumbled in his ear. "And the security people are going to see me fucking my husband into this wall."

I shoved myself inside of him after a few shorter thrusts to pave the way. He banged a fist on the wall and moaned. "Oh god."

I grabbed both of his hands and held them high above his head while I pounded into him and grunted into his ear. "Been teasing me all night with this ass. Even slicked up and stretched yourself, didn't you? Wanted me to fuck you. Wanted me to pound your ass and make you come where everyone could see who owns you. Whose ass is this, Blue?"

"Oh god," he whimpered again. "Yours. I'm going to come. Tris, Tris, oh god."

The sound of voices came through the door behind us just as I reached down to cup a hand over his dick to catch his release. His ass squeezed me tight as he shouted out my name and shot into my hand, and it pushed me over the edge. I vaguely heard the rattle of a doorknob turning as I released deep inside him.

I heard a man's voice behind us murmur, "Holy fuck that's hot."

Shit. I raced to pull Blue's pants up. I was still covering him with my body so anyone looking would have only seen me, and I was still fully dressed. Once Blue's pants were done up, I quickly did mine before turning around to see three guys grinning widely at us and holding the door open.

"Sure you wouldn't rather take the elevator? Because we're more than happy to ride up with you," one of them said. "Or down for that matter."

"Or just ride *you*," the other teased.

"Or go down *on* you," the third added under his breath.

Blue snorted and blushed deep red. "No, thanks. Stairs are good for the heart. Or so they say."

One of the guys held out a fist to bump Blue's before they turned around to presumably take the elevator instead. I pulled my sweet husband up the stairs behind me, both of us still in a bit of a postor-gasmic haze. By the time we made it to the door of our room, Blue was shaking his head.

"I can't believe you just fucked me in the hotel stairwell."

I followed him into the room and closed the door behind us. "Hey," I said, reaching for him and pulling him around to face me. "Are you upset?"

His blushing face beamed up at me. "Are you fucking kidding? That was hot as hell."

I leaned in and kissed him softly, taking my time exploring his lips and cheeks and chin. By the time I nibbled my way down his throat and began unbuttoning his shirt, he was fully hard again.

Blue's voice hitched. "I-I thought... I thought that was it. The stairs... and, and we'd just go to bed after..."

I pulled back and stared him down.

"Not until I peel that jock off you with my teeth. Take your clothes off, beautiful."

JUDE'S LULLABYE

1

JUDE

I was riding in a taxi through the streets of Barcelona when I saw the image that inspired me. There was a cartoonish tiger painted on the side of a building that I knew my son would have loved. I made a mental note to tell him and Derek all about it when I FaceTimed them later that night, but after that, I hadn't been able to stop thinking about the silly thing.

I imagined a whole family of tigers in the same style. If only I'd been an artist—a painter or illustrator. And stupid me had taken an entire day and a half before realizing I *was* an artist. The only difference was the way in which I expressed my vision.

After that, every night of my international tour was spent giving everything I had to my fans on stage and everything I had to this song afterward and into the small hours of the morning.

The soft tune and sleepy animals described in the lyrics haunted me until I could no longer sleep from wanting to perfect it for Derek and Wolfe to hear when I returned home. There was still something missing, something barely out of reach keeping it from being just right.

It was a lullaby... one of many I'd written since Wolfe had come into our lives two years before. But instead of lulling me to sleep like it was meant to, it was robbing me of it until I could barely get myself through the final week of my international tour. I'd just stumbled back to the hotel after playing a show in Berlin and was aching with the need to call home.

"You there, sweetheart?" Derek asked through the laptop screen in his deep, comforting voice. Just the sound of my kind, familiar husband made my stomach clench and my eyes smart. I was so fucking tired.

"I'm here," I said, leaning back into the crisp sheets of the hotel bed. "How did Wolfe do today?"

Derek's eyes brightened and his lips widened into a smile. "No way. You first. Everything is fine here. Your son is taking a nap after spending a big morning with your parents at the zoo. Tell me how the show went."

Now it was my turn to smile. "It was great. You were right. I'd forgotten how much I loved playing this venue. The crowd was on fire even when something went wrong with the rigging."

Derek's face turned stormy. "What happened with the rigging? Are you okay? Where was AJ? He should have call—"

I felt a laugh bubble up. "Slow down, He-Man. Everything's fine. No one was hurt. AJ handled it. The crowd thought it was a special effect, and Dante had words with the manager of the venue about it. He's been amazing. They both have. It was a good idea to send them in your place. They've had a ball sightseeing in all the European cities so far. I try to sleep during the day, and they play tourist. Win-win."

"AJ had better be getting enough sleep to be on his toes guarding you at night," he grumbled. "It should be me there watching your back."

"I'd rather you be there watching Wolfe's back," I reminded him. "He had enough upheaval on the domestic tour when we lived on the bus for six weeks. There was no way he'd be okay with both of us ditching him for three whole weeks for this international part. And you know how I feel about dragging a toddler across so many time zones."

"I know, but I miss you," Derek said, pouting. "Our bed is cold without you in it. I don't like it when you aren't here with me."

I reached out and drew my finger down the image of his handsome face, imagining the rough stubble I'd feel if the real Derek were beside me.

"I miss you too," I whispered. My eyes filled, but I did my best to blink away the traitorous tears. Derek would lose his shit if he knew how run-down I was.

"Baby, maybe you should get some sleep," he said. Crinkles of concern marred his forehead. "You look worn-out. What did you eat tonight?"

I took a shaky breath and tried to smile. "Something called a kartoffelpuffer. Don't ask me what was in it. It was vegetarian. That's all I know."

He studied me for a moment in silence, and I knew he was trying to decide whether or not to continue his lecture about me taking care of myself. He must have decided against it.

"Take your hair down," Derek said in a gruff voice. I could see his arm moving and knew he was most likely sneaking a hand into his boxer briefs to stroke himself.

I pulled the band out of my hair without thinking. When Derek told me to do something, I did it. And if it was a command that would increase his sexual pleasure in any way, I did it double time.

My thick hair fell out of its messy bun and around my shoulders. Derek made a growling sound that filled my cock up instantly. I set the laptop on the bed next to me and shucked off my own underwear.

This was going to be fun.

Seeing my sweet husband looking so tired and beautiful across the miles made my stomach hurt. Jude Marian had always been my kryptonite, and witnessing him in need was enough to bring me to my knees every time.

He needed me.

I'd known the minute I saw him on the iPad screen that he was doing his best to hide from me just how homesick and exhausted he was. I was sure one good snuggle with Wolfe would set him to rights, but I also expected he'd kick my ass for going against his wishes and bringing the little dude with me to surprise him.

Wolfe or not, I was going to Paris to get my man no matter what he said. Ollie had agreed to stay with the baby so I could fly over in time to catch the final show of the tour. That way, at least he'd have my shoulder to sleep on all the way home.

During our FaceTime session several nights before, he'd fallen asleep almost before his orgasm had even finished wringing him out. I'd watched in amused surprise as he'd collapsed into his pillows with his hand still around his deflating cock. Within seconds, the light, familiar Jude snore had kept me company instead of my usually energetic post-show husband.

The guy was running on fumes, and seeing him like that made me crazy. When we'd first gotten together, he'd been wrecked from a crazy tour. The difference in a Jude at full power and the shell he'd become after giving everything to his fans was brutal. Back then, he'd sworn he'd take a break from touring to have a normal life again for a while. And he had. We'd taken time to begin our family by having Wolfe, and the past three years together had been a dream. But we'd both known this time would come. It was time for him to get back to doing what he loved. The songs were coming out of him, and his band was champing at the bit to put out a new album and get out on the road to promote it.

His assistant and best friend, Ollie, had been a godsend. She'd requested the change from Jude's assistant to Wolfe's nanny, and we'd accepted with a giant cheer. The woman was everything to us. I wasn't sure what we'd do if she ever decided to move away.

I shuddered and put the idea out of my mind. I was way stronger than she was. The woman was not leaving, even if I had to tackle her and beg.

"Why are you looking at me like that?" Ollie asked from across the kitchen.

"Like what?"

"Like you're mentally measuring me for a taxidermy project."

"I'd never kill you," I said. And it was true. "And I've never been a fan of taxidermy."

"Why does that not reassure me?" She finished cutting up some green grapes and put them on Wolfe's high chair tray next to the lima beans he'd already been making a mess with.

"He hates lima beans," I muttered, looking down to make sure my passport was packed.

"No, *you* hate lima beans. BJ loves them," she corrected.

I looked up with a grunt. "Don't call him that. You know I hate it."

"Babycakes Junior. Jude's little one. Should I call him JJ instead? Or DJ?"

I slid the passport back into the front pocket of my backpack. "How about Wolfe? Why not Wolfe?" I felt like I'd crossed into whining territory. I needed my Jude before I completely lost my marbles.

"Did you pack the lube?" Ollie asked without skipping a beat.

"None of your business, nosy wench. When's what's-his-name getting here?"

Ollie handed Wolfe a sippy cup of water. "Drink some of this, baby boy. Who's what's-his-name?"

"Your flavor of the month."

"I'm not seeing anyone right now."

I sighed. "Fine, don't tell me. I'll just ask Jude."

She rolled her eyes. "As if he tells you everything."

That stopped me in my tracks. "What do you mean? Of course he tells me everything. I'm his husband."

Ollie stared at me for a beat before she looked back down at Wolfe. "Right. My bad."

"Hold up. What does Jude not tell me?"

"Nothing. He tells you everything."

"Why aren't you looking at me when you say that?" Now she was intentionally pissing me off.

She looked up and met my eyes. Her entire face was the very definition of coy. "Why don't you ask him? After you've thoroughly yanked his joystick and pressed his trigger button, of course. I'm sure he'll tell you."

I narrowed my eyes at her. "He'd better."

She laughed, the sound automatically making Wolfe laugh too. His toothy grin was covered in mashed-up lima beans, and his cheeks were so chubby I wanted to gnaw on them. That kid was the best thing that had ever happened to this family.

"I love it when you act like you're the dominant one in the relationship," Ollie said. "It's so cute."

I walked up and pulled my son out of the high chair, lifting him into the air and making faces at him.

"You be a bad boy for Ollie, okay, sweetheart? Yucky diapers and late nights, okay? I love you soooo much." I leaned in and blew raspberries into his neck, soaking in the sound of his high-pitched baby giggle and imprinting it on my memory. "I'll bring Daddy back."

"Dada," Wolfe said, kicking his legs with excitement before I slid him back into his chair.

"Yeah, Dada." I gave him one last kiss on the top of his head, taking a moment to inhale the baby scent of him.

Before I got to the door, Ollie's voice called out from behind me. "Think fast!"

I turned around and caught what she'd tossed at me.

A TSA-approved travel-size version of Buttjuice lube from Sally the Lovejunk Lady. As if I was going to slide that sucker into the little zip-top baggie in front of everyone at the airport security portal.

I rolled my eyes before sneaking it into my checked bag instead.

3

JUDE

The morning after the Berlin show, I'd awoken scratching my belly and realizing every hair there was glued together. "What the fuck?" I'd grumbled, looking down. Instead of an image of my sleeping husband, the laptop had shown a blank screen. I'd fallen asleep on him within seconds of climaxing.

Again.

I'd checked the time and noticed it was ten in the morning in Berlin, which meant it was one in the morning at home. I'd sent Derek a quick text to apologize before running downstairs to meet my brother Dante for breakfast.

And just like that, we'd been on to another city, another radio station interview, another night of performing. Everything in my body ached, and everything in my heart yearned to be home with Derek and little Wolfe. I missed my family so much. I wondered if I'd made the right decision to leave them behind for this portion of the tour.

Several nights later we played our second-to-last show of the tour to a sold-out crowd in Paris.

When I walked off stage, I high-fived everyone to avoid sweaty hugs. I was drenched. My jeans were stuck to me, and the button-down shirt I had on felt like it was glued to my back. The only thing I wanted was a shower followed quickly by a video call home.

Dante's smiling face was there waiting as I walked toward my private changing room. He handed me a cold bottle of water and a small towel. "Great job, Jude! They loved it. Hurry up though, we need to get back to the hotel ASAP."

"Why? I wanted to take a shower."

"Make it a quick one, then," he said with a weird wink.

As I passed through the corridor, tons of our backstage crew slapped me on the back or offered me a fist bump and a smile. I thanked them all and swallowed down as much of the water as I could as I walked, hoping it would perk me up enough to keep me going a few more hours. AJ walked ahead of us and opened the door of the private room. "Thanks, man. I'll be out in a minute. Just let me shower and change."

"You're small. Make it quick," AJ said. "I don't wanna be here all night. I have plans with your baby brother."

"Ew," I said with a shudder. "TMI, dude."

As soon as the door closed behind me, I dropped my smile and pressed my back against the cool door before letting myself slide to the floor in a heap.

I was almost done. Only one more show, and it was over for at least another year. I could go home to my husband and my baby.

My face fell into my hands, and I let my exhaustion get the best of me, finally.

The tears came quickly, but it seemed like before the first one even fell, there was a familiar grunt of frustration from across the room.

I looked up to see Derek Marian striding toward me from the door to the little bathroom.

Fuck. I was hallucinating. I buried my face back in my hands and sobbed. I missed him so fucking much.

"Baby, shit," he said. "Don't cry. You're killing me."

I whipped my face back up again. "You're really here?" I scrambled up and launched myself at him, half-afraid I'd fly right through the apparition and hit the wall on the other side of him.

"I'm really here. I'll always be here, Jude," he murmured into my hair as he caught me and held me tightly against him. "I missed you so fucking much, baby."

"Derek," I sobbed. "You came?"

I wrapped my legs around his big body and held on to him like a lifeline. With the exception of a mischievous toddler, this man was my entire world. "You're here," I whispered into his neck. "Oh, thank god. You're really here."

He walked us over to the cheap little love seat against the wall and sat down.

"You're soaking wet," he murmured. He brought his big fingers up to unbutton my shirt. I ran my hands up his chest, but he batted them away. "Let me do this. I can't concentrate with your hands on me."

"I love you," I said softly, sniffling and trying to dry my eyes with my shoulder.

One corner of his mouth turned up. "Yeah, I know."

I reached for his fly and ran my hand over the familiar bulge there. "You're dirty too, you know."

"Huh?" he asked, pushing the shirt off my shoulders and chucking it on the floor. He moved his fingers to my belt, and I sucked in a breath. My husband's hands on my body sent every drop of blood to my dick every time.

"Huh?" I asked.

Derek looked up at me with a knowing grin. "You called me dirty."

"Take a shower with me," I begged. "Get naked with me."

"Baby, not only am I getting naked with you... I'm also going to teach you never to leave me like that again and never to lie to me about how you're doing. But we're not going to do it here. When I get my hands on you, we're going to need hours and hours."

The deep rumble of his voice revved me up until my breathing was unsteady and my chest was heaving. Derek's fingers fumbled my fly open, and he shoved me off his lap to rip my jeans down. The sticky jeans automatically brought down my underwear, leaving me standing in a pile of boots and damp denim. "Get your boots off," he growled.

"Fuck," I muttered, squeezing my cock. "Don't make me shoot right here in your face." I leaned over to untangle my feet from the mess and almost tipped over. Derek's large hands landed on my bare hips to steady me. While they were there, he took the opportunity to cop many feels of my ass.

"You can shoot in my face when we get back to your room."

"Jesus."

How the hell did he expect me to be able to untie my boots while his finger was inching down my crease?

"Dammit, Derek," I snapped. "Stop distracting me."

Within moments, I was bare-assed naked and slung over his shoulders. His large paw mauled one of my ass cheeks, and someone around here was making desperate, begging sounds.

It may or may not have been me.

"We need lube," I said in a moment of panic. "Try..." I scrambled to think if he could ask Dante or AJ if they carried that shit around in their wallet.

"Not yet." He set me down on the bathroom floor and reached around me to turn on the water. I could feel the soft fabric of his shirt against my shoulder blades. I turned to inhale his armpit. He smelled like a combination of sweat and airplane.

I started to ask about the lube again, but a warm hand clamped over my mouth from behind, shutting me up and making my knees crumple.

Fuck yes. *Fuckkk* yes. This was the Derek I wanted right now. The one who manhandled me, and he damned well knew it.

His lips grazed the edge of my ear. "I want you to be quiet and get clean as fast as you can. Pay special attention to your ass, baby, because I'm going to eat it the minute we get to the hotel."

Oh my god.

"Mm-hm," I whimpered against his palm and stuck my ass into

his thighs. I reached down to stroke myself, but his grunt of disapproval stopped me in my tracks.

"Mine. You know better than that, Jude Marian. Hands to yourself."

When the water was the right temperature, he nudged me into the small space and slid the tiny plastic door panel closed behind me. The water felt amazing, but Derek's hands all over my body coated with slick body wash would have felt even better.

"Hands against the wall, Jude," he commanded. "Spread your legs for me. That's it. Good boy."

I turned around to see him leaning into the stall with a soapy hand.

I wiggled my ass at him, making him grunt again. Sometimes he got so grunty and growly during sex, I accused him of turning feral. He didn't think it was funny.

But it was so true.

His hands came around to stroke my dick and fondle my balls. I hummed in pleasure. A minute later, his slick fingers entered me, and it was tight enough to remind me how long we'd been apart.

"Fuck," I bit out. "Did your hands grow? What the hell?"

The sound he made almost made me come. It sounded like he was being tortured.

In the very best way.

His fingers disappeared and the rough scrubbing of the rest of my body resumed. I groaned in annoyance.

"More fingers," I whined.

"Wash your face and your hair. Let's go."

I did as he asked, going as fast as I could once I realized he really wasn't getting naked and joining me, but when I stood ready in the open shower doorway waiting for a towel with my angry purple dick at full mast, I saw the look in his eyes.

The one that meant good things for me.

"Dammit," he muttered, sinking to his knees. My damp hands went into his short hair as his hot mouth enveloped my cock. It took about three seconds for me to shoot into his throat while his hand clamped over my mouth to keep me from alerting every crew member outside the little room what we were doing in there.

As if they wouldn't know. Every single member of Jude and the Saints would recognize how long I'd gone without my husband and what that would mean the minute we saw each other again. Especially Dante and AJ.

Fuck. "My brother told me to hurry," I said.

Derek snorted, licking the edges of his mouth before smirking up at me. "How convenient for you to remember *after* you get the orgasm."

I leaned over and kissed him, tasting myself on his tongue. "Hurry up, GI Joe. Last one naked in the hotel bed is a rotten egg."

4

———————

DEREK

When we entered his suite at the hotel, Jude was subdued and pensive. Normally, performing made him energized and manic, but tonight he was calm and quiet.

"One more show and the tour's over," I told him. "You going to make it?"

He turned to me with a raised eyebrow. "Of course. Why wouldn't I?"

I stepped forward and pulled his shirt up and off, tossing it on a nearby sofa. I pushed him down on the soft surface and bent over to remove his canvas sneakers.

"You're exhausted, baby. I haven't seen you this far gone since Wolfe's newborn days. I'm worried about you."

I finished removing his shoes and started on his pants. He leaned back against the sofa and watched me with half-lidded eyes.

"I've been working on something."

"Ahh. That explains it. Keeping you up at night?" I worked his jeans down over his slim hips, revealing the little yellow boxer briefs he'd put on at the venue. My husband had the most amazing body of anyone I'd ever met. He was small but fit as hell from rock climbing.

His arms were sculpted, and his legs showed off the regular running we did together most mornings at home.

"That and missing you. It's hard to sleep without you," Jude admitted in a low voice. "I don't want to do this without you again."

"C'mere," I said, scooping him up and carrying him to the bedroom. His arms went around my neck, and his head leaned into my shoulder. When I got to the big, plush bed, I set him down in the middle and stood back to remove my own clothes. Jude's arms came up to cross behind his head.

"Show me what you got, big man." His grin was flirty despite the exhaustion. He shucked off his underwear and tossed them before grabbing for his cock with one hand and massaging his balls with the other. He spread his legs wide on the bed.

Once I was naked, I crawled up toward him from the foot of the bed, dropping kisses from his ankle to his hip and beyond. By the time I got to his belly button, his dick was hard and bobbing. I drew a wet stripe up the shaft with my tongue before leaning up to take his mouth in mine. Jude's hands clasped the back of my head and held me to him, his legs wrapping around my back and squeezing me tight.

"Want you," he breathed against my mouth.

"How do you want me, baby?"

"Want you to wreck me. Want to feel it. Don't want you to be gentle."

I knew what he meant. Some nights he wanted to be worshipped and made love to, and other times he wanted to be owned and fucked. Thank god tonight was the latter. I'd been holding back when all I'd really wanted to do was take charge and dominate him. But when I'd seen how tired and vulnerable he was, I wondered if that had meant he needed coddling and caring.

I guessed not.

"Turn over on your front and cross your wrists above your head," I told him. "Do it now."

He scrambled to do as I said, taking the position like a pro. I briefly considered using something to tie his wrists to the headboard, but decided against it since he actually preferred me controlling him with what he'd termed my "no nonsense" voice. He'd once referred to it as my "leather daddy" voice until I'd used a little vibrating dildo to teach him I didn't prefer that term since I was nobody's daddy.

I ran a finger down his side before I fetched the little bottle of lube from my bag and a few towels from the bathroom. Jude knew better than to move a muscle while I was out of the room.

When I came back, I saw him slightly humping the mattress.

"You trying to get yourself off without me?" I asked.

"N-no."

I almost chuckled. "Liar. Pull your knees up under you and show me that hole."

"Oh god," he whimpered into the bedding. "Derek."

"Pull up, baby. Do as I say."

His knees slid up as his little round ass raised into the air, exposing his hole and the familiar sac hanging down between his legs. I reached out to fondle his sac and leaned in to lick down his crease. His skin tasted like soap.

"Derek," he croaked as my tongue invaded him.

I smoothed a hand up his back and back down again while I licked and sucked and probed his ass with my mouth. Every so often I gave one of his ass cheeks a smack and squeeze. His legs began to shake as his incoherent noises of pleasure became more desperate. At one point, he tried to sneak a hand down to his cock, and I growled at him to put it back up by the headboard.

Finally, when I was so hard from tasting him and turning him on that I could hardly feel anything except the throbbing in my cock, I lurched up behind him and grabbed the lube. I slid some into him, scissoring him open as gently but firmly as I could before lubing myself up and beginning to push in.

I wiped my hands on a towel and tossed it away before leaning over him again and using my body weight to remind him I was planning on fucking him into the mattress.

I shoved in farther, stretching him wide and causing him to grunt and curse. "Is okay?" I managed to ask.

"Fuck me," he barked.

I took that as a yes. I reached up with one hand to hold him down by the back of the neck before I hammered into him from behind.

"Fuck yes!" Jude cried, arching his ass up to me even more. The sensuous curve of his spine topped with the brown tangle of his long hair was a familiar sight that never failed to rev me up. I kissed along his shoulder and down the back of one arm.

"I love you, Jude."

"Show me," he grunted.

I fucked into him harder. His hand scrambled back to clutch at my thigh as if he could pull me closer. I moved the hand on his neck around to the front and pulled us both up on our knees until he was sitting on my lap with my hand around his throat and my lips beside his ear. "Ride me. Show me how much you want it."

Both of Jude's hands came back behind my head as his back arched, and he used his leg muscles to bounce himself up and down on my cock, grinding on it every time he came down. I wasn't going to last much longer.

His skin was coated in a fine sheen of sweat, and he smelled like my familiar, beloved husband. His hair was all over my face, and I grabbed it in one fist to keep from getting it in my mouth.

"Fuck me, baby," I panted at him. "Take your pleasure. Come for me."

"Derek!"

One of Jude's hands scrambled for mine until they were locked together with fingers intertwined. He clasped them both to his chest and shouted as I reached for his cock with my other hand to stroke him off.

When his orgasm hit, he threw his head back on my shoulder and cried out my name. His body squeezed me so tightly, I couldn't hold back. I pressed us both forward again until he was on his hands and knees, and I thrust into him, one, two, three times until finally shooting on the fourth with a mind-blowing release. We stayed locked like that for several beats before I fell over onto my side to keep from squashing him.

We were covered in sweat and gasping for breath. I reached out to push the hair back from his face.

"I'll never get tired of seeing and hearing you come," I told him. "You're so damned beautiful."

Jude's eyes locked on mine. "I love you so much it hurts sometimes, Derek."

He looked sad. I grabbed a towel and wiped us down quickly before pulling him into my arms. "It shouldn't hurt, baby."

"I don't want to be away from you and Wolfe again like this. Maybe I'm weak, but—"

I cut him off. "That's bullshit and you know it. You're not weak."

"It's just... these are the important years for Wolfe, and I don't want to miss them. Three weeks is too long. I can't even imagine how military families handle it. How? You grew up like that. How did you guys manage when your dad was gone?"

"We didn't see him much, so we weren't close. That made it easier."

I realized my mistake the minute the words were out of my mouth.

5

JUDE

"Exactly! I don't want it to be like that with our kids. I want them to know me. Hell, I want them to be sick to death of me because I'm all up in their business."

"You want a family like you have," I pointed out.

"Exactly. Is that so wrong?"

"It's most people's dream, Jude. You know that. Just ask Mav, Griff, or Dante. Hell, look at how your parents have even taken Ammon in recently."

"Yeah. But we can't accomplish that by dragging our brood along in a luxury coach all the time, now can we?"

"Baby, Wolfe is hardly a brood."

I suddenly realized Derek was here and I could tell him the secret I'd been keeping. I'd wanted to tell him in person, and now I could!

"Wait right here."

I scrambled off the bed to find my iPad, racing back to the bed after clicking it on and scrolling through to find what I was looking for. I climbed back onto the bed and sat with my back to the headboard.

"Here, look," I said excitedly, turning the screen so he could see the image.

He studied it for a second. "What am I looking at?"

"It's an ultrasound picture!"

"I see that, but what... wait." He looked up at me with raised brows. "Did we... did we get matched with someone already?"

I nodded. "Yes! I've been dying to tell you, but I didn't want to do it from so far away. But it's twins so..."

"So?" Derek's face had gone bright with excitement. "Twins! Holy crap. Twins!" He sat up and cupped my face to kiss me. "Jude, we're having a baby!"

"Babies," I corrected. "So you're okay with twins?"

"Of course I'm okay with twins. Jesus. If your brother Pete can do it, we certainly can. Plus, you know your mom will freak, and oh my god, Ollie. Ollie is going to lose her shit."

I bit my lip and gave him my best apologetic face.

"You already told her."

"I had to tell somebody. It was killing me."

Derek rolled his eyes. "You tell *me*. I'm your somebody, Jude Marian. Jesus."

I crawled into his lap, leaving the iPad open on the photo of our unborn children next to us on the bed. "I couldn't stand the idea of telling you and not being able to touch you," I admitted. "And now you know why I'm done touring. These are the years to be together at home with our family. Tomorrow is my last tour show, Derek."

His hands came up to cup my face again. "You know I support you no matter what. Now, tell me about the babies. Tell me everything."

"Do you remember meeting Solome and Ernie at the fund-raiser festival last year? Teddy introduced us because he knows Ernie through work."

"Yes. Aren't they the ones who travel?"

"Right. She's a reporter, and he's a photojournalist. They travel all over the world researching and reporting stories. Well, they found out they were pregnant despite using protection. They thought long and hard about it before deciding to have the baby and give it up for adoption. They're Catholic, so I'm sure that had something to do with it. Anyway,

Teddy told them that you and I were on the list to adopt, and she contacted me super excited to talk to me about us adopting the baby. I didn't want to tell you about it until I felt like it was a sure thing, you know? And at that point they didn't even know it was twins. When she found out about that, she panicked and thought we'd change our minds."

"And you think they're sure about giving them away?"

"Yes. She said both of them came from huge families, and one of the things they had in common was the desire to be child-free and travel unencumbered. Their jobs are their babies. They both admitted to getting plenty of kid and baby time not only from their siblings growing up, but also from the myriad nieces and nephews they have now. They're very sure."

"Twins, Jude," he said again with a soft smile. "We're going to be daddies again."

"Wonder what Wolfe will think," I said.

"Let's call him and tell him good night," Derek suggested. "Obviously we won't tell him about becoming a big brother until closer to the time, but we can FaceTime him and maybe you can sing him a lullaby."

I thought about the lullaby I'd been working on, and suddenly the solution came to me. The song wasn't about a family of tigers at all. It was about an entire, varied, and wonderful collection of different animals.

I leaned over and gave Derek a long, lingering kiss. "Let's get some clothes on and make the call in the other room. I need to get my guitar."

That night the song poured out of me the way it was meant to be all along. With Ollie, Wolfe, Derek, me, and the image of our soon-to-be new babies propped next to us on the table, I felt loved and surrounded by my entire family. I thought of my siblings—bio and adopted—my parents, my great-aunt and adopted great-aunts, the spouses of my siblings who'd become like siblings to me themselves, my nieces and nephews—human and furry—and the various people who'd come into our world and become a part of it. We were a wild, crazy bunch from all over the place with different likes and needs. But we had each other.

And we had love.

The following night I closed my last tour show with a solo acoustic performance of my new lullaby to a standing ovation. Little did they know it would be my last tour concert for a long time.

It was time to go home and sing the *Love Menagerie* to my own little tigers.

BEACH MUSIC

1

BEAU

Was there anything hotter than a sweaty man running on the beach with an adorable dog loping alongside him? No, there was not.

And even hotter than that was when the man was the very same sexpot who'd given you a nice, thorough deep dicking the night before.

I noticed one of our neighbors do a double take at me as she walked past our boardwalk. After waving a friendly hello to her and getting an odd look in return, I looked down at myself only to realize the tiny Speedo I had on wasn't doing much to hide the giant erection I was sporting for my husband. No wonder she almost tripped over a tiny seashell.

Mav came pounding up the steps behind Jessie, and it was a toss-up who was going to cover me in the most amount of sand. I raced to the nearby outdoor shower to rinse off the dog before she went inside the house.

"Where are you going?" Mav shouted after me with a laugh.

"Sand dog," I called back before luring Jessie into the big wooden stall with kisses.

Mav followed her in and closed the door behind him before kicking off his running shoes and shucking down his jogging shorts.

I gulped.

"Yeah?" he teased, reaching for his dick and stroking it. "You like that?"

"Mpfh," I said with a sniff, turning around to hide my impossible-to-hide woody. "Just cleaning the dog, that's all."

His laugh was deep and easy which brought a smile to my own face. If Maverick Marian was happy, then I was happy. Every single time.

I leaned down to rinse the sand and seawater off our baby girl in the cool spray. Even though it was early, it was still too hot outside for a warm shower.

Mav moved up behind me, smoothing his hands across the exposed skin of my sides and stomach while pushing me under the spray. "Is that what you kids are calling it nowadays?" he murmured into my ear. His hand moved down to grasp my cock through the front of my suit. "I'll be happy to help you clean your dog, sweetheart."

I choked out a laugh. "Stop. You went too far. There's an actual dog here who's completely innocent." I finished rinsing her and gestured for her to walk to the other end of the large shower area before doing her big body shake.

She didn't listen.

Maverick turned me around and kissed my wet lips. "Innocent, my ass. That girl has seen things..."

I kissed him again. "Stop. Jesus. Don't remind me we're corrupting her. The poor thing."

Mav's hands snuck down the back of my suit and gripped my ass. "Why you wearing this?"

"Mm," I said, indulging in a few more kisses. "I was going to go for a swim before work."

He kissed me some more, running one long finger down the cleft between my cheeks until it brushed my hole. I sucked in a breath. "No you weren't," he whispered roughly into my ear. "You were hoping for a repeat of last night."

He was right.

"You're wrong," I said. "I'm all about eating right and exercising. I was just going to swim some laps."

"You ate an entire pizza last night, followed by three cupcakes."

I pulled back and frowned at him. "How dare you? That was... that was..." I swallowed. "That was carbo-loading for the marathon sex we were going to have. See? *Exercise.* Duh."

He laughed and pulled me close again, using those magical hands to make my Speedo disappear. I heard the familiar sounds of the dog sighing and settling down on the deck to wait. Poor innocent girl.

Maverick spun me and shoved me up against my favorite part of the shower wall. My shoulder collided with the carving of the two rabbits that represented us and our home on Rabbit Island. I traced the Mav rabbit with my finger.

His deep voice rumbled against my bare back. "I love you more today than ever before."

I closed my eyes and savored it. "Sucker," I teased.

He sucked up a mark on my neck. "Damned straight."

The wiry hair around his dick scratched against the skin of my ass before he reached past me to the shelf that held the soap, shampoo, and lube. The lube we never remembered to hide when friends visited. Mav's sister Simone called it the lube shower. Tilly called it the sex shower, and Granny called it the perfect view since the room she stayed in when she came to visit looked right down into it.

We'd found that out the hard way.

Once we were both lubed up with Mav's magic fingers, he shoved inside me in one full thrust.

"Fuck," he grunted, bottoming out with his hands on the wall on either side of my face. I reached back to hold him close.

"Fuck me into this wall, Maverick. Like you mean it."

"Fuck," he repeated, pulling back and slamming his hips into me again.

I gasped as his dick filled me up and my own erection grazed the wooden slats of the shower wall. As I reached down to stroke it, Mav moved faster. He knocked my hand away with a grumbled *mine* and held it in his firm, familiar grasp.

I ran my hands up the wall until my fingers caught the top edge, and then I just held on. Maverick's free arm moved around my front to hold me tight as he stroked me with his other hand.

My head tilted back until it landed on his shoulder. I muttered words of desperation and need as if he hadn't already spent hours the night before with his dick in my ass. But with Maverick, I couldn't get enough. I wanted him all the time. Even when I wasn't in the mood for sex, I wanted him touching me and holding me.

I could count on the fingers of one hand how many fights we'd had in the few years we'd been married. We were best friends and lovers, life partners and family. It had been Maverick Marian for me since childhood, and my dreams of building a life with him had finally come true.

"Stay with me," he breathed into the skin of my cheek.

"I love you." I moved my hand up into his hair. "Love you so much. Fuck!"

His dick struck my gland just as his finger raked over my frenulum and shot fucking rocket grenades through my nerve endings.

"Fuck!" I screamed, banging my fist on the wall.

Maverick grunted and shoved into me several more times before finally stilling. He held me to him as the cool spray continued to mist around us.

"God, I have the best life ever," he murmured before pulling out and slapping me on the ass. "Let me make you some eggs and toast before you have to head out to the jobsite."

Before he could do his usual quick wash routine, I grabbed his wrist and pulled him back, wrapping my arms around his waist and leaning my face against his upper chest for a tight hug. We stood wrapped around each other for long minutes while the sound of the shower and the squawks of nearby seagulls filled the air. The brightening daylight shined down into our little private oasis, lighting up the wet wood with sunshine sequins.

He was right. We did have the best life ever. It was a life pieced together with stolen moments like these, mundane nights on the couch watching the news, weekends spent strolling through flea markets for rare or unique salt-and-pepper shakers, and long strolls on the beach with our sweet Jessie. Maverick was my rock. But he was also my fire. And our love lit up our lives the way Rabbit Island's Fourth of July fireworks lit up the night sky.

I looked up at his handsome face, dark with beard shadow and full of familiar affection for me. My stomach flipped over.

"Thank you for loving me," I said.

His eyes crinkled with a smile. "Easiest job I've ever had."

And he leaned down and kissed me until my toes curled and we were both late to work.

BIRTHDAY SONG

1

DANTE

For my twenty-fifth birthday, I got an RV.

Or so I thought.

"Um... Angel, darling, what the fuck is that?" I asked, standing in my underwear on the front porch of the small cabin at the vineyard where I thought we'd be spending our week of summer vacation.

A shiny, bright, turquoise and white polka-dot camper sat front and center in the driveway. The thing was so large, it blocked the view of the road beyond. I was surprised it didn't block out the sun.

"Isn't it adorable?" AJ asked, sliding up behind me and putting his arms around my middle. I ignored the fat morning wood nudging my ass because this was serious. Someone had made a big mistake.

Namely, my husband.

"We live in an apartment in the city," I informed him.

"So?"

"That is a camper van."

He stepped around me and dangled a set of keys in front of me with such excitement, I thought he'd mistaken them for keys to something miraculous, like... like something other than a kitschy camper even HGTV would think was overdone.

"Not a camper van," AJ corrected. "A complete glamping *experience.*"

I stared at him. "Somebody slipped you something. We need to get you to a hospital."

His crooked grin was too cute for words, but I couldn't let it distract me from the matter at hand. "Angel, sweetums, why do we have a complete glamping experience in the driveway instead of the nice, reliable Prius we own?"

He skipped down the porch steps to the front walk and did a little dance, shaking his ass in his basketball shorts and grinning like a loon. "Because we're going on an adventure! C'mon. Check it out."

I followed him to the camper because, let's face it, I'd follow that man anywhere. When he unlocked the side door and led me into its pristine interior, I saw a more tasteful and subdued decorating scheme than I'd imagined from the exterior.

"Oh. That's cute," I admitted, stepping farther in to the tidy space and reaching a hand out to feel the soft velvet of a creamy white throw pillow on the built-in couch by the door. A vase of fresh yellow flowers hung in a holder next to the little kitchen sink and a pink tea towel hung over a cabinet door with the phrase "Glamping is my jam" embroidered over the image of a fat strawberry jelly jar.

AJ turned to face me with a lecherous look on his face. "Come see the bedroom."

"Is there candy in there? Are you luring me into your lair for nefarious purposes?"

I followed him toward the back of the vehicle because, again, I would follow that man anywhere. When he opened the door, revealing a large, lush bed taking up almost all the space in the small room, I decided maybe blowing our savings on a giant aqua party bus hadn't been such a bad idea after all.

When I stretched out on top of the cushy duvet and starfished around a little bit to feel the smooth cotton on my bare skin, AJ's eyes darkened.

"Don't distract me," he warned, pointing a finger at me and circling it around to indicate my body. "With all of that."

I bent my knees up and let them drop open, reaching down to palm my cock through my briefs. "All what?" I asked, batting my eyelashes. AJ was a sucker for the virgin routine. We'd spent many a night role-playing innocent Dante and devilish Angel.

He growled. "No. *No.* It's your birthday. That means presents."

"I was hoping your penis was the present. And you were going to put the present in my butt."

AJ snorted. "Stop. You're ruining the moment."

I sat up and reached for him. "I hope you didn't buy more than this RV. I'm seriously happy with the penis present."

AJ blinked at me. "I didn't buy the RV. Are you crazy? It's a rental."

A breath of relief whooshed out of me. "Thank fuck."

His eyes widened comically. "You thought I *bought* this? For your *birthday*?"

I shot him a look. "Jeez. Fine. Apparently I had grandiose delusions of a big gesture for my quarter-century celebration. You don't have to make me feel like an idiot."

AJ began laughing, closing the little bedroom door before crawling up next to me and yukking it up into my armpit. His hot breath tickled me, but I refused to break out of my epic pout to giggle.

I closed my eyes and concentrated on the cool bedding underneath me and the warm stripe of sunlight warming my thigh. This was nice. Things had gotten so crazy lately between work at Marian House and AJ's own travel schedule, I'd needed a break. I'd needed time alone with him.

I ran fingers into his dark brown hair. "Thank you for renting me a party bus," I said. "It's not that I'm not grateful. I'm just surprised. I thought we were spending the week in the vineyard so we'd be here for my family's big birthday plans."

AJ pressed a kiss to my side before leaning up to meet my eyes. His smile was soft and sweet. "That was a lie. I wanted to surprise you. We're taking this bad boy on a tour of Yellowstone. I have the whole trip mapped out."

I shoved him back and sat up with excitement. "For real? I've always wanted to see Yellowstone. Jamie and Teddy make it sound incredible."

AJ fell back and crossed his hands behind his head on the pillow. He wore a smug grin. "I know. Why do you think I planned it? I'm like the gold medal of husbands." He gasped and clutched his chest. "Dante, do you know what this means? You're a gold medalist in marriage. It's true. Congratulations."

I rolled over to straddle him. "And you're a weirdo. It's true. Congratulations."

He reached for the back of my head and pulled me in for a deep kiss. The kiss turned into heavy grinding and making out like teenagers until someone lost their underwear and someone else lost their shorts.

Then it was full on frotting and humping until both of us were covered in spunk and sweat and the pristine bedding was no longer pristine.

I turned to AJ with a grin. "When do we leave?"

"In the morning. Your parents made me promise to at least stay for a birthday dinner tonight. Everyone's coming to celebrate with us."

I let out a satisfied sigh. Best birthday ever.

"Can we sleep in the camper tonight?" I asked. "Maybe christen it with that penis present you promised me?"

AJ grinned back at me. "Absolutely."

That night we proceeded to get hammered with my family. Granny and Irene had invented some kind of Jell-O shooter that knocked me on my ass. AJ and I were lucky to make it back to the RV in one piece, much less find our way to the bedroom.

Which is why we didn't notice when the camper van started moving.

AJ's shout woke me up from a dead sleep.

"Tilly, what the hell?"

Her bossy voice called back from the driver's seat. "Shut your trap. I gotta buy-one-get-one at the casino in Reno. The girls are meeting me there. You can drop me off and finish your National Forest Fuck-fest without me."

We sat side by side in the bed staring up at the back of her head.

I slowly reached for AJ's hand and clutched it in a death grip.

"We're never having sex in an RV again," I whispered slowly.

He turned to look at me. "Agreed. But... after this trip, right? We'll start that new plan *after* the trip."

I thought of a week alone exploring Yellowstone in this big clean glamper with the love of my life.

"Yeah, okay. We'll start it after the trip."

AJ's giant, knowing grin appeared as he toed the bedroom door closed with a solid click. "That means we can have sex right now."

I waffled for a second before he leaned down to take my soft dick into his hot mouth.

"Oh fuck," I said, sucking in a breath. "That's... okay, yeah. Yeah. Good." My libido was way stronger than my fear of an octogenarian being able to hear us over the sound of the road noise.

As soon as he got a good rhythm going and my head was in the clouds, the speakers in the walls started blasting music.

The song was "Lollipop" by the Chordettes, one of Tilly's favorites from the 1950s.

I groaned and shoved AJ off. It was going to be a long ride to Reno.

HARD ROCK

1

———

AMMON

I remember the first time I officially met Mark Hayes. He scared the crud out of me. It was after the lunch rush at Marian House, and I was wiping down tables before leaving for a performance on the other side of the city. I had my earbuds in and Massenet's "Meditation" on repeat. Sometimes after a crazy loud meal at the youth shelter, I needed the quiet company of my favorite classical music to calm my racing heart and help me breathe again.

It wasn't like I was a stranger to loud noises or anything. I'd grown up on a farm with plenty of loud machinery and boys horsing around from time to time. But the enthusiastic free-for-all of the inner-city shelter... well, let's just say it had taken some getting used to. I'd had to learn some coping skills from my counselor. One of the things I'd learned was that I was more successful when I approached challenges with a steady mind and calm heart.

And playing my violin in front of hundreds of people at a different school's recital hall was definitely a challenge. It was hard enough performing in my own school's practice salons. I was scared out of my mind. It was the reason I'd insisted on volunteering today at the shelter. If I could just keep busy until the moment I had to walk on that stage... maybe I wouldn't die of fright or vomit all over my shoes.

So with my earbuds in and the mournful notes of the violin calming my soul, I nearly jumped out of my skin when someone tapped my shoulder.

I jumped a foot in the air which yanked my earbuds out and sent my phone clattering onto the table in front of me. My heart exploded into my throat as I made a gasping, choking sound and clapped my hand over my mouth before saying a bad word. Old fears of immediate punishment still controlled my tongue, but it was a near thing in the case of being scared out of my wits.

"Sorry," a deep voice said. I peered up at the stranger with wide eyes. He was huge. Jacked-up muscles and height for days. He even had ink going up the side of his neck and a mean-looking scar across one eye. Whatever had happened to cause that scar had thankfully left the striking green-brown eye unharmed. If the big, dirty-blond man hadn't been wearing a fancy business suit with a neatly trimmed beard and dark hair styled neatly, I might have been scared he was some kind of ruffian who'd come in off the street.

"M-m-may I h-help you?" I managed to squeak out.

His forehead crinkled in concern, and he dipped his head down to peer at me. I noticed his eyes were brown and warmer than I would expect from someone so... rough-looking. "Are you okay?" he asked in a softer voice that made my stomach squirm like a bucket of tadpoles.

I felt the flaming heat on my cheeks and knew without looking that my neck was probably embarrassingly splotchy. I nodded even though I was definitely not okay. Despite the suit, the man was still scary as heck. Tattoos covered both hands and some of his fingers, and even though I knew from my friend Nico that ink didn't mean the guy was some kind of moral reprobate, it still made my stupid brain jump to old, hard-wired conclusions.

Ye are the temple... If any man defile the temple of God, him shall God destroy...

I blinked up at him, trying to shove Paul's Letters to the

Corinthians down into one of the many, many suitcases that comprised my personal baggage.

The stranger stepped back and pulled a chair out before sitting down. It was an odd move, but at least it gave me more personal space to breathe.

"I'm here to pick you up for some kind of music practice," he explained, confusing the heck out of me. "My name is Mark Hayes." He eyed me carefully before adding, "I work for Joel Healy at On Your Six. Simone had an emergency at the vet clinic and asked me to swing by and pick up Ammon Marian. That's you, right?"

Ammon Marian.

Even after three years of living with Rebecca and Thomas and an additional two years of officially owning the name, I still reveled in it every time someone called me a Marian.

I nodded again, filing his words through my mental filters to make sure everything checked out. My facial expression must not have been convincing because Mark reached for his phone without breaking eye contact with me.

"I'm going to call Joel so he can vouch for me, okay? Simone is in surgery, and Joel is in—"

"Canada," I blurted, realizing suddenly I knew who he was. Mark worked for Joel, and he'd been around a few times here and there, only... he usually wore ripped-up jeans and graphic tees, not to mention a motorcycle helmet or baseball cap pulled low over his face. And he always wore sunglasses. Now I could see why. The angry scar cut a vertical line across one eye, from just above his eyebrow to the top of his cheek. I'd never noticed it with the sunglasses on, not to mention the fact he always had some woman stuck to his face.

Mark's face relaxed into a smile, and I wondered if I might hyperventilate from how much it changed his face. He was... well, maybe beautiful wasn't a good word to use on someone who clearly wanted to be seen as a tough guy, but he was more attractive than any man I'd ever seen before in person. No wonder he always seemed to have a woman on his arm. He probably had to beat them off with a stick.

"You have a nice smile," I said, my heart hammering against my ribs. Since when did I tell another man he had a nice smile? Did I have a death wish? "Sorry," I said quickly, squeezing my eyes closed. "I didn't mean..."

"Thank you," Mark said kindly. "I..." He sighed. "I really needed to hear that today. Thank you."

I opened my eyes and looked at him, noticing for the first time that he had scrapes on the back of one hand. I wanted to ask him if he was hurt, but I kept my mouth pinched closed. There was no telling what I would blurt out if I let myself converse with him. Instead, I nodded again and simply said, "I'm Ammon."

He held out a gigantic paw, rough-palmed and edged in black ink. I stared at it before putting my hand in his to shake. As soon as the heat from his skin touched mine, something inside of me went soft and stupid. The man terrified me still, but for the first time in my life, I wanted to hold that fear close and take it home with me.

2

MARK

He was the most beautiful boy I'd ever seen.

Ammon Marian was an angel on earth, and he even looked the part with a slender, almost frail frame and white-blond hair that fell partway over one eye. He was smaller than most men his age, and everyone at the youth shelter seemed to treat him with an extra helping of care. There was just something about him that made him seem... vulnerable. Innocent. Untouchable.

Everything about him called out to the part of me that ached to protect, the part of me that had gone immediately into the personnel rescue business after leaving the navy. But Ammon didn't need my protection. He had a million new brothers in the Marian family, and his almost brother-in-law Joel Healy was the ultimate protector and my boss. I had no business feeling protective of this young man who was pretty much a stranger to me.

Yet...

I couldn't stay away.

The first time I saw him, he was sitting in the grass playing with a puppy in the Marians' front yard. His face was alight with happiness as the little dog licked his face and pawed at his chest. It was one of those cheesy moments where, I swear, the sun shined down on just him. Like... like God himself was working the spotlight and wanted to make sure I saw what an incredible creation He'd made.

But I'd only been there to drop off my boss for his family get-together. He'd invited Raisa and me to stay for dinner on the drive over, but I'd already made our excuses. It would have been awkward to change my mind simply because I'd had a religious experience. Besides, the blond boy with the puppy had looked almost like jailbait, too young to be any business of mine. And, oh yeah, I'd been newly engaged to be married to the woman staring impatiently at me from the passenger seat of my truck.

After that, I'd noticed Ammon several more times in passing. He volunteered at Marian House where he always seemed to keep to himself and stay in the background. He hung out at Simone and Joel's house sometimes where I once saw him curled into a small ball in the corner of a large sectional sofa, fast asleep under a blanket. My heart had squeezed so tightly at the sight, I'd almost embarrassed myself with a sigh of longing.

It was embarrassing, my attraction to this young man, not to mention completely inappropriate.

For the better part of a year, I'd done my best to hide it. Even if I hadn't been engaged to Raisa, there were other big blaring obstacles from this fantasy ever becoming a reality. He was too young. Too sweet. Too special.

And he was a *Marian*.

Imagine having a crush on someone who literally had fifteen brothers and brothers-in-law watching out for him, not to mention a feisty sister who took shit from no one. Even without Raisa in the picture, there was no way I'd even be able to ask him out without facing the third degree. Hell, two of his brothers-in-law were body-guards for god's sake. One of them had even been Ammon's rescuer several years before when he'd been smuggled out of a religious cult in Utah. I happened to know AJ was extremely protective of Ammon, and neither he nor my boss would take kindly to my interest in the kid.

So I'd pretended he didn't exist.

Until Simone asked me to do her a favor one day and drive Ammon to music practice at a university hall across the city. Joel was out of town, Simone had gotten caught up at work, and I was the one at On Your Six who wasn't on assignment at the moment. Unfortunately, the reason I wasn't on assignment was because I'd been at yet another command performance for Raisa's parents. The business networking brunch at their country club had been excruciating. Her dad was convinced if I met enough of his golfing buddies, one of them would take pity on me and hire me into an entry-level position at one of their companies or firms. It had taken me a while to put it all together, but when I'd finally realized he was bound and determined to get me into a "respectable" job, I'd lost my shit. I'd been under the impression we'd been at the brunch to help *Raisa's* career, not mine.

What made the whole thing worse?

Raisa had simply stood there like a puppet, smiling prettily in her pristine business suit and nodding along with everything her asshole father had said, including an introduction to a plastic surgeon friend of his and the request that he begin crafting a plan to fix my ugly face. His exact words had been, "Nobody wants to have their clients scared off before the ink has dried on the contracts, right?" And there'd been nervous laughter all around.

"Speaking of ink," the doc had said, eyeing my skin with a glint of excitement, "I can get some of that off while we're at it. You definitely don't want any of that showing if you're hoping to move into the corporate world."

Raisa's dad had laughed and slapped the doc on the shoulder. Raisa herself had actually let out a soft snort of agreement until I shot her an incredulous look.

When we'd finally extracted ourselves from the event and made our way to the parking lot, the gloves had come off, and it hadn't been pretty. Her expectations had been made abundantly clear, and it became obvious I wasn't at all the man for her. Which, honestly, had been a relief. I hadn't known until pulling out of the parking lot of that shitty club that my attachment to Raisa had been one born more out of desire to start my "real life" than to forge a future with her specifically.

I wanted a family, and Raisa didn't. I wanted to have time away from work to have some fun, whereas Raisa was chasing partnership at her father's consulting firm which included too much travel and overtime. I liked staying in and watching movies while Raisa thrived in the club and trendy restaurant scene. As I watched my engagement crumble to dust in a parking lot surrounded by meticulously land-scaped greens and near-silent golf carts, I suddenly remembered a question my friend Anton had asked when I'd announced my engagement.

"Raisa? Really? I thought you wanted the white picket fence?"

At the time, I'd scoffed and explained she'd want it eventually, she just needed to establish herself in her career first. But Anton had given me that look, the one that expressed confusion and disbelief. I'd come this close to telling him maybe I wasn't cut out for that. I was hired muscle, a scarred soldier with no college degree or refinement. If someone like Raisa Monroe was willing to have me on her arm, I'd take the chance and run with it.

Stupid. Why would I have wanted appearance more than substance? And why hadn't I seen how incompatible we were from the beginning? How had I never known her desire to change me into a more "respectable" partner?

Needless to say, seeing Ammon's beautiful face after the morning I'd had was a balm to my soul. There was a calm strength about him that seemed to be contagious. And when he put his soft, pale hand in mine, I had to brace myself against the strong need to pull him in and simply hold that peaceful presence against me, letting his sweetness seep into my very bones.

After hearing Raisa's parents suggest needing to change my unac-ceptable appearance, I couldn't help but see the contrast between pure, kind Ammon Marian and myself. I'd grown up in West Engle-wood in Chicago where I'd had to choose between a life of crime, bullshit dead-end work, or entering the military the first chance I got.

My pops had begged me to get out any way I could, so I'd followed his wishes and enlisted in the navy.

I'd made something of myself through hard work and sheer stubbornness, but inside I was still that street kid who knew how to use a broken beer bottle in a dirty fight and could identify the headlights of a cop car in two seconds.

Seeing my dirty, rough palm anywhere near the flawless fingers of this angel was an abomination. I didn't belong in his orbit, just like I'd never truly belonged in Raisa's.

"Mr. Hayes?" Ammon asked in a timid voice.

His formal manners distracted me almost as much as his ice-blue eyes did. "Mm?"

"I need to grab my violin case out of Dante's office. Will that be okay?"

I cleared my throat and pulled my hand away, trying to remind myself I was here for a simple chauffeur job. "Yes, of course. I'll meet you by the front doors."

Once we were settled in my truck, I tried to focus on the directions to the recital hall he'd given me instead of the slightly floral scent of him. Ammon's small form looked tiny in the large cab of my pickup. When I glanced at him for the third or fourth time, I finally realized he was dressed more formally than before.

"You're wearing a suit," I said in surprise.

He glanced at me and nodded while his cheeks turned a light shade of pink. "Yes, sir."

Christ Almighty, what that did to me.

"Just Mark, please," I corrected. "I'm only thirty-one. Hardly old enough for mister and sir."

"Sorry." Ammon turned away to look out his window. His shoulders curled in, and hands rested together neatly in his lap. "Old habits," he murmured.

I knew a little about the religious cult he'd escaped several years before, but I didn't want to think too much about it. The idea of what he might have been through there made me feel helpless and heartbroken. I preferred to concentrate on how well he seemed to be doing now in college and with the Marians.

And I longed to get to know him a little better, even if we weren't going to be as much as friends to each other. I tried again. "Does your college have a dress code?"

Ammon glanced at me. "Not for classes, no... but, um... I... I have to kind of... give a performance. And... it's better to wear a suit for that."

That was news to me. "A performance? Simone said it was practice."

He paused for a moment before admitting the truth. "I didn't tell anyone about it."

"Why not? Ammon, they all would have been there. Are you kidding? The entire Marian clan would have shown up to support..." My words petered out when I realized that was exactly the point. "Oh. You didn't want them there."

Ammon's fingers plucked at an invisible piece of lint on his cuff. "I didn't want them to see me mess up." He looked back out the window.

I wanted to reassure him that wouldn't happen or remind him that the Marians would cheer like crazy even if he couldn't play a single note. But I got the feeling he wouldn't hear that from me, so I chose another direction.

"What are you playing?"

The corner of his mouth curled up as his shoulders relaxed. "Brahms Violin Sonata No. 3 in D minor. Do you know it?"

I loved that he gave me that much credit. "No. Tell me about it."

He launched into an explanation about how it was played by violin and piano. His enthusiasm lit up his entire body with energy and pleasure.

"The pianist is a student named Li Jun. He's amazing," he continued. "You should see his fingers on the keys. It's like..." He stopped speaking and glanced up at me. "You don't want to hear about this."

"I do. Tell me more. How do you get paired with the piano guy?

Do you pick someone from your class, or are you assigned to work on a piece together?"

Ammon glanced at me through white-blond lashes while the pink blotches on his cheeks deepened. "I, ah, requested him. I mean, he... Li Jun... is the best pianist at the school, so he was an obvious choice. But I was surprised he accepted."

"Wow. You must be really good if he wanted to perform with you."

He looked away again and mumbled something under his breath.

"What was that?" I asked.

He let out an adorable huff of frustration. "I'm okay, I guess. Or maybe he wants to make sure he's the better musician in a duet, so it was an easy decision."

I couldn't help but grin at his self-deprecating conclusion. "Or maybe he thinks you're an amazing violinist and wants to play with the best."

He made a pfft sound that almost startled a laugh out of me. Simply being in his presence like this made me feel giddy. It totally erased the bad morning I'd had.

Ammon continued. "Or maybe he only accepted so I'd finally go out with him."

I did a double take. "What?"

The pale skin of his neck streaked pink. "Well, he's asked me out a few times. And, um... touched me."

The truck came to a stop with a sudden jerk, and I realized I'd pulled over into a gas station without even fully registering what I was doing. I threw it into park and turned to face him. His eyes were wide in shock.

"He what?" I asked as calmly as I could.

3

AMMON

As soon as Mark whipped the truck across two lanes of traffic and into the gas station, I grabbed for the center console with one hand and the side door with the other. Now, with him leaning toward me, I could feel the heat of his big body against my left hand and arm.

"Not like that," I quickly amended, realizing the way I'd made it sound. "I mean... I just meant... he..." My heart fluttered up into my throat, and I felt like I was in some kind of trouble. The feeling was as familiar as waking. "Never mind. It's fine."

"Try again," Mark said. His tone was patient but firm. I reminded myself he wasn't mad at me, simply making sure I wasn't being taken advantage of. Joel would have done the same thing. Maybe it was in their nature as professional protectors.

"He... he does things like brushes against me when he walks by and squeezes my shoulder when I have a good idea. Sometimes he puts his hand in my hair. You know, normal stuff. But, also, kind of not normal, since we're just peers and not even really friends."

Did I sound like I was touch-averse? I quickly tried to backtrack. "I don't have a problem with being touched or anything. But not... at school. If we were dating, or whatever, it would be fine. I'd like it.

Probably." I shrugged and blushed some more. "I'm sure I would. Touching's nice. With the right guy. Or so I've been told."

Kill me now. Please. Why didn't I say "person" instead of "guy" for goodness' sake?

I peered at Mark out of the corner of my eye, a move that was quickly becoming my favorite thing. Sneaking peeks at a man like him was dangerous, but I had to imagine if he was friends with Simone and any of the Marians, he wouldn't do anything to hurt me.

The big man's jaw ticked. Maybe he wasn't as comfortable around me as I'd hoped.

"Anyway," I continued nervously. "It's fine. It just makes me flustered when I'm trying to play the violin. My hands shake and... it makes me feel nauseous. But after today, we won't be playing together anymore. As much."

"What do you mean 'as much'?"

I shrugged. "He's always asking me to practice with him, but it's not the same as performing together. Not as intense. For this concert it's been kind of crazy the amount of practice we've had to do to prepare."

Mark's knuckles turned white on the steering wheel. "Are you interested in him that way? As something other than a... peer?"

I looked down at where I'd clasped my hands together in my lap. The familiar calluses on my left-hand fingers grounded me. I thought about the slightly sick feeling I got when Li Jun flirted with me. Was that nervous excitement? Some of the kids at the shelter described having a crush on someone as fluttery feelings in your stomach. Was that the same thing as a creepy-crawly feeling on your skin? "I don't know. No?"

The silence between us turned jangly and strange. I finally got the nerve to look up at him. Mark's eyes locked onto mine. "Why not?" he asked softly into the space between us.

My stomach was full of tadpoles again. Only this was different from how I felt around Li Jun. This felt... not as sickening and scary. More... curious and expectant. Even though Mark was big and tattooed and everything, I knew a friend of Joel and Simone's would never hurt me. I was safe with him. And it was like drawing a clear breath for once.

"Li Jun has a big ego, and he likes appearances. That's not quite right... it's more like... he's a peacock. He struts, only not physically, more like he wears his success like a fancy suit. Sometimes I think he flirts with me because he likes the idea of two top musicians in the school being together. Like... a status symbol or something?" I rubbed one of my calluses with a finger on my right hand. "Not... not that I'm a top musician or anything, but he seems to think I am since I'm first chair in the conservatory's orchestra."

Mark's lips peeked out of his dark beard with a grin. "That's amazing, Ammon. Congratulations. I don't know much about classical music, but I do know first chair means you're the best."

I shrugged and willed my cheeks to cool off. "Lots of practice, I guess."

He chuckled which made his eyes crinkle. I wondered if he'd ever been on the cover of a bodyguard magazine. Was there such a thing? If so, maybe I needed a subscription. On second thought, if anyone ever saw it, they'd think I was even crazier than I already was.

Mark's voice took on a nice rumble. "Sounds like an understatement, Ammon. I don't think you get to be first chair at a prestigious music school just because you put in the time. I'd imagine it takes talent too, right? Little bit?"

He was teasing me. And the sound of my name on his tongue made me feel like I might actually run out of oxygen before the truck got back on the road.

"Um," I began. "Can we get going? It's, uh... It's just that I get really stressed if I'm not early for performances."

Mark seemed to shake himself before quickly shifting the big truck into gear and pulling back onto the road. "Sorry," he murmured. "But... you'd tell me if someone was bothering you, right?"

I looked at him funny. "I don't even know you."

"No, I mean, you'd tell Joel. Or one of your brothers. Or Simone."

I shrugged. "Probably not. They're a little overprotective."

"Ammon. They're protective for a reason. They care about you."

He was right. I knew he was. The Marians treated me like I was the most precious jewel in their crown. And it was amazing—better than amazing. It was the kind of love and attention I'd always wanted and never received. But it was also stifling. They didn't mean to, but their attention on me made me feel like I needed to live up to this impossible expectation, like I needed to be worthy of everything they'd done for me and given me over the past few years. I owed them everything, and I was scared of letting them down. Sometimes I wanted to have the privacy and space to fail without all of them noticing.

"Yeah," I admitted. "I know."

I didn't say anything else the rest of the way to the recital hall. When Mark pulled up to the recital hall and shifted into park, he reached over and lightly grazed the arm of my suit coat. "Hey. I'm sorry. It's none of my business. I was just trying to…"

I forced a smile at him, too nervous about the upcoming performance to do much more. "It's okay. I know I'm ungrateful, and they'll be heartbroken when they find out they missed this. But I just…" I shook my head. "Never mind. Thanks for the ride."

"Wait," he called as I opened the door and began to climb out. "How are you getting home after?"

"I can take the bus," I said with a wave of my hand. "I just can't take it before a performance. Too much… Anyway, too much. Thanks again."

I reached behind my seat to get my violin case. Mark turned around and pinned me with a glare. "You're not taking the bus home. I'll be here when you're done."

A familiar voice behind me called out my name. *Li Jun.* "Ammon, you're late. Let's go."

Mark's eyes narrowed almost imperceptibly. "You're thirty minutes early," he said under his breath. I didn't have time to argue with him if I wanted to stay as calm as possible before the performance.

"Okay. It'll probably be an hour and a half. I'll meet you out here when I'm done. But if you're not here, I'll understand."

"I'll be here. And break a leg, or whatever the violin equivalent is. Break a bow?"

As I walked toward the entrance to the performance hall, I couldn't help but crack a smile.

4

MARK

I finally found a parking lot north of the SFSU stadium and walked back down to the music school's theater. As I walked, I thought about that skinny-ass dude who'd whined to Ammon about being late even though he wasn't late.

The very idea of that asshole touching a sweet kid like Ammon made me crazy enough to grind my teeth.

When my phone rang, I barked a greeting a little too harshly. Simone's voice laughed over the line. "Who pissed in your cornflakes today?"

"Do you know this guy Li Jun who goes to school with Ammon?" I asked.

There was a pause before she answered with a laugh. "The piano guy who keeps trying to pop our sweet Ammon's cherry?"

Christ. I ran my hand through my hair. *None of your fucking business.*

Simone's voice turned serious. "Mark, what's going on? Is Ammon okay? Did something happen?"

I shook my head at my own stupidity and almost laughed at the real-world example of the Marians' tendency to overprotect Ammon.

"Sorry. It's fine. We made it here with plenty of time to spare, and I'm going to wait for him and bring him home."

The smile returned to Simone's voice. "You're the best. Above and beyond the call of duty as usual. I'll be sure and report it to the boss man."

"No need. I'm happy to get out of the office for a while. Did your pup make it through surgery?"

She proceeded to catch me up on the emergency that had kept her away as I made my way across campus. It took all of my self-control not to blab about Ammon's performance because I knew she'd want to be there for it.

"Hey, Mark. Why were you asking about Li Jun? I know he's a big-deal piano player who goes to the conservatory with Ammon. We think he has a big crush on Ammon, but that's about it."

I realized I'd completely overreacted. Ammon may have been sheltered, but he was an adult. I knew from Joel that all the Marians, including Ammon, had been encouraged to take the self-defense lessons offered at the shelter or the more extensive ones offered at the company I worked for. On Your Six took self-defense lessons very seriously, and Joel would have insisted on Ammon having at least the basics before he started college in the city. Besides, the piano player I'd seen at the theater was almost as tiny as Ammon himself, and Ammon was smart enough to know that one threat to the man's fingers would make him do anything Ammon wanted.

"Never mind. He's just an ass. It made me wonder about Ammon's other friends at school," I said stupidly. What the hell did I care? I didn't even know the kid. I was essentially a temporary chauffeur. That was all. "Is he doing okay? Socially, I mean?"

There was silence on the other end as I felt my stomach drop. What the hell had I been thinking?

"Well, well, well," Simone tittered. "If it isn't our little Markie-Mark developing a crush on a teeny tiny baby."

Now my stomach dropped for real. "How old is he? And I'm not developing a crush for god's sake."

In my job, lying was all in a day's work.

"He's twenty. But he has an innocence factor of a thousand as you probably know."

She was right. I had no business sniffing around that sweet college kid. The man deserved someone kinder than I was, softer... more refined and educated.

I coughed. "Yeah, I get it. He's definitely not my type. Besides, I'm not interested in taking some poor kid's virginity, Simone." *More lies.* "I just got the sense he was a little isolated. That's all. And maybe he'd enjoy taking that Krav Maga class that Mario is starting up. There are some good kids Ammon's age in that group, and I just thought..." *Stop talking, you idiot.* "Maybe it'd be a good fit."

Simone wasn't stupid, but she was generous enough to let me get away with my bullshit martial arts suggestion.

"That's a great idea. I'll ask Joel about it and see if he can convince Ammon to give it a shot. Maybe it would help give him some confidence. The poor guy's still so skittish. Last week even my dad scared the crap out of him by accident, and my dad is about as scary as a newborn kitten."

I was almost to the theater and could see people flowing in through the front doors. Thank god I was wearing a suit so I didn't look so out of place with the other concert-goers.

"Why's he so skittish?"

"Super shitty childhood. One of those extremist religious sects where the elders felt threatened by the teenage boys. They used to beat him and starve him on the regular, but when Ammon started showing signs of being gay, the abuse became life-threatening. I only know how bad it was because Joel was the one tasked with getting him out. If it hadn't been for an astute postal worker putting two and two together that the social worker was part of the same church as Ammon's family..." She stopped and responded to a question someone in her office must have asked. "Sorry, Mark. I need to go. Thanks again for doing this. We owe you one."

"I'll have Joel pick up the beer tab next time out," I promised her.

"Cool. Bring Raisa too. We never see her," she said distractedly. I couldn't bear telling her that there would be no more bringing Raisa to anything, and the reason they never saw much of her was Raisa's own discomfort around so many people who were different than she was. I guess deep down I knew that when she said "different" she meant *gay*.

"Take care, Simone."

I ended the call and joined the crowd entering the theater for the performance. After taking a spot near the back, I looked down at the program someone had handed me on the way in.

The photo of Ammon stared up at me. He wore a tuxedo, and his big blue eyes took up half his face like some kind of anime character. He was pretty and delicate, but I had to assume the kid was like an iceberg with tons of strength below the surface. After everything he'd endured growing up and all of the mental fortitude it took to pursue a serious musical career, the young man must be stronger than he appeared.

But looking at the photo of his beautiful face reminded me of how bad it must have been for him before he was rescued from that cult. His fine features and smaller build made him a natural target for any group who thought a real man had to be hairy and packed with muscles.

I ran my finger along the side of his face in the photo and smiled to myself. I'd often wondered what had helped Thomas and Rebecca Marian decide who to bring into their family from all the incredible youth at the shelter, but looking at Ammon's photo, I finally felt like I understood. It was a combination of horrible circumstances that had severely impacted their childhoods and the inner drive to overcome them and make something of themselves.

All four adopted sons were hard workers, more in need of love and emotional support than anything money could buy. Simone had once said they each went above and beyond pitching in when they lived at the shelter. They did it to prove their gratitude. And finding Ammon volunteering there today, three years after showing up on the Marian House doorstep with nothing and despite his college classes and part-time job he probably had, proved he still held that commitment deep in his heart.

When the musicians were introduced, I settled in to witness my very first classical music performance. The music theater in San Francisco was a far cry from the community center where my friends had used the old upright piano to bang out annoying noise when they were bored.

The guy who'd griped at Ammon in the parking lot glided onto the stage with his chest puffed out. After making a production of taking off his suit jacket and folding it over the piano bench, he took his seat to begin warming up. Then Ammon appeared. He looked even smaller from this distance, and his creamy skin glowed pale under the bright stage lights. The dark brown wood of his violin gleamed, making it clear the instrument was well cared for.

As he began to press the bow to the strings, I realized my hands were sweating. I wanted him to do well. I wanted him to be proud of himself for a job well done.

I shouldn't have worried. The alternating playful and mournful tune was breathtaking, and I wasn't sure I'd ever had reason to use that word before unless describing the experience of jumping out a plane.

Even Li Jun had my begrudging respect because the man had mad skills on that piano. The combination of the two instruments wielded by such capable musicians was beautiful and emotional. The people around me were just as riveted as I was.

Seeing Ammon with a half-grin on his face and his eyes sometimes falling closed while he played was both surprising and compelling. I wanted to stand right next to him and feel the energy and passion flowing off him as he pulled the notes out of thin air.

When they took their bows, the audience went politely nuts. I guessed it was mostly made up of local musicians and students who could appreciate it, but from the look on Ammon's face, the audience reaction was a relief. A sheen of sweat gleamed on his skin, and I imagined his arms must have felt like jelly after thirty minutes of playing at the top of his game with no break.

I snuck out the back before he could see me or any of the other attendees could wonder what a scarred and tatted guy like me had been doing at a classical concert, and I spent the entire walk back to the parking garage wondering how on earth I'd started the day discussing elaborate wedding plans with my sexy, successful fiancé over coffee and would no doubt finish the day by fantasizing about a sweet male violinist who volunteered at a homeless shelter.

One of those things made me nervous as hell, and the other felt as easy as breathing.

When I pulled up to the curb and helped load Ammon's violin into the back seat, I flashed him a big smile and began to tell him just how much his performance had moved me.

5

———————

AMMON

The following day at work, I had a hard time concentrating on what I was supposed to be doing. Mrs. Callahan had already snapped her fingers twice at me when I'd missed instructions about how to trim the greenery.

"Sorry," I muttered again before picking up the snips.

Mrs. Callahan's daughter, who everyone called Pinkie for some reason even though her name was Elizabeth, snickered at me. "Tell me all about it," she whispered. "Or should I say, tell me all about *him.*"

I glanced at her out of the corner of my eyes. "Nothing. There's no him."

"Bullshit. You're blushing."

I blew the hair out of my eyes. "I'm always blushing."

"Then why are you so distracted today?" she asked before adding some delicate stems of freesia to the arrangement in front of her. I handed over some of the greenery I'd trimmed so she could use it as filler.

"If you are rude to someone, but only because you were distracted and tired, do you think that person would assume you didn't like them?" My attempt to sound nonchalant should have been used as a comedy trophy.

Pinkie gave me a look that strongly implied compliance to her earlier request to spill the beans.

"Fine. I... I caught a ride home after my performance yesterday—"

Pinkie grabbed my arm. "You had a performance yesterday?"

"Not important. Anyway, I caught a ride home with this guy, only I was really tired and sweaty. And, like... sometimes I feel a little buzzy in my head after I've been on stage, you know? My brother Jamie once explained about adrenaline crashes and how they can mess you up like that. But I don't know if this guy—the guy who gave me the ride—would know that. Or he would, I guess, but maybe he wouldn't think that would explain a violinist being an idiot after only a thirty minute piece."

Her brows drew together. "You don't think Li Jun knows what it's like after a performance?"

I stared at her. "What? No. I mean, yes, he probably does, but no, it wasn't Li Jun."

She slapped my chest with the back of her hand. "Get out! Oh my god, tell me everything and don't leave out one single detail."

I glanced around to see if anyone was looking. "Nothing. It's just... he works with Joel, and he's... very nice."

Her throaty laugh drew a frown from her mom, but it didn't stop Pinkie from laughing even harder and demanding more details. I sputtered out a few nonsensical details like the color of his truck and the way his hands struck me as strong and capable. By the time Mrs. Callahan came back to ask for my help out front, my face was a deeper red than the roses I'd been trimming.

I followed her to the customer service counter where a young man in a suit stood impatiently. Mrs. Callahan gestured to me. "Ammon is our wordsmith. If you need a poetic turn of phrase, he's your man."

The guy looked relieved. "Great, because I'm terrible at this stuff, and my boss really wants to get it right."

I pulled out a notepad from one of the nearby drawers and reached for a pen. "Who are the flowers for, and what message are you trying to convey?"

"They're for her fiancé. She wants to say she's sorry for their fight. Oh, and also, Happy Birthday."

I nodded and began toying around with an idea. After a minute, I passed the notepad to the client.

He skimmed it quickly and grinned. "Perfect. Man, you're good. Thanks for this."

"No problem," I said with a smile. "And we'll make sure the arrangement has some purple hyacinth in it to symbolize apology. Let us know if you have any other floral needs in the future. We appreciate your business."

After he left, I returned to the back to find Pinkie laying out our sandwiches for lunch. "Mom's right, you know. I don't know what we'd do without you. The reason half our clients stick around these days is your magical words."

I shrugged. "It's kind of cheesy, don't you think? I mean it's all the same kind of ideas from Jane Austen books and bodice-ripper romance novels."

"You read bodice rippers?" she asked with a wink.

"Snuck them, more like. My bio mom had a million of them stashed in a cardboard box in the laundry room. Those books helped me realize I was gay. I remember one called *Master of Desire* that had this big beefy hero on the front. Man, he was so muscular and tan... and the smaller woman in his arms was blonde... I used to imagine I was her. The hero's name was Draven, and he was her father's sworn enemy. Draven takes the woman for a year as part of a peace deal or something, I don't remember. All I remember is wishing like heck Draven had come to steal me away instead."

The memory of sneaking the book outside under my work shirt and finding a tree to sit under was a good one. It had taken a few years for the constant nauseous fear part of the memories to fade and allow the highlights to shine brighter. The feeling of dappled sunlight warm on my face and the coolness of green summer grass between my fingers came back to me with the memory of the book, and I closed my eyes to savor it. Sometimes I allowed myself to miss the rural landscape of my childhood—the smell of a barn in use and the sound of my siblings laughing and splashing in the creek—but I loved the city too. San Francisco energized me and gave me a place to finally be anonymous if that's what I wanted.

There was power in anonymity. I could be whoever I wanted to be without feeling like my reputation would be irreparably harmed. I could try things on. One time I'd taken the bus to the wharf and imagined I was a tourist. I'd bought a T-shirt and visited all the corny spots a true San Franciscan would never be caught dead in. Another time I'd accepted Ginger's invitation to a professional football game and had even worn some Raiders' gear and cheered when everyone else had like I'd known what was going on. Everyone around me had probably thought I was normal, and for those few hours, I'd felt like I was.

And one time I'd even gotten up the nerve to go into a coffee-house in the Castro wearing a Pride T-shirt and flirt with one of the other customers. 'Course, as soon as he'd asked me back to his place, I'd panicked and bolted, but at least I hadn't puked or gotten beat up, or lied and said I wasn't gay.

That was what San Francisco did for people. It gave us room to breathe, to try, to simply *be*.

And that was a million times better than the stark loneliness of Tabiona, Utah, where all thirty-eight families in town had known exactly who my parents were, my grandparents, my siblings and cousins, and most especially, they'd known who I was *supposed* to be.

But none of them had ever really known who I actually was. Heck, most days, even *I* hadn't known. All I'd known for sure was that I was a sinner, and I was going to hell if I didn't become something impossible.

Times had changed though, and Tabiona was a million miles away.

I was finally beginning to believe that, regardless of what anyone else said, I was worthy. It was okay to fail. And I didn't need to always see myself through someone else's eyes, especially ones who found me lacking.

My brain helpfully supplied the memory of a sparkling pair of green-brown eyes from the day before.

Mark Hayes.

I sighed like a lovesick adolescent and spent the rest of my shift daydreaming that the gorgeous arrangement of white lilies, soft pink roses, and bright purple hyacinth we'd sold to the last customer was secretly for me from the man who'd told me my music had wrecked his heart and pieced it back together again.

After floating home that afternoon on clouds of my dreamy body-guard crush, I let myself into Jude and Derek's kitchen instead of heading up to my apartment over the garage. "Anyone home?" I called out.

Little footsteps got louder until little Wolfe rounded the corner and launched himself at me, saying my name like the ending to a prayer. "Amen!"

I laughed and spun him around, holding tightly to the chubby happy boy who made me feel like I was the most fun person in the world. "Hey, buddy. How was your day?"

Derek and Jude walked into the room at a much more sedate pace, smiling when they caught sight of me. Jude reached for a stack of mail on the counter and handed it to me. I didn't miss the concern in his eyes. "You got a certified letter from a Utah address."

All the bubbly feelings I'd been having that day popped and skittered away.

6

———————

MARK

When I returned to the office after lunch with the guys, there was a giant floral arrangement on the front desk. Our receptionist was newly pregnant, so I assumed her husband was spoiling her a little in their excitement.

I was wrong.

"Flowers for you, hot stuff," Cherie said without looking up.

After turning to the guys I'd been to lunch with, I noticed none of them paying attention to her. "For who?" I asked.

She looked up and rolled her eyes at me with a smirk. "You, Mark. None of those other guys are hot."

Considering one of them was her husband, I coughed out a laugh while I heard his exaggerated gasp of surprise.

"You wound me, woman," Damien accused, walking around the reception counter to hand her the salad he'd brought her from the restaurant. "How's your stomach?"

The sound of their conversation faded into the background as I pulled the card out of the giant arrangement and opened it.

My Love,

I want to be your shelter instead of your storm. Please forgive me. You deserve celebration today and every day. Happiest of birthdays!
   Raisa

I BLINKED and read the words again, my heart thumping at the unexpected sweetness of her words even though my birthday wasn't for another two months. The soft scent of the flowers pulled me closer for a better sniff.

Why did smelling these flowers make me think of Ammon Marian? And why was I thinking of someone else when I should have been thinking of my ex-fiancée?

My phone buzzed in my pocket, and I pulled it out to see another text from Raisa, bringing the total message count since yesterday up to twelve.

Raisa: *We need to talk. 7pm reservations at Inota's. Meet you there.*

My stomach soured. How could the same woman who'd written such a sweet message with the flowers be so presumptive? And how many times did I have to tell her I didn't like the Hungarian restaurant where I'd gotten food poisoning only four months before?

Me: *Can't. Working late.*

I slipped the phone back into my pocket and scooped up the heavy vase of flowers before heading to my shared office. When I finally settled behind my laptop to work on more of my expense reports, my phone buzzed again.

Raisa: *On your birthday? Are you just playing hard to get? Don't do that. Let's be adults.*

I had no idea what she meant, but I also didn't have the patience to ask her to clarify. Instead, I sent a quick text informing her it wasn't my birthday, and then I focused on knocking out the last of my expense reports so I could get in a workout before preparing to teach an advanced-level self-defense class that evening.

Three hours later, my boss poked his head into the room. "Got a minute?"

I was the only one there since my three office mates were out on assignment. After closing my laptop, I gestured for Joel to have a seat in the chair in front of the desk.

"What's up?"

Joel studied me for a minute, and I did my best not to squirm in my seat. I'd always gotten along well with the man, but he could also be a hard-ass when he wanted to be.

"What's going on with you and Raisa?"

It took me a minute to switch gears. I'd assumed he was coming into my office to discuss business. "We broke up. Why?"

"You called off the engagement?"

I nodded. "Yesterday. Why? How did you hear?" Since I wasn't one for drama and gossip, I hadn't even mentioned anything to the guys I worked with.

Joel sat forward and leaned his elbows on his knees, clasping his hands together before meeting my eyes again. "Raisa called me. Said you were really upset and probably needed some time off to get your head on straight."

I felt heat fill my face, and blood thundered in my ears. I was going to kill her. "No, sir." The words came out through clenched teeth. "That is absolutely untrue. And I apologize for the inappropriate phone call."

Joel let out a sigh. "Mark, I'm no longer your CO, okay? This is me asking as a friend. How can I help?"

He was a good man—had always been a good man—and I knew he meant it. "Do you have a time machine? Because I could really use one right now to go back and reject her advances that night in the bar."

Joel cracked a smile, bringing back memories of his tanned skin in the desert crinkling with laughter during a particularly ridiculous game of poker on deployment years before. He'd hardly allowed himself to cut up with the rest of us, preferring instead to remain ever-vigilant with eyes constantly roaming the horizon. But during the few times he'd allowed himself to relax, I'd seen the lighter side of him.

I swallowed and continued. "Her parents made it pretty clear yesterday that I wasn't good enough for her and needed a few upgrades. She didn't disagree. Honestly, the breakup has been a long time coming. I've never felt comfortable in her world. She leads me around like a pup on a leash, and that's not how I envisioned my relationship going down."

"You're hardly anyone's pup," Joel said with a teasing glint in his eyes. "But if you're not good enough for her, why parade you around?"

"I'm her one rebellion. Like... if she has this vice, she's not the same as all the other elite women. She's edgy and cool. Hell, I don't know. Maybe she just likes keeping Mommy and Daddy on their toes."

Joel's eyes met mine. "Do you love her?"

I thought about it for a moment as if I hadn't already spent hours trying to break it down like some kind of mission debrief. "I thought I did, but then I realized that when I'm with her, I'm still holding things back, still holding my breath and waiting for the exact kind of judgment that came yesterday. Hell, Joel. It almost makes me wonder if I fucking manifested this shit because I was so convinced I wasn't good enough for her in the first place."

Joel looked thoughtful for a moment before sitting back in his chair. "Hm. I never really understood what you saw in her. Don't get me wrong, she's smart and beautiful. But she never seemed your type, not that I know what that is. I just could never figure out why *her*. For some reason I pictured you with someone sweeter. Less corporate rat race and more..." He shrugged. "You deserve someone who dotes on you. She's not a doter."

I snorted at the word which brought out Joel's grin again. "No. She's not a doter."

He tilted his head. "It makes sense now. One of my friends in high school got asked to the prom by our team's quarterback. This guy was everything. You know the type. Anyway, my friend was in awe of his popularity and accepted right away even though they were the worst match ever. The date was a disaster. When we asked her what she'd been thinking, she shrugged and said she'd felt validated for once in her life. It was almost like an entry on her resume, as weird as that sounds."

Something about that made sense to me. When Raisa had wanted me, it had made me feel worthy. I closed my eyes and blew out a breath. "Can we not do this? I already feel like an ass as it is. The only thing that could possibly make it worse is talking about my feelings with a fleet admiral."

Joel stood up and stretched. "Fair enough. I also wanted to give you an assignment. One of Simone's brothers needs an escort on a trip."

My ears perked up. "Really? Why? And why me instead of Derek or AJ?"

"The kid refused. Says his family is too overprotective. Imagine that."

Warning bells clanged in my head. "Kid?"

"Ammon. The guy you took to—"

"I know who Ammon is," I snapped. Suddenly my skin felt too tight. My new assignment was protecting Ammon Marian? "What's he need personal security for?"

Joel's eyes grew large in surprise. "Ah... it seems his biological father has finally been indicted on child abuse charges, and they want Ammon to testify. Considering what we learned about the man and his friends during Ammon's rescue op... I think Derek's right to be concerned about Ammon's safety if he goes back there."

"Then maybe he shouldn't go," I suggested. "Surely they have what they need to put that fucker away without Ammon's testimony. The guy hasn't even been there in several years."

Joel's eyes got even wider. "That's not our decision or any of our business. He's going and Derek has arranged for us to provide appropriate support so Ammon gets in and out without being hassled. What the hell's wrong with you? Maybe Raisa was right, and I should give you some time off. I could always assign someone else—"

I opened my mouth to argue, but then he finished his sentence and the words hit me right in the gut.

"But Ammon specifically requested you."

The argument died on my tongue as my stomach twisted with stupid excitement. "Really?"

He nodded. "The only way he'd agree to someone going with him is if it was you instead of anyone from his family. I already emailed you everything we have on the town, the religious group, and the asshole he'll be testifying against. We'll meet first thing in the morning to go over everything before wheels up at ten. The district attorney wants to meet with Ammon midafternoon."

My head spun with the sudden influx of anxiety on Ammon's behalf. Most importantly, how was he feeling about all of this?

After asking Joel a few more questions, I had to excuse myself to get changed for the self-defense class. It took all of my willpower to stay focused on my students when all I wanted to do was dive into the file Joel had sent me on Ammon's situation.

When I finally got home and opened my laptop, my heart stuttered to a stop. AJ's notes from the rescue were professional and succinct, but they detailed years of abuse. Ammon and his siblings had grown up in a dirt-poor household where their fundamentalist religious sect redirected any food stamps or welfare income the family received to the general church coffers. The result was complete control of the family by church leaders.

The children were considered free labor and forced to work in the nearby hay fields owned by the church. The girls were groomed to be young mothers and caretakers, and the boys were indoctrinated into church belief and policy with hours of rote Bible memorization and repetition instead of any standard education as required by law. All of that was fairly expected until I got to the medical records.

On Your Six did a deep dive before committing to rescue a victim from their situation. We had to make sure removing a minor from an abusive situation was legally defensible. That meant collecting reams of paperwork proving the system had failed them. In Ammon's case, On Your Six had been informed by a postal worker that there was a kid in trouble and all of his previous calls to law enforcement about the family had gone unanswered.

It turned out that the local sheriff and the social worker assigned to the case were in the same church as Ammon's family. It was no wonder none of the cases involving church families had borne fruit. On Your Six gathered medical records from Tabiona Medical Clinic, Uintah Basin Medical Center, Heber Valley Hospital, and Park City Hospital. None of these medical facilities had enough evidence of abuse on their own, but when put together, the records showed an obvious pattern of, not only physical abuse, but deliberate attempts to hide it by spreading the visits out to different facilities in the region.

Ammon's injuries over a ten-year period included things I couldn't even stomach reading about. Broken bones and bruising blamed on "horseplay" and "boys being boys." One visit had such severe bruising and contusions that it was blamed on a single car accident (for which there was no police report). Photos accompanied some of the records, and I saw a tiny, terrified version of the beautiful, thriving young man I knew today. It made my chest pull tight and my eyes smart. In every report, there was a note about the father answering for the boy with the explanation the boy didn't speak much due to "shyness." While the Ammon I knew was definitely shy, it was more likely the father's desire to control the narrative.

I tossed the laptop to the side and pulled my knees up in front of myself before tightening my arms around them to keep myself from bolting straight out the door to stand guard outside Ammon's apartment over Jude's garage through the night.

I tucked my face down against my knees and tried to slow my breathing down. I had a job to do. Regardless of my emotions, I needed to focus on the mission. Escort Ammon safely through his testimony. Provide support to him based on *his* needs, not my own.

I could do this. Ammon deserved someone to look out for him, and if his family couldn't be there to do it, I'd try my hardest to be the next best thing.

7

AMMON

By the time Jude and Derek pulled up to drop me off at the private airport terminal, I was shaking with nerves.

"I changed my mind," I said through nearly chattering teeth. "Wanna stay here."

Jude grabbed me and pulled me into a tight hug, his body firm and warm against me. "You're the strongest man I know. You can do this. Please let us come with you. Ollie has the kids and—"

I cut him off. "No. I already told Mom and Dad I needed to do this on my..." My voice drifted off as we both realized what I'd said. As many times as Thomas and Rebecca had invited me to call them Mom and Dad, I'd still resisted. I hadn't wanted to upset the apple cart of their already perfect family.

Jude pulled back and met my eyes with a tender smile. "Finally. Thank god." His hands came up to cup my face just as Mark strode into view out of the corner of my eye. "You're my brother. Mom and Dad are yours too. We love you, Ammon Marian. And don't ever forget you have a big, pain-in-the-ass family here for you, no matter what."

Great, now my chin was wobbling too. All I could do was nod. Jude pulled me into another quick hug and then stood back, reaching blindly for his husband's big hand. Derek held on to Jude with one hand and ruffled my hair with the other. "No one's going to fuck with you with this guy on your six," he said gruffly, nodding his head toward Mark.

I glanced at the man I'd agreed to let take me to Utah. There was so much care and concern in his eyes, I could hardly stand it. It was everything I'd ever wanted to see in a man like Mark, but it was for all the wrong reasons.

I nodded again and mumbled a thanks before reaching for my bag. Mark grabbed it before I could. After swinging it onto his shoulder, he put a hand on the small of my back to direct me toward the small airplane in front of us. The touch felt strong and sure, and I breathed out slowly, allowing myself to let Mark take charge. One of the reasons I'd finally agreed to let someone accompany me was so I didn't have to keep track of all the logistics while I was busy freaking out about seeing my biological family.

When I settled into one of the leather seats on the plane, Mark stored our bags and took the seat next to me, leaning over to fasten my seat belt like I was a toddler.

"Sorry," I mumbled.

"S'okay," he said softly.

I felt the warmth of his breath against the skin of my neck while I tried not to notice his fingers working just above my lap. I shuddered and closed my eyes, feeling so raw and exposed, I was sure I'd burst into embarrassing tears at any moment. Part of me wanted to crawl into the larger man's lap and beg him to hold me tightly with his big muscular arms.

My biological father's voice grated in my memory. I was never really sure how he knew a Johnny Cash quote since we weren't supposed to listen to that kind of music, but he repeated it often. *Life is rough, so you gotta be tough.*

I swallowed and tried to slow my breathing down. By the time we took off, I was doing better. Mark took something out of his bag and handed it to me. "Ever done one of these?" he asked.

The colorful squares of the Rubik's Cube filled me with forgotten longing, and I laughed. "No, actually. I'm one of the rare people who've never tried one. Always wanted to though."

Mark grinned at me. "Go for it. I'm terrible at it. Maybe you'll fare better."

I spent the rest of the flight concentrating on learning how to manipulate the rows to get the colors to line up. It didn't occur to me until we landed that if Mark was terrible at it, there'd been no reason to carry a Rubik's Cube with him when he traveled. Besides, what kind of adult brought a toy on a business trip anyway?

He'd brought it for me. To distract me from the difficult task ahead.

And it had worked like a charm.

I looked up at him with newfound appreciation. When he caught me staring, he winked, and I thought maybe I was going to faint dead away from a raging case of puppy love. Or... at least I thought that's what it was. The tumbling feeling in my gut, the sweaty palms, and my apparent inability to meet his eyes anymore were pretty good indicators of my silly crush on the man.

In addition to being straight, Mark was engaged to be married. When Jude and Derek had discussed who could accompany me to Utah, the subject of Mark's fiancée had come up. She was some kind of corporate consultant with a firm downtown which meant she was smart and successful. Educated.

As we moved from the airplane to the SUV waiting for us on the deserted tarmac of the Duchesne airstrip, I felt my face fill with heat in the cool dry air. Mark was used to being around successful and poised people like that. If he wasn't hanging out with all of the highly decorated ex-military men and women Joel hired at On Your Six, then he was probably spending time with his highly educated girlfriend and her other smart friends.

I thought about how many hours of remedial schoolwork it had taken me just to be able to catch up to high school students my own age. That first year in San Francisco had been spent half-sleep-deprived while I scrambled to pretend to be normal. I still wasn't there, and I always felt behind. My one solace was the music I'd been playing since I was a small child. My biological mother had been the piano player at our church, and one of my biological father's other wives had played the violin. One of my half sisters and I had been the only ones able to learn both, and we'd practiced every chance we got.

"You're being very quiet." Mark's low voice filled the cab of the vehicle, jolting me out of my memories. "Are you doing okay?"

I swallowed around the nerves and memories threatening to choke me. "I wish I'd brought my violin." It was a silly thing to say, but sometimes simply wrapping my fingers around the neck and feeling the familiar bump of the strings over the fingerboard helped me slow down and take a breath.

Mark was quiet as his eyes stayed focused on the road ahead. I knew the drive to the county office building couldn't be more than five or ten minutes, so there was no time to panic.

Try telling that to my stomach.

I clenched my hands together so tightly they turned white. Someone needed to say something before I threw up.

"Tell me about your wedding," I blurted.

The vehicle jolted a little to the right as Mark turned to gawp at me. "My wedding?"

I sucked in a breath. "Jude and Derek said you were getting married. When? Is it going to be fancy or..." What other kind of weddings were there? Casual?

I sounded so ignorant.

"Ah, no," Mark said. "Not fancy. Not anything, really. We broke up."

The words dropped like lead bricks into the dim interior of the SUV.

"Oh. Sorry." Apparently, I was so messed up, I could even offend my bodyguard without trying very hard.

Mark passed the county office and continued on toward the center of Duchesne. Before I had a chance to point out the missed turn, he glanced over at me.

"Hungry? We have time to kill, and I'm starving."

I shrugged. "Yeah, but I don't know if I can eat. Besides, good luck finding anything decent here. I think there's a Burger King."

He found the Burger King a minute later and pulled into the lot. Once we were seated with our meals, I couldn't help but snicker.

Mark looked up from taking a bite of his Whopper. "What's so funny?"

I glanced at the three giant burgers in front of him and then at the small one in front of me. "You must work out a lot."

Cripes. Did that sound like a come-on? Did he think I was flirting with him? "I, uh... I just mean..."

He winked at me and swallowed. "Part of the job." Mark flexed his biceps like a weight lifter model. "The better to guard you with. Mwah ha ha."

I almost snorted out the sip of Coke I'd taken, and just like that, he had me relaxed and laughing the rest of lunch.

8

———————

MARK

The sound of Ammon's giggles muffled behind his hand was probably the best thing ever. His face was flushed and his eyes bright. I realized in a heartbeat that I'd do anything to keep those laughs coming, especially in light of the stressful situation he was facing.

When we couldn't put off our appointment any longer, I gathered up our trash and hustled us back out to the truck. Once inside the vehicle, the tone was somber again. I turned to face him as he clicked his seat belt closed.

"Would it be okay if I sat with you during the meeting?" I asked as gently as I could. "I promise not to say anything or get in the way, but—"

"Yes," he said quickly. "Yes, please. That... that'd be nice. I mean... it would be nice to have someone there who..."

"Who's on your side," I finished for him.

Ammon nodded and blushed some more. "Yes. That. Thank you."

I wanted to touch him, give him some kind of physical reassurance like a hand squeeze or pat on the shoulder. Which was a lie. What I really wanted to do was give him the tightest hug possible and then continue to hold him close throughout his entire ordeal.

But that was a little creepy to say the least.

We drove in silence the few blocks to the county offices where the meeting with the prosecutor was scheduled to happen. I knew from the assignment memo that we weren't expecting to run into anyone from Ammon's biological family today, but it still wasn't going to be easy for him.

As we made our way from the parking lot to the entrance, I placed my hand on his lower back and kept my eyes open out of habit. Even though we weren't expecting trouble, I was here for a reason, and I didn't plan on letting anything happen to Ammon on my watch.

We entered the building and checked in with the security guard on duty before being shown to a small conference room where a young man and an older woman in suits were waiting.

As soon as they stood, I felt Ammon tense beside me, but before I had a chance to ask him about it, the woman stood and reached out a hand. "I'm Dorothy Ernst, and this is my paralegal, Nathan Kincaid. It's nice to meet you, Ammon." She shook his hand and turned to me, unable to hide the surprise she felt upon seeing my scarred face. "And you are...?"

Ammon didn't say anything, so I reached out my hand with a smile. "Mark Hayes. I'm a friend of Ammon's. Just here for moral support."

The paralegal frowned as he looked between Ammon and me, making a big production of eying the scar on my face and curling his lip up. The disgust in my appearance was clear and reminded me of the experience at the club with Raisa. "I'm sure that won't be necessary. Let me show you to a waiting area where you can—"

I kept up the smile but cut him off. "No, thanks. Ammon, why don't you take a seat?" I led him to a seat on the other side of the table and held out the chair for him. "Are you okay?" I whispered as I leaned to help push the chair in.

The slightest shake of his head set my nerves on edge. "He's... he's..." Ammon swallowed and tried again, only this time he faced the young man and forced a smile before speaking at a normal volume. "Nathan is a member of my church. I mean, *the* church. My parents' church. Right, Nathan? We grew up together."

Dorothy didn't seem to pick up on the importance of that statement. "Oh, well, isn't that something? How wonderful. It's always nice to see a friendly face in times like these. Why don't we get started?"

I glanced at Ammon before leaning over to whisper again. "Do you—"

"I'm fine," he said between a smile full of clenched teeth. Clearly he was lying, but I had to respect him to know his own comfort zone. Instead of forcing the young paralegal out of the room the way I wanted to, I settled in next to Ammon and stayed quiet while Dorothy began explaining the case.

"Ammon, your father has been arrested and charged with thirty-two counts of aggravated child abuse, one count of child abuse by choosing prayer in lieu of proper medical treatment, three counts of child bigamy, and—"

A broken sound came out of Ammon at the last phrase, and I reached for his hand under the table without thinking. He gripped my hand and moved a little closer to me before nodding for her to continue.

Dorothy gave a sympathetic smile before continuing. "Fifteen counts of the commission of domestic violence in the presence of a child, and one count of assault against a healthcare provider."

She looked up at Ammon, who'd somehow become even more pale than he normally was. I could feel his entire body trembling through our connection under the table.

"I know this is going to be difficult for you, but we'd like to ask you several questions before I tell you what we think happened. Is that all right?"

He nodded and spoke in a soft voice. "Yes, ma'am."

"When was the last time you saw your father, Donald Allred?"

Ammon cleared his throat and sat up straighter but didn't loosen the grip on my hand. "Three and a half years ago on the day after my sixteenth birthday."

Dorothy made notes on a legal pad, but I noticed Nathan's eyes remaining focused on Ammon.

"And was there a particular reason you left home that day?" Dorothy continued.

Ammon shifted in his chair. "Yes, ma'am. I actually left home the day before. When I woke up on my birthday, he told me to leave. And when I didn't move fast enough, he grabbed me and forcibly removed me from the house."

"Why did he ask you to leave?" Dorothy asked. I bit my tongue against the desire to correct her. He hadn't asked Ammon to leave, he'd kicked him the fuck out.

"He told me that I had two choices. I could marry Jenny Kimball or I could be excommunicated from the church and turned away by my friends and family."

I glanced over at him, shocked by his words. Nothing about the pressure to marry at the age of sixteen had been mentioned in our notes at On Your Six from his original rescue.

Nathan spoke up. "So it was your choice to leave?"

I whipped my head around, but Ammon squeezed my hand and answered before I could say anything. "No. It was not my choice to leave."

Nathan looked confused. "But you loved Jenny. Why didn't you just marry her?"

I felt like I was watching a tennis match. Ammon displayed an eerie sense of calm as he answered Nathan's ridiculous question.

"Because I'm gay. And because I was sixteen years old. And because Jenny was fourteen at the time which also made it illegal."

Nathan's eyes widened at Ammon's casual outing of himself.

Dorothy reached out and patted Nathan's arm. "Let's get back to the point, shall we? When your father kicked you out of the house, where did you go?"

Ammon's eyes flicked over toward me before focusing back on the tabletop in front of him. "I hid underneath the trailer. I... I was still in my pajamas and..." He tried pulling his hand from mine, but I gripped it even tighter. "And I was bleeding. I didn't want anyone to see."

Now Ammon wasn't the only one trembling, only I was trembling with rage. I wanted to get my hands on this abusive monster and beat the fuck out of him to give him a taste of his own medicine. But first, I planned on helping Ammon stay strong and get through this deposition as quickly and painlessly as possible.

"Why were you bleeding?" Dorothy asked.

Ammon looked up at her. "You'd be surprised how many obstacles there are between the back bedroom and front door in a small trailer with a family of seven living in it. My biological father made sure I hit all of them on the way out. With my face."

The words settled heavily in the conference room while Dorothy scribbled notes onto her pad and Nathan continued his study of Ammon.

Finally, Nathan asked the next question. "Why didn't you call the authorities?"

Ammon's eyes narrowed slightly at him. "I did."

Dorothy's head shot up. "There's no record of such a call. Are you sure?"

"Yes. I'm very sure. The call was answered by the 9-1-1 dispatcher, Michael Simmons. He's a member of my father's church. He advised me that if I required help, I needed to ask my father instead of getting a 'third party' involved in family business."

Nathan pressed on. "Why didn't you call the police directly instead of—"

I made a noise in my throat and locked eyes with him. Was he seriously implying a hurt, bleeding minor should have had the foresight to call multiple numbers to find help after being beaten by his own father? Was he for fucking real?

Ammon surprised me with a wry chuckle. "Because the chief of police of Tabiona at the time was Vernon Kincaid, brother to Hank Kincaid and uncle to Nathan Kincaid." He glanced at Nathan. "Do you want me to give examples of the kind of help Chief Kincaid was known for?"

Nathan began to sputter. I couldn't keep my mouth closed anymore. After a quick, whispered apology to Ammon, I spoke up. "I think it would be appropriate for Nathan to step out for the remainder of this interview."

For some reason, Dorothy looked surprised. "Because his uncle is the chief of police?"

This fucker was still active in his position?

Ammon murmured, "It's fine."

"It's not fine," I countered before looking back at Dorothy. "Because he seems to have a bias here. He's implying the victim should have made better choices which at the very least is obstructionist and at most is harassment."

She looked at her paralegal and patted him on the arm again. "Let me handle the questions, and you can help take notes, okay?"

Ammon squeezed my hand again, presumably to get me to stand down. I reached for a bottle of water in the center of the table and set it in front of him. "Do you need a break?"

When he turned to face me, his expression softened. "I'm okay. Thank you for staying with me."

I reached out, intending to brush back the hair that had fallen over one eye, but I caught myself just in time. My hand hung between us awkwardly for a minute before I rested it back on the table and curled it into a loose fist.

He was a client. At most, a friend. This sweet young man wasn't mine, and he sure as hell didn't need another asshole taking charge of him. I needed to respect his wishes and be there as support only, not a bulldog intent on ripping all comers to shreds.

Dorothy asked several more questions about Ammon's departure from Utah. Ammon answered with the approved script On Your Six gave to all of its rescue victims. A friend of a friend had offered to pick him up and take him somewhere safe. When Dorothy pressed for the name of the friend, Ammon refused to answer, claiming rightly that it was irrelevant to the cases involving his biological father.

Then she moved on to questions about Ammon's childhood and how life in the house was with his biological father. He detailed years of abuse, explained the connection between the "discipline" and the followings of his father's church which was a known extremist sect too far gone from any mainstream religion to be considered more than a cult.

When Dorothy finally had everything she needed from him, she explained what had happened to lead them to charging him.

"Jenny was rushed to the emergency room with pregnancy complications."

Ammon's head shot up. "Is she okay?"

Dorothy nodded. "She's fine now, but when she came in she was crying for your father and referred to him as her husband. He didn't have proof of marriage, but he had medical power of attorney signed over from her parents when she was fifteen. It took a while for the social worker to get the whole story, but they eventually learned that this was her second child in less than three years and that there was another young woman living in the house in the same situation."

As Dorothy spoke, Ammon lost what color he had before finally bolting out of his seat and racing from the room. I took off after him and found him retching in the men's room. I squatted down next to him as best I could and rubbed circles on his back.

"Go away," he said through a sob.

"Not happening," I replied softly, handing him a wad of tissue for his mouth.

"I don't want you to hear all of this. To see me like this."

His body was warm and solid under my hand. "You don't want me to hear how brave you were? How strong you are now? You don't want me to learn how far you've come and how incredible it is you're healthy enough to come back and make sure no one else has to go through this the way you did? You don't want me to see how sensitive and caring you are when you hear about people in pain?"

He wiped his mouth and chucked the tissue in the toilet before flushing. I stood up and backed out of the stall so he could rinse his mouth at the sink.

Once he was done, he turned to look at me for several beats, and without saying a word, he walked straight into my arms.

9

AMMON

I just needed a hug. At least that's what I told myself. But as soon as the big man's strong arms were around me and my face was mashed against his wide chest, I felt like one hug was never going to be enough.

I wanted to move in and set up shop, live against his warm strength for the rest of my freaking life. Being held by Mark Hayes was like finally finding my home. It wasn't even sexual—not that I didn't find him unbearably sexually attractive—but it was the solid comfort and complete absence of judgment that made me feel the same kind of rightness with him that I had when I'd found the Marians.

We stood like that for several minutes without speaking before Mark finally pulled back and smiled down at me. "Let's finish up so we can get the hell out of here. I saw an ice cream shop in town we can hit on the way to the hotel."

I smiled and nodded, reaching up to wipe the remaining tears from my face before taking a deep breath. "Lead the way."

The rest of the meeting was fairly straightforward since I didn't have any personal knowledge of most of the charges involved in the case. My testimony in two days' time would be used to establish a long-term pattern of behavior. Dorothy warned me about being cross-examined and gave me some pointers about how to stay calm and focus on giving simple, clear answers. By the time we left there, I was exhausted. Mark must have sensed it because instead of driving to the ice cream shop, he headed straight for the nearest hotel.

Somehow he managed to get two rooms connected together, and I had just enough energy to unlock my internal door and thank him for everything he'd done that day before I stripped down to a T-shirt and underwear before collapsing on the bed.

I heard the low rumble of Mark on the phone in the other room as I drifted off to sleep. Hopefully he wouldn't let me nap too long, but I was too zoned out to set an alarm or anything. I fell asleep quickly and slept hard, so when my phone woke me sometime later, I didn't know what day it was, much less what hour.

After fumbling my phone out of my pants pocket on the floor, I mumbled a hello. Had I been more awake, I probably wouldn't have answered without looking to see who it was.

"Ammon?" a girl's voice asked. It was familiar, but I couldn't place it while I was still half-asleep.

"This is he," I said out of habit.

"Can... can you come get me?"

"Who is this?"

During the pause, the door between our rooms slammed open and a half-naked Mark stormed through. "You okay? What's wrong?"

My jaw dropped as I took in miles and miles of inked muscles and a tight pair of black boxer briefs with a very impressive bulge in the center. I'm pretty sure I made an embarrassing whimper-choking sound, and I for sure dropped the phone.

Mark knelt on the floor by my feet and handed me the phone. "Who is it?" he asked with a frown.

As soon as I put the phone back to my ear, my brain engaged. "Ruthie?"

I covered the phone and whispered to Mark, "One of my sisters."

He stayed where he was, his hands resting on my bare knees. If I hadn't had the voice of my little sister in my ear, I would have been fighting back an embarrassing erection.

"Ammon, I'm scared without Daddy here. I want you to come home," Ruthie said. "They said you were here close by."

"How did you get this number?" I asked, still fighting to organize my brain cells.

"Mama had it. Mrs. Kincaid gave it to her when she dropped off a casserole."

I could tell from Mark's facial expression he'd heard her and wasn't happy about the news.

"Where's Gideon?" I asked, hoping one of my brothers was still around to help out.

Another pause. "He took off last year when Daddy—"

I cut her off before she could tell me something that was going to upset me even more than I already was. Just hearing the tremble in her voice was bad enough. It brought back so many memories of nights spent hiding together in our room with furniture pushed in front of the door.

"Boo, who else is there with you?" I asked her. The childhood nickname came back without thought. I'd spent hours and hours discussing my biological siblings during counseling sessions back home in San Francisco, but it had been like talking about characters on a television show. The therapist had called it a kind of compartmentalization that was commonly used to avoid cognitive dissonance. Like a kind of brain-based defense mechanism. Hearing Ruthie's voice was like opening the television set and walking right into it.

"Mama is crying and Laidy is asleep. Beth and me are trying not to wake up the babies. I think..." Another pause while sounds muffled in the background. When she came back, she whispered even more softly. "I think Zeke and Noah are gonna get mad at us if they... oh no! Gotta go!" The call cut off so fast, I pulled the phone out from my ear to stare at it.

Mark reached for the phone and set it down on the bed before moving up to sit next to me. "What do you want to do?"

I looked around the dark room. The only light came from the

direction of the bathroom. The clock on the bedside table read one in the morning.

"When I was rescued and brought to Marian House, I started seeing a counselor," I began. "The first thing she helped me do was report the conditions my siblings lived in. The brainwashing and physical abuse. The overcrowding and poverty. The lack of proper medical care."

I took a deep breath and let it out. "The social worker who'd been assigned to us was a member of the same church, so in all the years growing up, we didn't stand a chance at getting help from her. But once I was free, I reported her over and over until I finally got help three levels up. They replaced her with a man who had a stellar record. Even then, the children still weren't taken away from my parents. You know why? Because my father is a smart man. He only ever hit us boys, and he always knew how to put on a good show when the law came around. He has reasons and explanations for everything. Boys like to roughhouse. Boys can be a handful. Boys need strong discipline. On paper he looks like a stand-up, god-fearing man who is trying his hardest to provide for his family and raise obedient kids."

Mark reached for my hand again, threading our fingers together as if they'd been made to fit that way. "I'm sorry. They... *you*... deserved better."

I nodded. "The worst part? All of my siblings lied for him. Every single one. They told the social worker I'd made it all up. They said he'd never raised a hand to any of us, and I'd been the one to start something with my dad that day. AJ and Derek even brought me back here one time to see them, and they all treated me like the devil. Said I ruined their lives by sending that awful social worker around asking questions. Then they all, every single one of them, said they never wanted to see me again."

Mark let go of my hand and moved to slide an arm around me, pulling me against his side with a gentle squeeze. I laid my head on his shoulder and let out a breath, remembering the worst part.

"And then my mother filed a restraining order," I admitted in a shaky voice, feeling the flush of embarrassment fill my face. "So even if I wanted to go help my sisters, I can't."

The quiet strength of the man beside me reminded me I wasn't alone. His large hand rubbed up and down the outside of my arm as he held me close. "They'll be okay," he said in a gruff voice. "Your father isn't there. He's safely behind bars." Mark paused before turning and lifting my chin until I met his eyes. "This isn't your fault. They're not your responsibility. You've done all you can to help them."

"I know. That's the second thing the counselor helped me with. Letting go and accepting I've done all I can for them. They're not my responsibility anymore."

"They never were," Mark corrected. "You were a child."

As much as I knew it to be true, it still helped hearing him say it out loud.

"Sorry I woke you," I said, suddenly cognizant of the fact both of us were in our underwear and I was practically sitting on his lap. If I spent too much more time thinking about it, I was going to humiliate myself.

His forehead wrinkled and he reached out to run fingers through my hair. I wasn't sure he even realized he was doing it, but my groin definitely did. I yanked at the bottom of my T-shirt to try and cover the front of my boxers.

Mark's deep voice didn't help. At all. "You must be starving. You slept through dinner."

I squeaked and jumped back a little. "St-starving," I stammered.

His eyes widened in surprise before he stood up and stretched. "Then let's go find you something to eat."

As I watched his muscular backside saunter back to his room, I had a dirty thought about what that something might be. My face flamed so hot at the thought, I raced to the bathroom to douse it with cold water.

It didn't help.

10

MARK

My feelings for this young man were only growing stronger. Every time he allowed me to comfort him, I savored it. If all he needed was a friend right now, I'd be the best damned friend I could be.

But I couldn't deny being attracted to him sexually. After updating Joel on our trip so far, I'd peeked into Ammon's room to check on him and saw him sprawled facedown on the bed, his tight little ass drawing my attention immediately. His body had been laid out like a sensual buffet. The normally tidy blond hair on his head had been messy already, and his light eyelashes had brushed the tops of his flushed cheeks. His skin had appeared creamy smooth with the lightest pale hair on it, and my fingers had itched to touch him everywhere.

Now, as I stepped into a quick cold shower in hopes of ridding myself of the inappropriate erection sitting next to him had given me, I couldn't help but remember the soft sounds he'd made in his sleep and the way his smaller body felt in my arms.

Even the cold water couldn't completely rid me of this obsession that was building.

I thought of how different Ammon was from Raisa, and it was

enough for me to laugh. How could the same person be attracted to two such opposite people? Where Raisa was brash and ballsy, Ammon was gentle and humble. Raisa demanded all the oxygen in a room while Ammon would give you his very own breath if you needed it.

As I dried off and got dressed for our midnight food run, I tried to think of ways to get him out of his head and help him avoid thinking about his sisters.

We had to drive all the way to Vernal to find a Denny's. The only other option was McDonald's, but I figured we'd had enough fast food that day already. The drive took an hour, and Ammon used it to his advantage.

"Tell me what happened with your fiancée."

So much for me needing to find ways to keep his mind off his family.

"What do you want to know?" I asked.

Ammon fiddled with his fingers in his lap. "I met her once. She's pretty." He turned to look out the passenger-side window. "Never mind. That's stupid and it's none of my business."

I glanced between him and the dark road ahead. "She's very pretty," I agreed. Ammon's lips tightened together. "On the outside," I added. "Turns out, she isn't as pretty on the inside."

He turned back to me with lifted brows. "Really?"

I shrugged. "She wanted me to change. Get rid of my ink and try harder to fit into her world. I spent too long figuring out who I am to try and change it. Plus, we had different goals. Honestly, I should have never asked her out in the first place."

"Why'd you propose to her if you were so different?"

I let out a soft laugh. "I didn't. She proposed to me in front of her entire family during a Fourth of July thing."

"But you said yes."

"Yeah. I didn't want to embarrass her, and I figured that was most likely where we were going to end up anyway, so why not go ahead and get started? I wanted a family, and I thought maybe if we married quickly it would help us get to the kids stage that much faster. It was stupid, I know."

"You want kids?" Ammon asked incredulously.

"Why is that so hard to imagine?"

"No, I... I'm sorry. I didn't mean to sound surprised. I just... I want kids too." He glanced at me with wide eyes. "I don't mean... I don't mean it like that... like, not that you wanting kids has anything to do with me wanting kids, of course. I just..."

I reached over and squeezed his hand with a smile. I kind of liked it when he babbled. "Relax."

He blew out a breath. "Now you're back at square one. Are you going to start dating again? There's... um... there's a woman at my school who..."

I laughed again. "So help me, if you're getting ready to set me up on a date..."

Ammon grinned at me. "Yeah. Too soon, huh?"

I drank in the sight of a happy-faced Ammon. "Not too soon," I said, meeting his eyes for a brief second. "Just not the right person. Maybe not the right gender either."

He blinked. "Oh."

I couldn't help but run my fingers into his hair again and mess it up. He made a feeble attempt to push me away with an indignant squawk, but I was too giddy to take my hands off him yet.

"Dude," Ammon said. "You're harshing my vibe."

I gawped at him. "I'm *what*?"

"Did I say it wrong? That's what the kids at Marian House always say."

I snorted. "*Dude*, don't ever say that again."

"What?" he asked with a cheeky grin. "I can be cool. I can be hip. I've been observing the popular kids."

After pulling into the Denny's lot and putting the vehicle into park, I turned to him and brushed his hair back into place. "Don't change yourself for anyone, Ammon Marian. You're perfect just the way you are."

Our eyes stayed locked together while the air electrified between us for several beats. His lips called to me, but I forced myself to ignore the temptation. This wasn't the time to put a move on him. He was vulnerable and shaken up, not to mention facing the upcoming testimony against his own father. What he needed right now was a friend.

"C'mon. Let's get some pancakes in you," I said. "Then you can tell me more about this punk Li Jun."

He sputtered as we got out of the vehicle, proclaiming it was a false equivalency since Li Jun didn't mean anything to him and they certainly weren't *dating*.

By the time we got settled in a booth and had started on our drinks, coffee for me and orange juice for Ammon, I was ready to press him for more details.

"Yeah, but do you *want* to be dating him?" I asked.

"What? No. *No*." His cheeks were pretty much a constant apple red in my presence now, and I loved every minute of it.

"Why not?"

He flapped his hand dismissively. "He's an egotistical musician. They're unbearable. His entire life revolves around his music. As soon as he finishes his degree, he'll be traveling wherever they offer him the most money and accolades."

"Isn't that what all musicians want?"

He shook his head emphatically. "Not me. I want stability and roots. Maybe it sounds silly since I'm only twenty, but I want to settle down. One of the things I did love about the way I grew up was the focus on family and kids. It's one of the reasons I feel like I won the lottery when the Marians took me in. I love helping Jude and Derek with the kids. I miss the craziness and the noise of a full house, seeing kids playing in the yard." He laughed. "Of course, I'll never be able to afford an actual yard in the city, but maybe if I ever meet the right guy, he'll want to move somewhere more affordable."

"What do you want to do for a living if not play the violin?"

The waitress crossed the near-empty restaurant to put our plates down in front of us, her eyes lingering on my face long enough to convince me she was at least a little worried I was going to dine and dash. I shot her a smile that almost made her dump a plate full of eggs into Ammon's lap.

"Oh, sorry, hon," she muttered at him before disappearing toward the kitchen again.

Ammon didn't seem to notice any of it. "I'm double majoring in violin and education. My hope is to teach music. I also play piano, and I'm teaching myself guitar."

"How'd you get so good so fast?" I asked before tucking into my food.

"The church. It's the reason I can't hate it too much. My biological mom taught me piano so I could help play it for the kids' choir at church. When the elders realized how easy it came to me, they taught me more and more until I was helping our pianist. It made the elders so happy, my dad let me go to the church and practice when my chores were done. One of my..." He glanced up at me before looking back down at his plate. "Um, one of the other ladies taught me how to play violin. I loved it, so when one of the church elders died, his widow gave me his old violin to have all to myself. Man, I loved that thing."

"Do you still have it?"

Ammon looked down at his plate with a laugh. "Didn't you hear my story earlier? I was lucky I wasn't naked when he shoved me out that door."

I winced, remembering the situation he'd described and the fact he'd left there with nothing. "Sorry."

He shrugged. "It was nothing fancy. Just sentimental is all. But as soon as Dante learned I could play, he asked his brother Jude if he could get his hands on a basic violin at a secondhand shop or something." He laughed again. "Can you imagine Jude walking into Goodwill and picking up some old student violin?"

I grinned and shook my head, swallowing a bite of french toast before reaching for my coffee. "What'd he get you?"

Ammon's sparkling eyes met mine. "A fifteen-thousand-dollar

Gibertoni. I refused to even touch it. The danged thing made me want to throw up. He finally relented and swapped it out for an intermediate Yamaha. But he's tried to give me the Gibertoni for Christmas every year since. I think I'm finally going to let him this year. Derek took me aside and begged. He said Jude won't stop whining about it, and it's gathering dust in his studio."

That sounded like the Jude Marian I knew. It must have killed him not to foster Ammon's talent himself with the help of the fiddle player in his band. But he was about as kind and humble as Ammon was, so I was sure he completely understood how best to approach the younger man.

We spent the rest of our midnight meal talking about the Marians and music before we finished up and got back in the car for the dark drive back. Once we were on the road, Ammon turned the topic back to me.

"What do you do when you're not... bodyguarding? Guarding bodies? Providing personal security services?" He groaned and leaned forward to lay his face in his hands. "Why does it sound dirty no matter which way I say it?"

"*Close* protection detail," I added in a sultry voice. When I got the giggle out of him, I mentally pumped my fist. "I also teach self-defense. In fact, there's a great group of people your age taking Krav Maga with my buddy Mario. I think you'd really like it."

Ammon lifted an eyebrow. "My age? You sound like a boomer."

"College kids, I mean."

The dark highway stretched for miles in front of us in a way that made it feel like we were the only two people on the planet. I liked it.

"How old are you?" he asked.

"Hmm, too old to remember."

Ammon rolled his eyes and leaned back in the deep leather seat, pulling his knees up and wrapping his arms around them. "I was right about the boomer thing, then."

I ruffled his hair again. "Thirty-two, kid."

"Hey!" he yelped, pulling away from me with a laugh. "I'm not a kid. I'm a *man*." He'd tried saying the last part in his own version of a sultry voice, but it sounded so ridiculous coming out of his mouth, we both burst into laughter until tears were streaming down our faces. Once we realized the retro radio station in the background was playing "Macho Man" by the Village People, I thought I was going to have to pull over to catch my breath.

We cranked up the music and sang along with '80s songs the rest of the way to the hotel. When we arrived, a thin band of sunrise was barely peeking up from the horizon behind us.

"You going to be able to get some more sleep?" I asked as I held the glass hotel door open for him. "We don't have to be anywhere today."

"Yeah, probably. But..." He looked up at me before his eyes skittered away down the hallway and down to the floor. The confident, singing friend from the drive home was gone again, just like that.

I reached for his shoulder and turned him back toward me. "But what?"

"There's this hike I used to like to do. It's a place called Crystal Lake. Probably... I don't know, maybe two hours from here? Anyway, I wondered if maybe I could borrow the car and—"

"We'll both go," I said quickly. As if I would leave him alone with his thoughts on the day before his father's trial. "I'd love to see it, and I haven't been on a hike in forever."

Ammon's lip curved up in a shy smile. "Yeah? You like to hike?"

I nodded. "And fish, and camp. I love the outdoors. Didn't really even learn that about myself till I joined the military."

We stepped up to our respective room doors, side by side. "Well," Ammon said. "I guess I'll see you when... whenever we get up. Sleep well."

"You too," I said. Even though I wanted to say so much more. Like how much I'd enjoyed getting to know him a little better, how beautiful and brave his heart was, how luminous his smile was. How, in just a few hours with him, I'd had more fun than any other person I'd ever dated and had felt more myself than I had in ages.

When I slid into my bed alone, I tried desperately to listen for him through the crack in the door between our rooms, but he must have already been settled in bed.

I fell asleep to the fantasy of his lithe body next to mine and the deep, solid conviction that when we returned to the city after his family ordeal, I would find a way to make my fantasy a reality.

11

AMMON

"All rise. The Court of Duchesne County is now in session, the Honorable Judge William T. Naylor presiding."

When my father was brought into the courtroom shortly after the judge, I closed my eyes and tried to remember the way Mark's muscular body had looked in front of me on the hiking trail the day before, the way the sun had felt on my skin, and the sound of our combined laughter when Mark had been spooked by a tiny little garter snake on the side of the trail.

It had been the perfect day, like two friends enjoying a day off together instead of a professional security escort and his needy client killing time before a trial. But now there was no escaping reality. This is what we'd come for. For me to testify against my father in hopes of sending him to prison for the rest of his life.

I had mixed feelings about it. On the one hand, he deserved to go to jail. There was no doubt he was a child abuser, master manipulator, and rapist. But he was also the sole breadwinner in the family. He provided for at least eleven people. What would happen to them when he went to prison? I certainly didn't have much extra money to contribute. While the Marians had been overwhelmingly generous with me, I tried my hardest not to take more than the tuition help they'd offered and the free room and board at Jude's place.

With my eyes still closed, I was surprised to feel Mark's warm hand take hold of mine. I blinked at him and saw his reassuring smile next to me.

I wasn't alone.

Letting out a breath, I leaned my shoulder into his. What I really wanted to do was climb in the man's lap and bury my face in his neck, but I refrained. Just knowing he was there to support me was comfort enough.

My father didn't notice I was in the courtroom, so when I was finally called to the witness stand by name, his head swiveled around in surprise.

I froze partway to the stand, locked in his narrow-eyed gaze as if I was a naughty child again caught doing something I shouldn't. All the same desperate, terrified feelings came rushing back as if time hadn't passed between then and now, as if this man still held power over me.

A throat cleared somewhere in the room, drawing my attention away for a split second.

Mark.

He crossed his eyes and flashed me a silly grin. It wasn't enough to make me bark out a laugh, but it was enough to remind me that this was life. And life was crazy. Ups and downs, scary times and exciting times. Even in the midst of something serious, it was okay to catch a break and remember that not everything would be this hard.

I continued onto the stand and took my oath, half-worried my hand would burn when I placed it on the Bible in front of my father. Considering just how far I'd strayed from the "accepted path" of my father's church, I couldn't think of myself as anything other than the worst kind of sinner today. My brain knew that was a lie, but old habits and thoughts were very hard to break.

While Dorothy led me through some basic questions about my identity, my father's eyes pinned me in place. I tried not looking in his direction, but it was hard. He'd always been the biggest presence in any room.

I tried focusing on Mark. When I'd first met him, I'd been intimidated and tongue-tied, but after spending so much time with him, I felt comfortable with him in a way I never expected to. I knew he wouldn't mind me using him as a focal point to get through my testimony.

"Tell me what happened the day of your sixteenth birthday," Dorothy said in a kind but clear voice.

I was grateful the rest of my biological family wasn't here. As soon as I'd entered the courtroom, I'd scanned every face for anyone familiar. Dorothy had explained they weren't coming because apparently my father had forbidden them to see him in this "farce" of a trial. I had mixed feelings about them not being here, but I was glad that at least Mark wouldn't see a row of three women—well, four now if what they said about Jenny was true—all claiming my father as their husband. The very idea of it humiliated me. I'd been raised by three women and had loved them each in their own way, but when push came to shove, none of them had stood up for me. None of them had fought for me. So, no. I was ultimately glad they weren't there.

But three of the church elders sat right behind my father with their own stern expressions and crossed arms. I glanced back at Mark and began to tell him the story all over again. As I spoke, his jaw tightened a few times, but he kept his eyes on me. He kept his expression open, and every time my eyes traced the scar that ran down over his face, I was reminded that I wasn't the only one who'd been hurt and come out the other side of it.

I didn't know what had happened to him exactly, but during the hike the day before, he'd mentioned growing up in a tough part of Chicago where it was just his dad and him. His mom had taken off when he was very little. I thought about the irony of him growing up without a mother and me growing up with several. My experience was a testament to the fact you could have plenty of mothering and not benefit from it any more than someone who'd grown up with no mother.

I tried focusing back on the questions Dorothy was asking. Thankfully, they were straightforward and expected.

It was when the defense attorney—my father's attorney—cross-examined me that everything went downhill. It happened slowly without my realizing exactly what was happening. It was like the fable about cooking a frog.

"Isn't it true that your father only demanded you marry Jenny Kimball because you'd had premarital sex with her and discovered she was pregnant?"

I blinked at the attorney in confusion. "Uh, no, sir."

"Are you saying she wasn't pregnant?"

I couldn't speak to whether anyone was pregnant or not. I only knew I was still a virgin to this day. "N-no, sir. I'm saying—"

"Strike that. Didn't your father discover Jenny hiding under your bed late one night?"

I remembered the night Jenny had snuck over to borrow my sister's purple sweater. I'd shared a room with two of my sisters and three of my brothers. All of us had been in there together, asleep until Jenny's and Mary's giggles had woken us up. When we'd heard the sound of my father's footsteps, we'd known we were going to be in serious trouble, so we'd told Jenny to hide. It had happened a full year before my sixteenth birthday and had nothing to do with why I'd been kicked out of the house.

"Yes, but—"

He cut me off with a raised hand. "Would you say your father was the type of man to take responsibility for his children's mistakes and offer a young, pregnant, unwed woman a home and support when she needed it most?"

Before I could unpack what he was asking, Dorothy stood to object. The defense attorney immediately withdrew the question, but the implication was already out there: I was the father of Jenny's baby. My father was the kind soul who'd taken responsibility when his good-for-nothing son had refused.

By the time the truly horrible questions happened, I was half-numb and trying desperately to escape to that little place in my head

I'd almost forgotten about. The place I went when real life was too hard, too scary, and I just needed a minute or an hour or a day to myself. My eyes stayed on Mark's face out of desperation, but my brain was so scrambled, I interpreted his growing anger at the interrogation as judgment against me, anger at me.

I couldn't handle someone else I cared about thinking the worst of me, so I completely shut down. I stared down into my lap and mumbled a yes or no to the rest of the questions. If they required a longer answer, I did my best to keep it as short as possible.

The character assassination was swift and brutal, and after it was over, I wondered how any human being who'd witnessed it could even look me in the eyes. All the hopes I'd had of continuing to foster a friendship with Mark were dashed. With only an hour's cross-examination, my father's team had reminded me I was nothing. I was a sinner, a whore, a disgrace in the eyes of God, and an ungrateful child whose goal in life had always been to find greener pastures.

It had been a long time since I'd felt so small and worthless, undeserving. And this time it was worse.

This time I had so much more to lose.

12

MARK

He was so fucking brave. But sitting there watching him disappear inside himself broke my heart into a million tiny pieces. I wanted to scream and cry, beat the shit out of both the attorney and the monster he represented, but if I wanted to be there for him when it was all over, instead of sitting in a Duchesne jail cell, I needed to keep silent.

While Ammon sat in that seat and maintained his pristine manners and humble respect for authority even as he was being trashed on the stand, I fell absolutely head over heels in love with him.

He was everything I'd ever valued in the world: kind, thoughtful, giving. He was, at times, light and laughter. But he was also darkness and pain. Watching him revert to the darkness was an education in how far Ammon must have come from the broken boy AJ had whisked out of there several years before. The hours spent in therapy and the loving effects of being surrounded by the Marians had brought him light-years beyond the pain and poverty of his childhood, the conviction that he wasn't good enough.

And I'd be damned if I was going to let him stay back there in that mental place.

He needed to know that he'd done an amazing job. The jurors believed him. Two of the women had even shed tears as he'd begun to shake and shut down on the stand. His father was going away, there was no doubt in my mind.

As soon as his testimony was done and he stumbled down from the witness chair, I wrapped an arm around him and led him straight to the SUV in the lot outside. He was even paler than usual, and his entire body shook. I murmured reassurances and praise at him during the short drive back to the hotel, but I wasn't sure he heard any of it.

I hustled him into my room, but before I could get him through the door into his own room, he pushed me down on my bed and crawled onto my lap, straddling me and sliding his arms around my neck before finally letting go.

"Oh, baby," I said, pressing a kiss against his temple and tucking his face under my chin. My heart screamed for him. If there was anything I could do to carry his burden, I would. Holding him seemed like the opposite. Not a burden, but the best gift the man could have given me in that moment. "Let it out, sweetheart. You're safe. I'm here."

I scooted us back until I felt the support of the headboard behind me, and I pulled his shaking body even tighter against me. He cried for a long time, enough to make tears fall down my own cheeks as I tried my hardest to calm and reassure him. My hands ran up and down his back and into his hair, and it was only the heavy weight of his emotion that kept me from hardening into a full erection with his body that close to mine.

But when he finally quieted down and pulled away to wipe his tears, my body couldn't help but react. He was goddamned gorgeous. His blue eyes sparkled brightly from the crying, his eyelashes were wet and spiky, and his face was flushed from being against the heat of my neck. His lips were full and deep pink as if he'd been biting them.

I let out a noise from my throat as I reached up to cup his face. Ammon's eyes widened.

"You're perfect," I said softly. "Please don't let anyone convince you otherwise."

I drew my thumbs under his eyes to catch some of the remaining tears. Ammon's eyes mapped my face before locking on my eyes. We'd already had so many moments like this where electricity sparked between us and a kiss seemed inevitable, but every time it happened, I'd forced myself to wait. I hadn't wanted to take advantage of him when he was vulnerable.

But this time was different because Ammon finally spoke up for what he wanted.

"Kiss me," he whispered. "*Please.*"

I leaned my forehead against his and closed my eyes. "You don't mean it," I tried, using all my strength to keep from taking everything of his I possibly could.

His hands moved over my chest. "I've never meant anything more."

"Ammon," I tried. "You're upset. You—"

His soft lips brushed against mine, tentatively at first before pressing in for a full kiss. But then he laughed, and I blinked my eyes open in surprise.

"I'm sorry," he said with another giggle. "It just... it feels so good. I can't believe you let me kiss you."

Ammon Marian laughing was the best thing on earth.

"Why wouldn't I let you kiss me when it's all I've been dreaming about for the past two days?" I asked.

His smile dropped. "What?"

Instead of answering, I leaned in and kissed him again, holding on to the back of his head and feeling the silky strands of his hair between my fingers.

Ammon moaned into my mouth, and I took the opportunity to press in with my tongue and taste him. Then it was my time to groan. He was just as sweet as I'd imagined, and every little indrawn breath and touch of his hands set my entire body on fire. I couldn't help but press my hard cock up against his ass. He squeaked and pulled away from the kiss, glancing at me with such surprise in his face, I almost laughed.

"You're... you have..." Ammon stammered and looked down at where our laps were joined before he glanced back at me with a scarlet face. "You're straight."

I shook my head. "I'm bi."

"But you..." He seemed to remember that bisexual meant I could have a female ex-fiancée and still get hard for a man. "You're... you're really bi?"

I nodded. "Right now I feel more Ammon-sexual though. In case you couldn't tell."

He wrinkled his forehead at me. "Have you ever been with a guy?"

I leaned in and kissed his neck. "Mm-hm." I pulled back and looked at him. "Have you?"

Ammon looked away and tried to squirm out of my hold. I held him still.

"Baby, stop," I said as gently as I could. "It doesn't matter to me either way. I just want to know so I'm careful. I don't want to do anything that makes you feel uncomfortable."

He leaned in and pressed his forehead to my chest. "Neverbeen-withanyone," he said all at once into my shirtfront.

My heart was so full, I wanted to laugh. I kissed the top of his head. "Then come up here and let me give you a proper first kiss."

He straightened up and looked at me like this was some kind of trick. "We already had a first kiss."

I cupped his hot cheeks in my palms and brought his face close to mine. "I want a do-over," I whispered against his lips. He made a little whimpering sound that went straight to my dick.

The kiss was everything. It was sweetness and desire, love and laughter, promise and expectation. It was the answer to a question I'd asked myself a million times before. Why had I never felt settled with anyone? Why hadn't any of the people I'd dated in the past felt just right?

Because I was meant to be here, with him. He was mine. I knew that as well as I knew how to salute a superior officer or as well as I knew how to draw a weapon and aim true.

We kissed until Ammon was breathless and begging. My hands had rucked up his shirt and snuck underneath to feel the warm smooth skin of his back.

"Please. Oh, oh, *please.*"

My dick was so hard it ached. Ammon's hips tilted into me, pressing his own hard cock against my stomach.

"Mark," he breathed. "I need..." He sucked in a breath. "I want..."

His chest raised and lowered with each gasping breath.

"Anything," I promised. "Anything you want is yours, sweetheart."

He threw his arms around my neck and hugged me tightly. "I'm scared," he whispered.

I pulled him away and cupped his cheeks again. "Hey, hey. No. Nothing to be scared about. We're not doing anything, anything at all, that you're uncomfortable with. Hell, if you wanted to go in your own room right now and be alone, that would be fine with me."

"It would?"

I didn't want to lie to him. "Okay, maybe it would be very hard for me to not peek in on you every few minutes, but yeah."

His lips curled up in a smile. "I definitely don't want to be alone right now."

I returned his grin. "No?"

Ammon shook his head. "But... but I'm not ready for more than kissing right now." He looked worried, like I was going to toss him off my lap unless he let me have his ass.

"Ammon. Please understand that I wasn't even going to try and kiss you yet because of everything you're going through right now. The last thing I want is to put any more pressure on you than you've already been feeling with this trial." I leaned in and kissed his nose. "I have an idea. Why don't you take a shower and change into pajamas? I'll go pick us up some sodas and snacks, and when I get back, we'll have a movie marathon. Maybe some rom-coms or action-adventure movies. What do you say?"

He nodded and smiled. "That sounds really nice."

I sat up and smacked his butt before nudging him off me. "Go before I start kissing you again."

He hopped up and headed toward the door to his room before turning back to me with a cheeky grin. "Would that be such a bad thing?"

I growled and lunged in his direction, but he squeaked and slammed the door closed between us with a laugh.

I was still smiling like a lovesick fool when I made my way outside into the evening half-light and noticed a young man sitting on the sidewalk next to the SUV.

When I approached, he looked up. "Are you with Ammon Allred?"

He was skinny and blond like Ammon, but he looked like he hadn't had a decent meal or shower in a while.

"Who's asking?"

The guy stood up, revealing the same petite frame Ammon had. They had to be related.

"I'm Gideon. His brother."

And then the kid wavered dangerously on his feet. I lunged forward to grab his arm to keep him from pitching headfirst onto the asphalt.

"Shit," I muttered, pulling out my phone. This kid needed more than a decent meal. He needed medical attention.

13

AMMON

At first I thought Mark might have gotten lost. It was a small town, but he'd never been there before. I tried not to think about how well he'd seemed to navigate the few days we'd already been here, but I knew he was used to traveling to new places.

After an hour, my stomach began to hurt as I worried he'd changed his mind about me and was staying away while he figured out a gentle way of letting me down. Maybe he'd gotten away from me long enough to realize how stupid it would be to get involved with someone who had my kind of baggage.

But Mark wasn't a coward, and he'd always been kind to me. Even if he didn't want to be with me that way, I didn't think he was cruel enough to leave me alone tonight.

I sent him a text after an hour and a half.

Me: *Did you get lost?*

My phone rang immediately with a call from him.

"Are you okay?" I asked as soon as the call connected.

"Baby, shit. I'm so glad you called. I've been trying to call your hotel room because I didn't have your cell number in my phone. I even tried to get the lady at the front desk to knock on your door. I was worried."

I glanced across the room at the hotel phone and noticed the handset askew on the cradle. "Oh, sorry. I think it's—"

He cut me off. "No, no, it's fine. I'm just glad you texted. I'm at the hospital."

"What?" I screeched, scrambling for my jeans. "What happened? Were you in an accident?"

"No, I'm fine. I promise. I wanted to come get you, but I didn't want to leave Gideon alone."

I put the phone on speaker and quickly changed out of my pajamas. "Gideon, my brother Gideon?"

"He's okay too. Take a breath, sweetheart. Everyone is okay, I promise. When I left you and went out to the car, he was waiting there. He was hungry and dehydrated, that's all."

"Where are you? The hospital in Roosevelt? I'm coming there." I pulled on my running shoes.

I heard someone speaking in the background, and then Mark said, "Hang on, he wants to talk to you. And don't leave yet."

"Ammon?"

Hearing Gideon's voice over the line made me feel like I was going to cry again. It had been so long since I'd heard it. "Gid? Are you okay?"

"No. Not really." His voice was a mixture of tears and laughter. "I miss you. Sorry I messed up your night. I just... I just heard you were here and I... I wanted to see you."

"Where have you been?" I asked. "Ruthie said you took off a while ago."

"Yeah. It's a long story, but, um... it sounds like maybe it's not so different from yours. Is... is Mark your boyfriend?"

I wondered if I was on speakerphone. "Uh, no. Not really? No?"

Great, now I sounded like a doofus. But Gideon's laugh was worth it.

"Well, he might feel differently, brother," Gideon said with a laugh. "He nodded his head with a maniacal grin when I asked the question."

"Really?" I asked in an unbearably high octave. I cleared my throat. "He did? Really?"

Gideon chuckled again, and it brought back good childhood memories of late nights giggling under the covers together. I missed him.

Mark took the phone back, and I could hear the smile in his voice. "How about you ask me that question when I get back. I should be there in about forty minutes. You must be starving."

"I'm okay, but what about Gideon?"

Gid's voice came back on the line. "I'm fine. They want to keep me overnight with an IV. Honestly, I'm going to enjoy sleeping in a decent bed. Mark said he'll bring you back in the morning and we can talk then, okay?"

"Are you sure?"

"Very sure. Let me hydrate and get some sleep. I'll be in better shape in the morning. And, Ammon?"

"Yeah?"

"I love you."

I sat back on the bed and let out a whoosh of breath. "I love you too. Sleep well. See you in the morning."

The sound of Gideon and Mark talking in the background came over the line before Mark came back on. "Still there?"

"Still here."

"I noticed a couple of pizza places around here. That good with you?"

I nodded and swallowed. Mark Hayes was a good man. "Yes please."

"Stay on the phone with me while I drive back?" he asked in a softer voice.

I kicked off my shoes and lay back on the bed. "Tell me what happened, and don't leave anything out."

As he made his way back to me, he told me about Gideon waiting for him by the car and then nearly passing out. Mark suspected Gideon had been living rough since leaving home, and he was fairly sure he'd been kicked out for being gay.

"Really?" I asked. "I didn't..." I thought back through what I remembered of Gideon. Had I seen any signs of his attraction to boys? He was only a year younger than I was and one of my fully biological siblings like Ruthie, Adelaide, and our brother Tommy. "I didn't know he was gay, but then again, he wouldn't have known I was either. It was too shameful, even to admit it to ourselves, much less each other."

"I hope you don't feel that way anymore," Mark said carefully.

"No," I said with a laugh. "Not after becoming a Marian, are you kidding?"

Mark chuckled too. "Good point."

He paused to order the pizza and then came back on. "Hope extra anchovies are okay with you," he said. "I like me some fishy breath when I'm kissing someone."

Even though I was in the room alone, I blushed. "You'd better not have."

"Yeah? You have plans for me, sweetheart?"

"Mm-hm," I said, reaching down to adjust myself. I needed to change back into pajamas if he was going to talk to me in that rumbly voice.

"More kissing, maybe?"

"Mm-hm."

"You're going to get me arrested for public indecency, Ammon Marian," he said in a low voice. "I'm not sure the laws in Utah are very forgiving, especially for someone who looks like me."

I knew he meant the tats and scars, but I chose to misinterpret. "Someone big and strong? Handsome?... *Sexy*?"

Lord only knew why I whispered the last word since I was the only person in the room. I shouldn't have been surprised when Mark barked out a laugh.

"How did it feel saying that word out loud?" he teased. "And how red are your cheeks right now?"

The tadpoles danced in my stomach, but this time it was nervous excitement. I was flirting with a man who seemed to like me back. I was flirting with a man who'd *kissed* me.

"Mark?"

"Yeah, baby?"

The tadpoles swam higher, nudging into my heart. "What if I wanted to do more than kiss?"

Silence descended between us for several beats. "Well, first, you'd have to be very sure."

"I am," I blurted. "I mean, I would be. I am."

I heard someone call Mark's name and assumed the pizza was ready. After some shuffling around and the sound of a car door closing, he came back on the line.

"And you'd have to know that at any point you could change your mind and that would be okay. *More* than okay."

I could hear the hesitant excitement in his voice, but he was being so careful. "I would. I do," I assured him.

After more silence, he spoke again. "I want you to know that I'm serious about you, Ammon. This isn't... I'm not interested in just messing around with you. I hope you know that."

He couldn't be serious, but I was going to go along with it on the off chance he was. Everything I'd learned about him screamed he was a man of integrity. I couldn't imagine him stringing me along just to get lucky. If nothing else, I was a poor bet for hot sex since I had to come off as a terrible prude.

But I still had insecurities, and the biggest one of them had a name.

"What about Raisa? I don't want to—"

"Shh. Raisa and I are over. I promise. Even if nothing happened between you and me, things with Raisa would already be over for good."

Was he saying something *could* happen between the two of us? The reassurance was nice to hear, and it gave me the guts to do something I never would have imagined.

Ask him out.

"When we get back to the city, will you go out on a date with me?" I blurted it, my tongue tumbling over the words as they raced to get out before I lost my nerve.

His warm laughter made me grin. "Sweetheart, just try and stop me."

We spent the rest of his drive back talking about where we would go, what we'd do, and places we liked most in San Francisco. By the time I heard him open the hotel room door, I'd changed back into pajama pants and made a picnic nest for us on his bed.

He strode into the room and slid the pizza box onto the dresser before growling, "C'mere."

I jumped off the bed and flung myself at him, wrapping my arms and legs around him and drinking him in.

"God, you feel so good," he murmured, tightening his arms around me.

I tangled my fingers in the back of his hair, relishing the freedom to touch him this way. The fact he still wanted me after having had several hours to reconsider was simply amazing.

I pulled back and met his eyes. "Is he really okay?"

Mark reached up to run a finger along my cheek. "Mm-hm. Promise. Mercy, you're beautiful."

My heart fluttered away with my breath.

"Stop trying to distract me," I whispered before leaning in to kiss him.

We kissed for several minutes before he set me down. "You need to eat. It's been hours."

As we ate, I asked him a few more questions about Gideon to make sure he was really okay staying overnight on his own.

"I'm surprised you didn't hear anything, actually," Mark said, taking a sip of his soda. "They sent like a million first responders, and everyone came screaming into the lot with sirens on and lights blazing."

"I took a really long shower," I admitted sheepishly.

Mark moved the pizza and sodas to the bedside table before pulling me over to straddle his lap. It was quickly becoming my favorite place to sit.

"And what exactly did you do in the shower that took so long?" he teased.

My face heated. "Um... n-nothing," I lied.

Mark's hands roved around to sneak under my shirt. I caught my breath as my heart hammered in my chest. His warm palms against my skin were everything.

"I don't believe you," Mark said before nibbling a line up the side of my neck. "Were you a dirty boy in there?"

I made a few embarrassing sounds as his lips found my collarbone and sucked. I felt it all the way down to my groin until I was painfully hard. "M-maybe. Oh... oh my goodness."

Mark snorted softly against my neck. "I think if I ever heard an actual curse word out of your mouth, I might pass out."

"I can say curse words," I said, sounding like a silly child.

Mark's chuckle vibrated against my chest. "Please don't."

"Damn... damnation," I tried, still way more concerned with how I was feeling than what I was saying.

His chuckle turned into a full laugh. "No."

"C-cock." Because that was all I could think about anyway.

His eyes met mine with so much heat in them, I finally understood the meaning of the word *swoon*.

"Is that a request?" he asked.

"Maybe," I said before closing my eyes and putting my hands over my face. "Oh my goodness, I can't believe I just said cock out loud to you."

Mark pulled my hands away and kissed each palm. His eyes twinkled with mischief. "Was it easier the second time around?"

I thought about it. "Yeah, actually it was."

Whatever anyone called it, mine was hard. It made an embarrassing tent of my lounge pants right there between us. I tried not to draw attention to it when really, it was desperate for attention.

I tilted my hips into him without thinking.

"Fuck," Mark groaned. His hands moved down to cup my butt and pull me in again. "You're driving me crazy. I want to touch you everywhere. Peel off these clothes and run my mouth all over you."

That sounded amazing. Every inch of my skin was on board with his wish. It was time to be brave. "Can we...?" I swallowed. "Can we do that, please?"

The answering look on his face almost made me come in my pajama pants.

14

MARK

With twin splotches of deep red on his pale cheeks and lips wet from my kisses, Ammon was the most beautiful human being I'd ever seen. His eyes were alight with desire, and the flutter of his thundering pulse moved beneath the thin skin of his throat.

I moved him around until he was lying on his back underneath me, his blond hair almost as light as the crisp white pillowcase below.

I started by kissing those flags of red on the apples of his cheeks. One by one, I dropped openmouthed kisses down his cheeks to his jawline as my palms moved under the front of his T-shirt to the warm skin of his abdomen.

He sucked in a breath. "Holy cow. Oh, oh *man*." The murmured words made me giddy. I moved my hands up to brush my thumbs over his nipples. "*Mpfhhh*."

Ammon arched back his neck, so I leaned in to suck on his exposed Adam's apple.

"So beautiful," I told him in a low voice. "So expressive and responsive. That's it, baby. Just lie back and feel good."

His eyes were glazed and half-lidded. He reached up to grab the headboard and arched his cock up into my belly.

"Please, Mark. I want..." He groaned and squeezed his eyes closed for a beat before opening them again and looking right at me. "I want you to touch me. Stroke me. Make me come. I want to come with you."

I sat back and reached for the hem of his shirt to draw it over his head. When he lay back down on the pillow, his hair was every which way. His slender chest was so pale, it was almost translucent, but he had some slight muscle definition in his shoulders and arms. I'd seen him at the gym at work a few times with Joel kicking and punching the heavy bags.

The rounded shoulders and biceps got their fair share of kisses as I leaned back down and explored his chest with my mouth. As I worked, Ammon's hips continued to push up into me, seeking friction for his dick. After I took my own shirt off, I could feel the damp patch on the front of his pants every time he thrust into me.

It only made me hotter and more desperate to see him and taste him everywhere, but I'd be damned if I risked going too fast for him.

After kissing my way down his belly to the top of his pajama pants, I looked up at him for permission to go further.

"This is at your speed, sweetheart," I reminded him. "We can stop here and I'll be happy to cuddle and kiss the shit out of you. We don't need to go any further than you—"

Ammon reached down and slid his thumbs into the waistband of his pants before shucking them off and tossing them aside. His slim, pink dick jerked up and down when I glanced at it.

"Mmm." I ran my hands along his thighs and leaned in to kiss the tip of his erection where the precum had left a sticky, smeared trail. "Mm-hmm."

Ammon's hands threaded into my hair, and his breaths came in short, panting sounds. "I'm not... I might not be able to... to last..."

After teasing his dick with my tongue, I sucked it all the way into my mouth and slurped it for several quick strokes with abandon. Ammon screamed and arched as he came.

"Oh god! Oh god," he cried, clenching his fingers into my hair. "*Aghh.*"

I swallowed down every drop before releasing him and licking him clean. He continued to make little exclamations as the final shock waves hit his body. I moved up to check in with him.

"Okay?" I asked softly, brushing sweat-damp hair from his forehead.

He looked at me like I was the second coming of Christ, wide eyes and mouth open in an O shape. It slowly turned to a lazy grin.

"*Mm-hmm.*"

I smirked down at him. "That good, huh?"

His own smile was shy and goddamned adorable. "I just got a blowjob from the hottest guy on the planet."

I laughed. "That right?"

Ammon's hands came up to hold the sides of my face. "Mm-hm. And now he's going to kiss me with that same mouth."

Desire pooled heavy in my gut as I leaned in to do as he wished. We kissed for several long minutes as Ammon's hands moved more bravely over my shoulders and down my back until his fingers began to sneak inside the back of my pants.

"Off," he muttered against my lips. "No fair."

I pulled away from his tempting mouth and reached for the button on my slacks. Ammon clapped a hand over his mouth just as a nervous giggle escaped.

"You're not supposed to laugh when a man takes his clothes off in front of you," I reminded him, lowering my zipper. I slid the pants down and cupped my dick through my boxer briefs, keeping eye contact with him. When I stroked myself, his eyes flared wider.

Finally he seemed to shake off his orgasm stupor and knelt up to help pull the rest of my clothes off, murmuring sweet little things under his breath like, "Off," and, "More," and "Wow."

When I was finally fully naked, he stared at my dick like it might bite him.

I reached out to tip his chin up so he'd meet my eyes. "It won't hurt you unless you want it to," I said gently.

He blinked. "Oh. *Oh!* No, I..." He looked back down and reached to give it a tentative stroke. He grinned. "It's distracting." He looked up at me. "Me likey."

I wasn't sure I'd ever laughed so much during sex before, but with Ammon it felt natural. I could be myself, and I knew he was being himself, even if it was a shy version of him.

"Good," I said, leaning in for more kisses. "Maybe that means you'll want to spend more time with it."

Despite the late hour, his cheeks were still smooth, void of any noticeable stubble. He was so young, but I couldn't seem to stay away. The idea of walking away from him to allow someone more appropriate, someone better, to have him was terrifying. I simply wasn't that selfless.

We knelt together on the bed with our tongues in each other's mouths until he pushed me down on my back and crawled on top of me. His dick had filled again and brushed lightly against my own. I arched up into him, seeking more contact with it.

"Do you want to, um, have sex?" he asked, pulling away again. "Like, um—" His eyes flicked away.

"No," I said quickly. "I mean, yes," I chuckled. "Of course I do. I want to feel you every which way there is. But no, we're not going to do anything more than we're already doing tonight, okay? Is that good with you?"

He looked back at me. "It's not that I don't want to. Actually, I do. Very much. But I don't want it to be bad for you and I don't know what I'm doing, so it would probably be a disaster and then there's the whole—" He flapped his hand around like I was supposed to know what he meant.

I pulled his face back down for a kiss to stop his nervous babbling. He moaned into my mouth as his entire body relaxed against me.

"This is good too," he murmured between kisses. "This is really good."

We kissed and felt each other up, humping together like teenagers until I remembered I had some good lube in my bag.

"Hold on," I said, scooting out from under him. "Hold that thought. Stay right there. Don't move."

I dug through my bag until I found it, holding it up triumphantly. When I turned around, Ammon was stroking himself on the bed.

"Oooh, bring that here. What is that?"

"Baby, if you tell me you don't know what lube is, we're going to have to slow way down and conversate," I said, knowing full well he had to know what lube was since he'd been present at several sex toy parties the Marians had thrown.

"Shut up," he said. "I meant which kind. There's one that I like that has an obscene illustration of a peach on it. Believe me, my brothers think it's hysterical to give me Love Junk gifts for every holiday."

I lifted an eyebrow and handed him the bottle before leaning down to run kisses up the inside of his thigh. His balls were dusky pink and naturally hairless. As my mouth drew closer, they tightened and lifted until Ammon's fingers tangled into my hair and pulled gently.

"Come up here or you're never going to get a chance to come," he said in a breathy voice. "It'll be the Ammon show. All Ammon orgasms all the time."

"I like that idea." I moved up his body and reached for the lube. "I love seeing you experience pleasure. I could watch you come over and over until the sun rises and sets again."

After slicking up my hand, I reached for his dick and pulled it against mine, moving my grip until I had both of our shafts sliding together.

Ammon's hands clutched my shoulders. "*Ffff...*" he began. "*Freak,* that feels amazing."

He was right. Understatement of the year. We thrust together, picking up speed until Ammon wrapped both of his hands around mine and squeezed.

"Mark, *hnghh*. Mark!" He squeezed his eyes closed and thrust one last time until his release coated our hands. The clench of his body and cries of his release finally gave me permission to let go. I came with a roar followed by several grunts as my body continued to feel pulses of my orgasm long after the initial climax.

"Oh fuck," I said, sucking in a breath. "Fuck."

I grabbed my undershirt to wipe my hands with and did a cursory clean of Ammon's belly before stretching back on top of him for some lazy kisses. His arms and legs wrapped around me in a possessive hold.

After a while, I slid off to the side so I didn't crush him. I rested my head on my hand and propped myself on my elbow so I could look down on him, laid out like a buffet on the bed.

I drew fingertips down his chest. "You blow me away," I said softly. "The first time I saw you, I had a religious experience."

He snorted and pushed my shoulder as if I'd made a joke.

"I'm serious," I said. "I thought you were an angel on earth. The sun shone down on you and I..." I sucked in a breath. "I thought I'd never seen a more perfect human being." Ammon's eyes widened.

I continued, reaching up to brush the hair from his face and then cup his cheek. "It scared me. You were so young. So sweet... I thought maybe there'd never be someone good enough for you, and I sure as hell knew it wasn't me."

"Why not? Why not you? You're amazing."

I shook my head. "No. I'm as flawed as they come. I've done so much stupid shit and made so many bad decisions. I'm not educated. I'm not good in social situations. I wouldn't know the first thing about religion or the Bible. I—"

Ammon's long fingers pinched my mouth closed. "Nope. I reject your self-judgment." He shoved me over onto my back and crawled on top of me, bracing his hands to either side of my head and leaning in to meet my eyes. "You're strong and protective, tender and sweet. You stand up for what's right and condemn what's wrong. You served your country. You make a living from keeping people safe."

He leaned in and kissed me softly on the lips before pulling back and smiling down at me. "You open doors for me and make sure I wear my seat belt. You keep track of whether I'm hungry or not. You sneak into people's violin concerts and donate your time to teaching self-defense at Marian House. You're a good man, Mark Hayes. And I feel like I won some kind of lottery to be the one here with you right now."

His words made my heart slam against my chest. I reached up to cup his cheeks. "I'm falling for you," I confessed in a rough whisper. "Total and complete freefall."

Ammon flushed and grinned wider. "Then we fall together, sailor."

15

AMMON

After the incredible conversation we had in which he'd confessed to falling for me, I fell promptly and rudely to sleep right there on his chest. I awoke sometime later to the low mumble and flickering light of the television. Mark's hands moved idly over my back and down to the top of my butt.

I was hard again and pretty much humping his thigh.

He dropped a kiss on my head. "Sorry I woke you."

I rubbed my face against his furry chest, enjoying the heady scent of soap and sweat on his skin. Mark's nipples pebbled as I moved my face across his skin.

"Not sorry," I said in a sleep-slurred voice. "Still dreaming."

He pulled me up for a kiss which I tried desperately to avoid due to horrific morning breath. "Mmpfh!"

"Lemme in," he said with a chuckle. "You're so sweet, even your morning breath probably tastes like cotton candy."

I groaned at him. "That was terrible. I can't believe you just said that out loud."

He grinned, flashing me enough teeth to show the little twisty one behind one of his canines. The move scrunched up his eyes, drawing attention to the scar across one of them. I reached up to trace a finger over it.

"Tell me what happened," I said softly.

Mark's hand came up to pull mine off so he could press a kiss to my fingertips and then hold my hand over his heart.

"I grew up in a really rough part of Chicago. My dad encouraged me to get out by any means possible—otherwise I was going to wind up in a gang—so I joined the navy. Well, the night before I left for RTC, the gang took offense to my decision, and I wasn't quick enough to completely avoid their blade." He showed me the back of one of his forearms that was covered with an intricate tattoo of a feathered wing. Looking at it this close allowed me to see something I hadn't noticed before. The skin below the image was scarred as well.

"Defensive wound?" I asked in surprise.

Mark nodded. "If I hadn't gotten my arm up, I would have lost my eye. Thankfully, a neighbor saw it happen and screamed that he had a shotgun and wasn't afraid to use it to clean up the streets. I can still hear him cocking that thing."

"What did your dad do? He must have panicked."

Mark shifted a little, bending up the knee that had been resting between my legs. His thigh pushed me up his body until my face was within kissing distance. "He did. But I was able to use the attack to convince him to move to Florida when I'd finally saved up enough money to help, so it ended up being a good thing. He loves it there. Met a woman and everything. Now stop changing the subject and gimme that mouth."

His strong hand came up to cup the back of my head and guide me in for the kiss. I lost track of how long I sucked his face and rubbed my skin raw against his rough stubble. I probably looked like a strawberry by the time I was done.

"I need to shower and feed you before taking you to see your brother," Mark finally said, moving me gently off him.

The idea of taking a shower with this man was enough to make me shudder with excitement. I escaped to my own bathroom first to use the toilet and brush my teeth. When I returned to his, the water was already steaming up the small room.

"Get in here," Mark growled from behind the curtain. An inked arm shot out to grab me, and I yelped out a laugh when he pulled me against his hot, wet body. He was a tower of muscles, one of the most... *masculine* men I knew in person. Once I got my feet under me, I leaned my forehead into the center of his chest and let the hot water beat down on my back.

Mark's hands were all over me. He'd grabbed the tiny soap sliver and was busy sliding it over every square inch of my skin. By the time he reached between my legs, I was breathless and begging, which had quickly become my new normal around him.

"I want to suck you," I said, sliding down to my knees. "Please. Let me try."

"Jesus," Mark muttered. "Not saying no to that. Anything you do will feel good, Ammon."

The sound of my name in his sex-roughened voice was enough to make me whimper as I tried to determine the best way to tackle his heavy erection. I reached my hands up to feel his hips and abs. The bumpy muscles were covered in dark blond hair with sparkling drops of water trapped in the trail below his belly button.

I followed the trail down with my tongue. It was sloppy and awkward, but the sounds Mark made and the way his fingers traced the sides of my face with such tenderness... well, they made me feel like it didn't matter I didn't know what I was doing.

And when he gripped my chin and pulled me off just in time for his release to hit me in the throat and chest, it was enough to make me reach for my own shaft and pull quickly until my release hit me just as hard as his had.

If it hadn't been for Mark's strong arms pulling me up and holding me against him for the rest of the shower, I would have slipped quite happily down the drain in my stupor.

Before I knew it, we were checked out of the hotel and on our way to the hospital in Roosevelt with drive-thru breakfast sandwiches and coffee in the center console.

"I didn't think you were a coffee drinker," Mark said before taking a big bite of his sandwich.

"I'm not, really. When I took a hard class in college, I finally figured out why people drink so much of it. I try not to get addicted, but sometimes it's just a morning that demands coffee, you know?"

"Every morning demands coffee, gorgeous boy."

My heart filled with his endearment. He was quick to call me baby and sweetheart. I'd never had that before, and it felt really good.

"You've never had my fruit and yogurt smoothies," I corrected. "Jude showed me how to—"

Mark held up his hand. "Ack, no. No Jude health nut mumbo jumbo. He once tricked me into eating brownies made of kale."

I laughed. "They're made of avocados."

He shuddered dramatically and clutched his heart. "I'd rather die."

We flirted and teased our way down the road until he parked on the hospital lot. Suddenly, my stomach jangled with nerves.

"How did he seem?" I asked, opening the car door to hop out. "Okay? Do you think he's in trouble?"

Mark came around the side of the SUV and reached for my hand. I wondered if he knew what a big deal that was in small-town Utah.

"I think he could use some family right about now," Mark said carefully. "And I just want you to know, I support whatever you decide."

I glanced over at him in confusion. "What do you mean?"

He shrugged. "If you decide you want to help him in some way, I'll be there too. Don't forget what Joel does. What I do. We help get people out of bad situations."

I reached up on tiptoes to press a kiss against his cheek. "See? You're a good man. Told you."

"Pfft." He blushed a little pink in the most endearing way.

We entered the hospital and went directly to my brother's room where I was shocked to see a skeletal version of him taking up only a tiny portion of the bed.

"Gideon," I cried, racing to his side. Despite being afraid of breaking him, I had to hold him in my arms.

We hugged and cried together until I heard Gideon giggle.

"You're all... I don't know. Trendy or posh or something," Gideon said, looking me over with a smile. "What are you even wearing?"

I looked down at the clothes I had on. The jeans were a gift from Jude on my last birthday, and the sweater was one I'd picked up on sale when Blue had taken me shopping before this semester started.

"Um, clothes?" I said, glancing over at Mark. His expression was affectionate.

"Babe, you're wearing two-hundred-dollar jeans and a designer top."

I blinked at him before turning back to Gideon. "I have rich, um..." I stopped myself before I said the word *brothers*.

"How are you feeling?" Mark said, cutting in to save me from an awkward situation.

Gideon sighed happily. "So much better. I can't thank you enough for your help. They said I have a vitamin deficiency, so they gave me some kind of infusion after you left. I also had a hot breakfast for the first time in forever. Whoever said hospital food stinks was lying."

I sat on the edge of his bed and held his hand. It felt cold and frail in mine. "When are they letting you go?"

Gideon's eyes shifted nervously. "Um, now? I think? I'm not sure. They said they could, ah, call someone to take me to Camp Preston-wood if I wanted."

It took me a minute to place why the name made my stomach twist. "The conversion therapy place the church runs up in Logan?" My voice raised so high at the end of the question, Mark's forehead scrunched in confusion.

Gideon's face flushed. "It's not like I have a choice," he said in a voice full of emotion. "I tried it on my own. Living, I mean. I tried living on my own and I'm just..." The tears spilled over and his voice broke. "I'm just so tired. I need food and a safe place to sleep. Maybe if I spend some time there, I can go back home again."

I looked at Mark for help before realizing it wasn't his job to solve this problem for me. Even if he was willing to be my hero, he wasn't the only one capable of helping others.

"No," I said defiantly. "You're not going there. You'll come home with me."

Out of the corner of my eye, I noticed Mark's soft grin. He stepped up behind me and put his hands on my shoulders, rubbing the muscles with his strong fingers. His voice murmured into my ear. "Good man."

I shuddered.

"Erm, anyway, so, uh, yeah," I said, trying desperately to ignore the sexy man pressed up against my back. He smelled like the soap from our shared shower. I closed my eyes and did my best to focus. "Um, what? What was I saying? Yes. California."

Gideon's eyes betrayed a glimmer of hope. "Are you sure? I don't want to be a bother. I can work. That is... if you can maybe help me find a job, or... I'm good with animals and kids... oh, but no one would want someone like me around their kids probably."

"Why not?" I asked, wondering how he could have changed that much in three years.

Gid's eyes flicked between mine and Mark's. "Because I'm... *gay.*" He whispered the word.

Mark snorted, and I rolled my eyes. "First of all, it's San Francisco. So the whole gay thing is..." I flapped my hand. "Secondly, I kind of got taken in by a big family there and, well... let's just say, they're really, really okay with the gay."

Mark snorted again, and I reached back to swat at him. "Shut up," I muttered.

He wrapped a muscular arm around my chest and pressed a soft kiss to the side of my face. Gideon's cheeks reddened even more.

"Let's go home," Mark said to Gideon and me.

I thought of AJ rescuing me all those years ago, of Thomas and Rebecca who'd taken me in as one of their own, my Marian siblings and their partners, who treated me like the doted-upon baby brother, my volunteer job at Marian House, my violin classes at school. I thought about my hopes of one day teaching children and maybe starting a family of my own.

I thought of returning to San Francisco and going out on a proper date with Mark Hayes, who I was basically already in love with and daydreaming of a future with.

"Home," I said with a nod and a grin. I looked at my brother's too-skinny face. "You're going to love it there. It's the perfect place for a fresh start."

16

"Jesus fuck!" I felt the blow before I landed on my ass.

Gideon slid to his knees and accidentally knocked me in the face with his glove while he leaned in to check on me. "Oh no! Oh, Mark! I'm so sorry, I didn't mean to knock you over!"

The very familiar sound of my boyfriend snickering came from the corner of the training room.

"Ammon Marian, zip it," I warned, pointing at him with my own glove. "You're next, by the way."

He held up his bare fists in an exaggerated defensive stance and made a silly face at me. "Ooh, tough guy tryna scare the poor little innocent student."

I glared at him. "Innocent, my ass." I noticed the big clock high on the wall as I jumped back up and shook off the well-placed hit Gideon had scored on me. "Wait. What are you doing here? I thought you had work until five."

"Babe, it's half past five. That clock is wrong."

"Shit, shit!" I glanced at Gideon, who knew why that was a problem. He winked at me and waved me out the door.

"Go. Derek's coming to pick me up to go to the new Disney movie with them and the kids."

Ammon looked back and forth between us. "What? Why? What's happening?"

I ignored him and raced to the locker room for a quick shower, yelling back over my shoulder what a good job Gideon had done in our sparring. He'd come a long way from the half-starved homeless kid I'd met almost a year before. Simone had taken him under her wing right away and had given him a job as a vet technician at her practice. He'd spent enough time with Simone and Joel to finally cave to Joel's insistence on self-defense classes. One thing had led to another, and he was one of Mario's best Krav Maga students.

Gideon was thriving. And seeing him happy made Ammon happy. And anything that made Ammon happy made me happy.

Which was why I was practically skipping with excitement about the surprise I had planned for him that evening.

I showered and dressed in record time and met Ammon in the lobby, where he was reading the card from the flowers Raisa had sent me for my birthday. Even though my birthday wasn't for another two months. It wasn't the weirdest thing she'd done in the past year to try and get my attention, but it was still weird enough.

When my shoes squeaked on the floor, Ammon's head shot up. "What the hell?" he asked.

I blinked at his use of a curse word. "Ignore those. It's nothing."

Ammon looked from the card to me and back again. "No, you don't understand. I wrote this."

"What?"

He waved the tiny white card in my face. "I freaking wrote this! Why is she sending you flowers? And why is she wishing you a happy birthday two months early?"

I slid my arms around him and nuzzled into his neck, inhaling the familiar combination of lilies, freesia, and roses mixed in with a little masculine sweat. It never failed to make my dick hard.

His words sank in. "You wrote the card? These are from your shop?"

I thought of the half-dozen sweet florist cards I'd gotten from her over the past year and how incongruous they'd been with her actual personality in real life. I also knew that Ammon's friend Pinkie called him the florist's favorite wordsmith. It finally made sense.

Ammon shoved me back, still mad as a snake. "Yes, I wrote this. The same asshole who comes in every month to order flowers on behalf of his, quite frankly, *asshole* of a boss..." He took a breath. "Came in and ordered these today. And by the way, this ex of yours sends flowers to half the men in the city. What a b-b-... witch!"

Another curse word and almost a third. He was on a roll.

"I love you," I said with a big grin. Cherie snorted from behind the reception counter. I shot her a look and turned back to my boyfriend. "You're the love of my life."

He narrowed his eyes at me. "I know that. You don't care that she's a... a... cheat? Some kind of... player?"

I shook my head. "Raisa is none of my business anymore. But you know who is?"

He tilted his head, his facial expression softening just a smidge. "Me."

I nodded and pulled him against me again, leaning down to take his soft pouty lips in mine. "You," I whispered against his mouth. "You're my business."

"Mpfh." His body melted into mine. "Say it again."

Joel's voice came from behind me. "Please don't. That's my baby brother you're molesting."

Ammon's chest puffed up a little the way it always did when one of the Marian men claimed him as family.

I turned to Joel, tucking Ammon against my side. "We're headed out. Wish us luck."

Joel winked at me. "You don't need it. But good luck anyway."

I led Ammon out the front door.

"Aren't we going to the vineyard for Thomas and Rebecca's anniversary weekend? Why did he wish us luck?"

I opened the truck door for him. "You'll see. It's a surprise."

While we made our way out of the city, Ammon chatted to me

about his day. "Oh my goodness, I totally forgot to tell you. Li Jun is dating... a woman."

"No way. Are you sure? How is that possible? I saw how he looked at you."

Ammon turned in his seat and pointed at me. "You're implying there's no such thing as bisexual, my bisexual friend."

"Boyfriend," I corrected with a growl. And hopefully fiancé soon, but I didn't want to push too many new things at him at once. I'd gotten the feeling he'd be more inclined to accept a proposal after his graduation in a few months.

"Live-in *lovah*," he teased.

It was true. I'd moved into his place over Jude's garage only four months into our relationship. Ammon had found out about my apartment lease coming up for renewal and had begged me to stop paying rent on a place I rarely saw. It turned out to be even more of a blessing than I'd thought because in addition to having Ammon in my arms every night, I'd also managed to save up money faster than I'd ever dreamed.

Which led us to this weekend. Yes, we were going to the anniversary party which was a front for a weekend of drunken poker and debauchery with a million Marians. But we were also going house hunting.

Ammon had been offered a job to teach music at Verona Elementary school which was where Blue and Tristan's kids would attend when they were old enough. Blue had offered us the use of the small cabin on the vineyard property, but I was ready to give Ammon more than that.

I wanted to give him his dream. While we weren't anywhere near ready to start our own family, we could at least find the home we wanted and begin making it our own.

When we finally struggled our way out of the city, suburbs, and across the Carquinez Bridge, I told Ammon some of my news.

"Joel said I can work remotely."

"What?"

I smiled over at him before looking back to the road. "Yeah. As long as I come to the office for important meetings and still go out on assignments as usual, I can work from a home office."

Ammon bounced in his seat. "Oh wow. Oh *wow*. This is great! We can set up..." He seemed to remember the little cabin at the vineyard was very little. "We... well, the good news is, when I'm at work, you'll have the whole place to yourself. Maybe we can fit a desk where the TV stand is right now."

By the time he'd twisted himself inside out trying to figure out how to make it work for me, we'd pulled up to a quaint blue cottage-style house with a pristine front yard and freshly painted white shutters. I knew from the online photos that it had an updated kitchen Ammon would love, and it had french doors that opened onto a wide, grassy backyard that was fenced in and perfect for Marian family cookouts. It was also within walking distance to his new school.

"What's this?" Ammon asked before noticing the For Sale sign in the front yard. He glanced over at me.

I leaned over and kissed him softly on the lips. "I want to buy us a house."

Ammon's eyes widened in surprise. "Really? Now?"

I nodded. "If we find one we both love. If not, we'll keep looking until we do."

He bit his bottom lip and looked back over at the house. "But... I don't have any money saved up."

I slid my hand behind his head and turned him to look at me. "I do. And everything I have is yours too. Please let me help us start our life together."

Ammon's eyes filled. "Really?"

I dropped kisses all over his face until I pulled him in for a tight hug. "You have made all of my dreams come true, sweetheart. Now it's time I do the same for you."

He moved over and climbed into my lap, wrapping his slender arms around my neck. "Will it have an office for you?" he asked with a flirty smile. His eyes were still bright from the tears.

"Mm-hm. And a music room for you." I leaned in and kissed the top of his cheek where it was warm from his excitement over my surprise.

"And can we still have naked Sundays?"

I laughed and nodded. "And naked Mondays, and Tuesdays, and—"

Ammon leaned in and kissed me.

And it was heaven.

YAKKITY-YAK

1

———————

JAMIE

"Not that one," Teddy warned. "It's not warm enough."

I rolled my eyes at him. "Dude, I used to live in Alaska. You think I don't know how to pack warm clothes?"

"Babe. That fleece has been washed ten thousand times. There's no more fleece left. It's just a mesh shell at this point. Bring the blue one instead." He turned back to his own backpack and shoved his rain pants deep inside.

"This wouldn't have anything to do with you preferring me wearing blue in photographs would it?" I teased.

"Mpfh."

"Because you know which one is the warmest? The orange one my mom sent me for my birthday."

He shot me a look. "Absolutely not."

Teddy hated orange. It was a joke between us, but I knew the truth. It reminded him of hunters, and he couldn't stand the idea of animals losing their lives to humans in the wilderness.

"Did you remember to take the joint supplement when you dropped Sister off?" I asked.

"James," he said. "How many times have we—"

I held up a hand to cut him off. "I know. But she's getting old, and I worry about—"

Teddy put down the socks he was folding and came around the end of the bed to wrap his arms around me. He wasn't wearing a shirt, and his bare skin felt warmer than any fleece. "I love you," he said softly before leaning in to kiss me. His kisses still left me dizzy and panting even after years together. "And I love that dog almost as much as I love you. Not only did I take the joint supplements, but I also took the heated bed, her favorite squeaky, some cans of the special wet food she loves, and a few of our T-shirts from the dirty-clothes hamper. Your mom thought I was crazy when I showed up with half the house in the back of the SUV."

"My parents love that girl," I reminded him.

"I know. And your dad made an absolute fool out of himself the minute she hopped down from the vehicle. I didn't even know his voice got that high."

Teddy dropped another kiss on my lips and moved back to his pile of clothes on the bed. I watched the muscles move under the skin of his shoulder and biceps and felt the familiar tightening in my groin I got when I looked at my husband's body. He was the kind of good-looking that stopped people in their tracks. Just last week a woman had literally run her shopping cart into the rear door of a parked car while staring at Teddy in front of our grocery store. He hadn't noticed a thing and had kept on talking to me about the ropa vieja he was planning on cooking for my parents the following night.

My sister Simone had been asked for her hot brother-in-law's phone number twice by people who knew he was already taken. She loved answering the inquiries by asking which hot brother-in-law they meant. She had six. And then when they inevitably specified Teddy, she still gave them her own boyfriend's phone number instead. She delighted in vexing poor Joel. None of us knew how the hell he put up with her.

Teddy's voice snapped me out of my thoughts. "What are you doing? I know I've got impressive guns, but seriously."

Then he flexed.

I rolled my eyes and threw a T-shirt at him. "If you must know, I was thinking about Joel," I corrected.

"Healy?"

"Yep."

Teddy frowned at the biceps bulge still flexed in a nice arc. "It's okay, big guy. We'll keep working. One day we'll be bigger than that stupid Navy SEAL."

I snorted. "Keep dreaming, Theodore."

He glanced at me, still frowning. "Do you seriously find him attractive? I mean, he's built and all... but..."

The pout damn near killed me. I bit my lip to keep from laughing more. "Babe. No. Of course not. I wasn't daydreaming about my sister's man."

He blew out a breath and relaxed. "Good. 'Cause for a minute there—"

I interrupted him. "He's straight. No sense in lusting after someone who won't recipro—"

Teddy tackled me onto the bed with a deep growl. "I'll show you reciprocate." He bit lightly into the side of my neck and sucked hard, clearly intending on giving me a hickey from hell to pay me back from the one I'd accidentally given him the night before he had to teach a photography class at UC Davis last month.

I tried to squirm out of his jaws. "The photos! We're going to Tibet! Think of the yaks!"

We both froze for a beat as my words echoed around our bedroom. Teddy's eyebrow raised, and the corners of his lips began to curl.

"Don't," I warned.

"Did you just—" Teddy began.

"Stop. Seriously. I meant... you know what I meant. The pictures. You don't want me to have a huge hickey in the pictures you take on our trip."

"Photoshop, baby doll." He leaned back in to nibble on the already tender spot on my neck, still mumbling. "Works wonders on love bites and handcuff marks."

My heart thumped hard in my chest, and my dick hardened. "H-handcuff marks?"

His hands circled my wrists and tightened. "D'you like that?" Teddy's deep voice was a rumble that went straight to my dick as usual.

The scratch of his stubble against the tender skin on my neck made me dizzy. I'd once asked my brother Pete how he could possibly stand to be straight and miss out on feeling the roughness of five-o'clock shadow or the smell of a man's hairy armpit. He'd waxed poetic about the softness and floral scent of a woman, but I'd glanced over at his wife, Ginger, before both of us had dissolved into a fit of giggles. There was hardly anything soft or floral about that woman. She was a powerhouse of snark, and most days she smelled like horse since they'd been cursed with daughters who were obsessed with riding.

"I must not be working hard enough," Teddy murmured into my skin. "Who're you thinking about now?"

I didn't dare mention my brother or sister-in-law.

"Horses," I gasped as he moved down and sucked hard on my nipple.

"Mmm, kinky bastard." He continued sucking hard marks down my front as I struggled for breath and pushed my hips up into his chest. "You like to ride, cowboy?"

I threaded my fingers into his thick, dark hair. "Don't. Please don't. You'll ruin it."

Teddy stopped what he was doing and looked up with an expression so intense, my boxer briefs shrank. "Sweetheart," he drawled, "I've never ruined sex in my life."

I hooked my leg around the back of his knee and hauled him off me, flipping us until he was on the bottom and I was on top. His grin was all-knowing, the smug bastard, and I ached to put him in his place.

"You once vomited on my dick," I reminded him. "Just as I was about to come."

He rolled his eyes. "You have a long memory. And your sister makes a strong drink."

"It was last New Year's, and you know Simone pours heavy when she's pregnant. Then there was the time you didn't realize the lube was frozen until you squeezed it onto my ass, and I screamed like a banshee."

"Spoilsport," he muttered. "Where's your sense of adventure? We were camping in the Rockies in early spring. Of course things were going to be cold."

I ground my hard-on against the bulge in his pants. "Or the time you reprogrammed Siri to respond to the word *fuck* by asking 'how hard, sir?' in Aunt Tilly's voice. And I totally lost my ability to orgasm for a week."

Teddy's smile widened, and I felt the vibration of his laugh through my chest. "That was epic."

I noticed the little wrinkles at the corner of his eyes and the mark on his left earlobe leftover from a piercing that had long ago grown in. Silver threaded through his dark hair here and there and, of course, it only made him sexier. I wanted him desperately.

I *always* wanted him desperately.

"We don't have time," I said instead. His eyes darkened with intent. I knew that look. The determined look. "Teddy..."

"Get naked."

"Babe... traffic..." I tried again. His eyes narrowed, and his nostrils flared. My dick throbbed in response.

After taking a shaky breath, I gave in.

"Want you inside me. Please," I breathed.

He stared at me for several long beats before ruining it. "Shh... I'll take care of everything. Just lie back and think of the yaks."

TIBETAN CHANTS

1

TEDDY

My ass was showing.

Well, not literally, thank god. It was cold as fuck out here. But when I got nervous, I turned into an ass. And poor Jamie was bearing the brunt of it right now. We were stranded on the Tibetan Plateau after our all-terrain vehicle tour had abandoned us. I pinned Jamie with a glare that must have looked an awful lot like blame.

"Don't look at me like that," Jamie said with a sniff.

"Like what? Like you're the one person I'd want with me at the moment of my death? That's a good thing, considering—"

He held up a hand. "You may stop talking now."

"You're so sweet with the permission. Remember that time I cut my hand helping your mom prep for Thanksgiving, and you were kind enough to allow me to visit the emergency room?"

Jamie turned in a circle, looking around as if an Uber driver was going to four-wheel their ass across the barren, snow-covered tundra. "That didn't happen," he muttered.

"False. I said I thought I needed stitches, and you said if I left, I'd ruin Thanksgiving," I said. "And then the blood kind of spurted near the potatoes, and you sighed and finally said I could go."

A bird squawked somewhere overhead. I looked up into the overcast skies, wondering exactly how cold it would get overnight and how the birds were lucky they could travel south if they wanted.

Jamie continued. "It wasn't that I didn't want you to receive medical attention. I simply thought Simone could fix you up at the house."

"I needed stitches," I reminded him.

"She's a veterinarian." He eyed me before adding, "And you're a dog."

"Am not."

He leaned over to dig his water bottle out of his pack. Even though he was dressed in bulky winter gear, I still took a minute to ogle his ass. My husband was the sexiest man alive, and not a day went by I didn't want to see him naked and run my hands all over his warm skin.

He stood up and caught me staring. "Did you just check me out?" he asked incredulously. "Seriously?"

I shrugged. "You have something on your pants."

Jamie's eyes narrowed. "I have your pervy eyeballs on my pants."

"Pfft, whatever. Where's a good place to bed down for the night?" I glanced around, wondering if it was better to stay near the cluster of toasty-warm but horribly stinky yaks or move toward the rocky hillside to get a break from the wind. A thick layer of snow covered everything around us, and it was already cold as hell.

Jamie's eyes widened. "Hell no. No. We're not actually stuck out here."

I lifted an eyebrow at him. "You're right. I'm sure the tour guide simply ducked into a convenience store for a quick pack of smokes." I gestured to the miles and miles of open wilderness around us. "He'll pop back around to get us in two shakes of a lamb's tail."

When Jamie got nervous, he used his arms to talk. They began waving around now. "I don't understand. Who leaves two American tourists in the middle of the Tibetan Plateau? How did this happen? Didn't you see him leave?"

I threw it back at him. "Didn't you?" I took his water bottle and sucked down a big gulp.

He sputtered, flailing the arm between me and the nearby rocky outcropping. "I was over there! Studying the lichen!"

"Lichen story," I muttered, trying to hide a grin.

"You're not funny."

Jamie was beautiful. His cheeks were pink with the cold, and his eyes sparkled in defiance.

I pulled him in for a quick kiss on the cheek. "Except that I am. I'm also excessively experienced in international wilderness travel unlike some people I know. So, really, who do we think is at fault here?"

"Still you," he cried, shoving me away. "It's not my fault. I'm plenty experienced in international wilderness travel as you well know. Plus, I wasn't the one who had to get a million photos of the snow leopard."

I stared at him in disbelief. "It was a black-necked crane *riding* a Tibetan snow leopard. Do you have any idea how much money I'm going to make off those images when we get home?"

"*If* we get home," he muttered before shivering again.

I reached out to pull him in for a hug, tugging his wool hat down lower over his ears before dropping a kiss on his red nose. "We'll get home. I know a guy. And by 'guy' I mean woman. And by 'woman,' I mean force of nature."

Jamie looked around us at the miles of barren, snow-covered plains. The partridge I'd spotted earlier was long gone, and the few cranes still hanging around nearby were decidedly ignoring us. I thought I saw the little sand-colored head of a pika pop up between some rocks, but I could have been mistaken. And if I even tried to claim a need to check it out, my argument that we were only here for Jamie's scientific curiosity and not my own photoshoot would be dashed.

Wasn't worth the risk.

"How're you going to call this force of nature?" he asked. "By coughing again?"

I looked at him in horror. "It's called throat singing. It's a Tibetan—"

"No," Jamie said, cutting me off. "That's not what you were doing. Children were crying, babe. Sorry, but there it is."

I studied him for a minute before pointing a finger at him. "Bet you that throat singing would get someone's attention out here on the plains."

Jamie's eyes rolled. Such pretty eyes with such ugly distrust in his life partner. Shame.

He huffed. "Bet you it would get the sleeping yaks' attention which is definitely not what we want." He flapped his gloved hands. "Do the thing. Call the lady."

I dug in my pack for the sat phone and dialed the number. When the woman answered, I tried to play it cool to buy us some time.

"Yeah, uh... it's me."

I could hear her rolling her eyes from thousands of miles away. "You're lost."

"Not exactly..." I glanced up at Jamie, who was staring a hole into me. I tried to ignore him. "We know where we are, it's just..."

"And where is that?" she asked.

I turned in a slow circle before licking my pointer finger and holding it up in the air. After a few beats, I nodded. "Tibet."

2

JAMIE

I tilted my head at Teddy. Sometimes he was adorably frustrating, and sometimes he was just frustrating.

"Give me the phone," I demanded.

He ignored me.

"We're about twelve klicks east-southeast of Coqen," he said with false conviction. I figured he was more or less correct.

"Tell her we're on the western coast of Zhari Namco."

"That's not how you say it," Teddy said to me. I clenched my jaws to keep from cursing at him in Lhasa. Or what would have been creatively made-up Lhasa.

Teddy turned back to the woman on the phone. "All we need is for you to call someone in Coqen and arrange for them to get a jeep or something out here for us."

The screeching on the other end of the line was familiar, but I couldn't place it. Teddy listened patiently before pulling out what I called his "now, now, darlin'" act.

"Hey, beautiful," he began in a smooth, deep sex voice. "No need to get angry and start throwing blame around. You know how your brother is. He catches sight of one little Tibetan partridge and the guy goes wandering off with his big nerdy magnifying glass—"

I stared at him in shock as the clues clicked together.

"You're on the phone with my *sister*?" I blurted in a screechy sound that bore too much resemblance to the one on the phone for my comfort.

Teddy placed his hand over the microphone and turned to me with his charming grin, the one that usually made me take off my clothes no matter where we were.

"Stop," I muttered, pointing in his face. "It's too cold for that smile. And besides, Simone? Really?"

"She has connections to Joel, who has connections with alphabet agencies. It's the best way to find safe passage in certain parts of the world."

He wasn't wrong, but still. "Don't tell her about last night," I warned.

Teddy spoke back into the phone. "Oh, Simone, wait till you hear about last night."

"Ass," I said, mentally kicking myself for even bringing it up. I walked farther away so I didn't have to hear him tell her how I'd made a fool out of myself when I'd misunderstood a question from one of the professors we'd met for dinner, and the misunderstanding had caused me to pontificate on the glories of barley grain in Tibetan cuisine for a solid ten minutes before the professor had clarified that his wife's name was Carly Reyne. The silence that had followed had been deafening until Teddy had leaned forward and said with his easy, sociable way, "Please excuse my husband. He was so excited about our visit, he immersed himself in the study of Tibetan culture the entire flight over. You know how professors can be with research." His wink had put everyone at ease as usual, and the dinner had progressed smoothly from there.

Charming bastard.

I glanced back over at him. His free hand was waving around wildly as he told some other story about our adventures so far. His smile was wide, and his eye wrinkles were just barely visible to the sides of his sunglasses. He really was very good-looking. And funny. And adventurous, and sweet, and sexy.

I let out a sigh. He was right. Even if we were left out here to die, I'd die happy. He was the one person I wanted to be with no matter what.

Movement caught my eye over his shoulder. The yaks were waking up.

"Teddy..." I began.

"And then he came sauntering out of the bathroom stark naked right in front of all of them," Teddy continued, holding nothing back with my sister. "Good thing the man has a nice dick."

The now-familiar screeching escalated again as Simone clearly disagreed with Teddy's decision to mention my unmentionables.

I grabbed Teddy's waving arm to get his attention. "Can we... not? I think it would be best if Simone actually got off the phone with you and arranged some transportation for us." I kept my eye on the waking yaks in the snow several hundred feet away.

The sound of thumping rotor blades hit my ears, and I turned to gawp at Teddy. How in the world had Simone gotten someone here so fast?

Teddy winked at me and said something to my sister I couldn't make out over the noise.

When the helicopter appeared, I noticed a decided lack of skis under its belly. Sure enough, instead of landing and picking us up, the helicopter hovered near the ground before opening its door and shoving something out.

Teddy and I stared as some sort of parcel thunked down into the snow. The helicopter's door slid closed, and the bird sailed out of sight.

"Huh," Teddy said, still holding the phone.

"What the fuck?" I muttered, making my way toward the parcel. It was a weatherproof duffle bag of sorts with nylon strapping around it. The Red Cross logo on the bag was faded and chipped as if the bag had been thrown out of multiple helicopters in our time.

"Ohh, presents! Think there's a hot pizza in there?" Teddy asked, slipping the phone into his pocket.

I unwrapped the parcel to discover a tent, sleeping bags, cookstove with fuel bottle, food bags, and a big bottle of water. There was also another sat phone, some extra clothing layers, and a small first aid kit.

"This doesn't look like a rescue," I said, poking through the meager items in the food bag. Lentils, pasta, oats.

Teddy nudged me out of the way so he could root through the supplies. "Babe, it's a super-fun sleepover kit. C'mon, let's get set up so we can snuggle in the tent. Is there by chance any lube in here?"

We yanked everything out of the bundle and found a spot close to some rock formations so that some of the wind would be blocked. Thankfully, the area was farther away from the yaks, who didn't seem all that thrilled to be sharing their land with us.

"Is this our life now?" I asked, shaking the high-rated sleeping bag out of its roll. "We just live on the Tibetan Plateau permanently?"

Teddy looked up from where he was snapping tent poles together. "Yes, Jamison. We live here now. Surprise."

Snow caught in his beard, and the red-and-blue striped wool beanie he wore set off his eyes. He really was a gorgeous human even though he could be frustrating as hell.

I ignored how sexy he was. "By any chance, did Simone say anything about sending a helicopter with skis next time?"

He finished fishing the pole through the pocket until the tent looked like an actual tent. "Our bus is returning tomorrow to fetch us. Don't worry. We only need to survive out here one night." Teddy looked up at me, the expression on his face unusually serious all of a sudden. "Plus, I wanted to talk to you about something in private."

I turned in a circle, taking in the miles and miles of uninhabited wilderness before meeting his eyes again. "Seems a bit extreme for a private conversation, but no one ever said you were subtle."

He grunted before shoving the tent spikes into the frozen ground and then stomping on them with a boot. Once the tent was set up, we both took a break inside to get out of the wind.

For a few minutes, the only sounds were the snick of untying laces and the thunk of heavy boots hitting the floor of the tent, followed by the swish of high-tech fabric as we yanked off coats and gloves. When we finally stretched out side by side on our sleeping bags, Teddy turned on his side and propped his head on an elbow.

"We should stop traveling."

I blinked at him in surprise. "Babe, the bus will be here tomorrow. We're fine."

His lips curved up. "No, doll. That's not what I meant." He reached out a hand to pull off my hat and run fingers through my hair. I luxuriated under his familiar touch. "I think it's time for us to consider starting a family."

Now I was really surprised. Theodore Kodiak Marian was a man made up of wanderlust and adventure. The idea of him settling down in one place was laughable.

He cupped my cheek. "Before you tell me what I do or don't want, please consider how I feel about our nieces and nephews."

"You adore them," I confirmed. "You take them on hikes and teach Pete's girls how to take photos. On Ella's last birthday you made a scavenger hunt through the vineyard for all the kids old enough to participate."

Teddy nodded, but I narrowed my eyes at him. "But when any of the babies needed a diaper change, you were suddenly the invisible man."

"Yeah... babies don't work for me," he said with conviction.

"Exactly! So what—" I stopped and met his eyes as his words began to make sense. "Adoption."

Teddy nodded. "Or even fostering. We've been fund-raising for Yolo Care since we moved to Davis. Remember when we did the big barbecue thing and we heard about the brother and sister who were adopted out to different families?"

My heart dropped. Teddy had been upset about that for weeks. We all had been. "They try not to separate siblings. You know that."

He nodded. "No, I know. But part of the reason they're able to avoid it is because they have adoptive parents open to older kids and open to taking siblings. And I think we should consider doing the same."

His words surprised me. All this time I'd assumed we'd spend our lives traveling the world and pursuing our careers. It had never made sense to bring a baby into the kind of lifestyle we lived. But... he wasn't talking about babies.

"Teddy," I began, unsure of where to start. "This is a big decision."

Teddy sat up and crossed his legs, reaching out for my hands with his. "That's why I wanted to get you alone with absolutely zero distractions."

I stared at him, noticing the only sounds around us were the muffled groans of the yaks in the distance and the wind buffeting the sides of the tent. "You stranded us on purpose?"

His grin never failed to flip my stomach upside down. "We're not exactly stranded. We have the sat phone, shelter, food, and an appointment with a stinky tour bus in the morning. I told Simone we were fine, but she knows where we are if we don't check in tomorrow."

I lurched up and pinned him to the ground, leaning over him and growling in his face. "You drive me fucking crazy. Why can't you be normal? Normal people talk about this shit over a nice bottle of wine with dinner."

Teddy's eyes sparkled with his usual self-congratulatory mischief. "You had normal. You didn't like normal. Admit it. You like the crazy. You crave the crazy. You wanna suck crazy's dick."

I narrowed my eyes at him. "You might have taken it one step too far."

"Or *did* I?" he asked, bouncing his eyebrows and arching his hips up into mine. There were so many layers of clothing between us, I had no idea whether he was even hard or not.

"Are you serious about this? What about your job? What about—"

Teddy grabbed my face with his hands and pulled me down for a kiss, soft and slow. The tenderness of the kiss took me by surprise, not because he was never sweet with me like that, but because it was a clear sign he was feeling emotional despite his joking around.

"I love you," he whispered against my lips. "I love you so much. I've been selfish keeping you to myself. It's time to share my incredible husband with children who need an amazing dad. You'll make a wonderful father. And my job can change. I'll cut down on traveling assignments and increase the classes I teach at the university." His eyes met mine. "I've already talked to Ed about it. He said they'd be thrilled to offer me full-time. I can add courses in digital imaging, lighting, and black-and-white analog."

I imagined more days with us walking to school together. As it was, he only taught one class there and was off on assignments much of the other time. It was lonely at home without him. The only times I could travel with him were during school breaks.

"You'll be stir-crazy," I hedged. This entire idea was too good to be true.

"I'll be well rested," Teddy countered.

I ran my fingers through his hair. "You'll get bored with me."

"Never. You're the best thing that's ever happened to me." His voice was deep and sincere. The words filled my heart and made me giddy. "I want a family with you. I want a life not spent in airports and shitty hotels. When I come home to you, I feel like I can breathe, like it's where I'm supposed to be. I've spent years traveling the world and taking pictures. Now I want to spend years putting down some roots and giving some children a much-needed family. Please say yes, Jamie."

He rarely called me by name.

I thought about the life I'd originally envisioned with my first fiancé. I'd wanted stability and children, neighborhood cookouts and trick-or-treating. But then I'd met Teddy, and he was worth exchanging that dream for another. We'd been living that new dream for several years now, traveling the world for our jobs and enjoying adventures like this one together.

But he was right. Something was missing. Every time we got together with my family, I envied my siblings their children. I wondered what it would be like if we had bedtime routines to get home to and school buses to wait for. When Teddy and I first got together, I didn't feel the loss of what I'd given up to have our exciting life, but these days, that loss had been sneaking in around the edges more and more.

"Are you sure this is something you really want?" I asked him, watching his eyes for the truth.

Teddy reached up and ran his fingertips through my beard scruff. "Our life is so good, and we have so much to share. Every child should have the opportunity to learn, to thrive, to be loved. I can't think of a better family to bring children up in than ours. I'm very sure of this."

My heart felt like it was going to fly out of my chest from a combination of nerves and excitement. "Okay, Papa Bear. Let's do this."

Teddy pulled my face down for another kiss, and I felt every bit of his relief and excitement in his touch. "Does that make you mama bear?" Teddy purred.

I let out a sigh. "Is it too late to change my mind?"

Teddy scrunched up his face in thought for a minute before replying. "Hm. No. I already submitted our initial applications."

I barked out a laugh. "Why doesn't that surprise me?"

Teddy's face softened again. "Because even when we settle down with a family, I promise to never stop surprising you. We're going to have more amazing adventures together, Baby Doll. They're just going to be different ones for a while."

I leaned in for another kiss. "And you can take pictures of our kids."

Teddy's hands were warm against my cheeks. "And you can teach them all about yaks."

POKER FACE

1

———————

TILLY

I was good at poker. My whole life had included telling lies to people's faces and convincing them things were one way when they were really another. Like right now.

Tonight, I was everyone's favorite, zany, irreverent Aunt Tilly.

And that was as easy as breathing.

"I fold," Tristan huffed, tossing down his cards on the vineyard lobby's new heavy wooden game table.

Blue opened his mouth to say something, but I cut him off. "If you make a laundry joke, you're banned for life. Ante up, princess."

Blue tossed in his bet as Simone's eyes narrowed at me. "You're bluffing."

She was right, but I'd be damned if I was going to confirm that. "You're right. Aren't you going to have fun spending my money. Now pony up."

She rolled her eyes and tossed her hand into the pile. "I'm going to get some ice cream."

We all watched her lumber out of her chair like a half-beached whale.

"Need a forklift?" Granny asked. "There've gotta be fifty beefcakes here and none of them could haul your fat ass out of that chair. Might want to cut back on the ice cream, if you want to know what I think."

Simone's nostrils flared. "I do not want to know what you think." Then her eyes filled with tears.

Shit.

Joel narrowed his eyes at Granny while he practically burst a blood vessel helping his wife out of the chair. "Mind ya business, old lady." He turned to Simone. "You okay, sweetie? Want me to get you some of that frozen yogurt you like?"

The tears spilled over. "You think I'm fat too?"

"No! No, gorgeous. Of course I don't. Seeing you pregnant with my child is the most beautiful thing on earth. Look at you, you're..."

We all looked at her as he paused to find the right words. She was winter-pasty with a few pimples on her face that I'd place bets on indicating she was carrying a girl despite what the ultrasound said. Her hair was half-in, half-out of a messy bun. She wore a navy blue On Your Six hoodie with smudges of pizza on the front from dinner. The old sweatpants hung low, beneath the behemoth belly. Even the warm light of the giant fire roaring in the stone fireplace nearby did nothing for her.

"Rode hard and put away wet?" I suggested helpfully.

"One mimosa shy of a brunch?" Blue added.

"Two aces shy of a full house?" Granny asked, looking right at me.

Dammit. The woman was a notorious cheater. I pretended not to notice her, but I honestly didn't care. It wasn't like I needed the money. It was more about knowing whether or not I still had the ability to pull one over on the people who loved me most. It had become almost automatic, which was depressing as hell.

I needed another drink, so I grabbed Joel's while he was distracted. By this point, Simone was full-on wailing and Joel had begun to panic.

"No! That's not... they're lying. You're... beautiful. Just... look at you?"

I laughed at his questioning tone. Even he couldn't say she was beautiful with a straight face.

Blue stood up and clapped him on the shoulder. "Maybe you'd better get the full-fat shit. It's going to take some major ice cream therapy to repair this damage."

Joel's shoulders dropped in defeat, and he put his arm around Simone to lead her to the kitchen. "I just thought the frozen yogurt was your favorite flavor," he said desperately as they walked away.

Finally, we could get back to the game.

I looked over at Irene and snapped my fingers. "Make it happen. We're burning daylight here."

She frowned. "It's practically midnight."

I flapped my hand. "Money. Go."

"Jesus," she muttered. "Fine. Rob an old lady blind, why don't ya?" She tossed in the cash.

I pinned her with a glare. "Your wife owns a jet. I'm not crying about your two-dollar bet."

Everyone gasped and stared at Granny. She looked up from her hand and pursed her lips. "What?"

Tristan was the one who explained. "She stole money from my grandfather and bought a couple hundred shares of Apple stock in 1980."

Everyone continued to stare at my tiny friend. Why the hell weren't they playing the goddamned game?

Granny gave Tristan the evil eye. "Explain the word 'stole' in that sentence, and be sure to use legal terms like marriage and shared assets."

Tristan held up his hands and laughed. "Dude, I agree that you had a right to that money, but you literally pilfered it from his billfold every night for years."

"Just because he was a cheap-ass bastard didn't mean I was gonna go into my retirement wearing clothes from JCPenney. I had plans. And those plans didn't include watching him drink away my future. Do you have any idea how bad I had it? Do you? I was a sharecropper's child—"

Irene reached out a hand to pat Granny's arm in a soothing gesture as if she'd done it a million times.

She had.

I needed to nip this bullshit in the bud.

"You weren't a sharecropper's child. Your dad owned a department store in Des Moines."

Now it was my turn to be on the receiving end of the evil eye. She also used the two-finger *I'm watching you* gesture to really drive the message home.

"You will pay for your disloyalty," she warned in what I called her mafia voice. "I swear on my mother's grave—"

Irene patted her arm again, then reached for her cocktail. "Your mother's body was lost at sea, sweetheart. Simmer down."

"Mpfh."

Blue looked back and forth between Granny and Irene with glee before turning to Tristan. "Thank you for marrying me. This will never get old."

"I'm getting old right now," I warned. "I'm going to be dead before this game finishes."

After being uncharacteristically quiet up till now, Derek spoke up. "Tilly, you'll outlive us all."

I liked that one. Jude could keep him.

I cleared my throat and leaned in, meeting the eyes of the remaining players. "Put in your damned money so we can get this show on the road. I have sex plans in an hour."

"Oh god," Tristan said. "Please."

Blue turned to him with a shit-eating grin. "That's what she's going to be crying out in the senator's room later."

Jude stifled a snort.

The look on Tristan's face was priceless, and he wasn't able to meet my eyes for the rest of the night. Even when I took his fifty bucks.

Later, I heard him whining to Blue about how I'd deliberately grossed him out for competitive advantage in the poker game. It wasn't true though. I really did have sex plans. But they were with myself.

I didn't have the guts to tell my family that Senator Harold Cannon had dumped my sorry ass three weeks before.

And I'd deserved every horrible accusation he'd thrown at me when he'd done it.

HAROLD

"Dad, you have to rally."

I lifted my head up from the book I was reading and tried to focus on my daughter. "What? There's a rally? For what?"

Wendy rolled her eyes and continued scrambling a big pan of eggs for the kids. We were at the house in Vail, and she was preparing a hot breakfast before they took off for the slopes.

"No. You need to rally, as in... you need to stop moping around and come with us today. You've been cooped up in the house too long. It's unhealthy."

I shifted in the overstuffed chair by the window which had unofficially become mine since it had the best light for reading. "I'm not moping. I'm engrossed in a biography of Nelson Mandela. I'll loan it to you when I'm done."

"Dad," she said more softly. "You haven't turned a page in that book for at least an hour. It's okay to be upset about Tilly. We all are."

"Wait," I said, putting down the book and straightening up into a stretch. I may have been in great shape for my age, but my back wasn't getting any younger. And since I'd stormed out on Matilda, I felt like I'd aged a thousand years. "Why do you all miss her?"

Again with the eye roll.

"She's spicy and energetic. Smart and interesting. More than that, she makes you happy, and that makes the rest of us happy."

My chest tightened. "You're right about those things," I said in a rough voice. Dammit, I'd sworn I wasn't going to do this. Breaking off our relationship had been my idea. She'd done something unforgivable, and I wasn't sure I'd ever be able to even look her in the eye again.

Wendy wiped her hands on a kitchen towel and came over to sit on the ottoman in front of me. She put her hand on my arm. "Dad, won't you tell us what happened?"

Where did I even begin? And how could I tell my kids the story without losing them forever too?

I shook my head. "I can't. I'm sorry."

She studied me for a beat before nodding and standing up. She returned to the giant stove, but instead of going back to the eggs, she pulled out her phone. After a moment, she spoke.

"Aunt Glenn?" Wendy's eyes met mine. "I need you to come to the mountains and help fix Dad."

Shit. Calling my sister was like pulling out the big guns. I made a frantic slashing motion in front of my throat, but she ignored me.

By dinnertime, Glenn was there. And by breakfast the following day, she finally broke me.

I waited until all the kids and grandkids were off on another frozen adventure before spilling my guts.

"She had a baby." The words came out in a whisper as if they'd somehow lose power that way. We sat side by side on the deep leather sofa in the family room where we could see both the warm flames from the gas fire and the large expanse of ski runs out the giant picture window. Tiny figures in various brightly colored parkas moved across the white snow, and the steady pace of the nearest ski lift was a reminder that life was moving on for everyone else even though mine had ended several weeks ago. "And gave it up for adoption," I added.

"Tilly?" my sister asked in surprise. "Matilda Marian? When? Who?"

Before I could answer any of her questions, she glared at me. The cheesy red holiday sweater she wore brightened the pink on her plump cheeks. "And you broke up with her for that? What, were you expecting her to be some kind of virgin at this age? Harry, what the hell? No, wait. You're pissed because she was an unwed mother and you're Mr. Perfect. Or, Jesus, you're not still worried about your reputation in the public eye, are you?"

I held up a hand. "Stop." I sighed and ran a hand through my hair. "It was mine. It *is* mine. I mean... *she's* mine. Her name is Kelly Hobbs."

Glenn processed that for a second until her eyes widened in understanding. "Tilly had *your* baby. Gave *your* baby up for adoption. And you didn't know?"

I shook my head, still incredulous that she'd kept it from me for so many years. We'd lost our virginity to each other at seventeen. At eighteen, I'd gone off to Princeton to make my parents proud. I'd tried having a long-distance relationship with Tilly through letter-writing and the occasional long-distance phone call, but halfway through my first semester she'd told me she'd met someone else.

I'd been crushed.

And now here I was all over again. Only this time, it was my own damned fault.

Glenn seemed to remember the circumstances of Tilly's and my breakup. "Oh," she said. "*Ohhh.* Oh, poor thing. Oh, Harry." She leaned in to hug me. When she pulled back, there were tears in her eyes. "She was trying to protect you."

I nodded and tried swallowing around a painful lump in my throat. "But she made the decision for me about my own child, Glenn. My own daughter. How could she keep something that big from me?"

My sister swiped the tears from her cheeks. "She was scared. She didn't want to hold you back. How could we not have known?"

I thought back to growing up in Bakersfield, California, in the

1940s. The population was less than thirty thousand, and it felt like everyone knew everyone. She couldn't possibly have had the baby in Bakersfield. Not that I'd taken the time to ask her very many questions. I'd been too angry, too hurt. I'd basically told her to go to hell and then stormed out.

It had been three weeks since I'd seen her lovely face. Since I'd kissed her soft lips before falling asleep next to her. Since I'd heard her call someone a dumbass in her elegant voice.

I sighed. "I don't know, Glenn. I can't even wrap my head around it."

We sat in silence for a bit and sipped our coffee. After a while, Glenn turned to me. "You said her name is Kelly? Have you talked to her yet?"

I stared out at the light flurry that seemed to be trying to gather strength. "Yes. She has advanced lung disease though. They don't expect her to make it to spring."

"What? That's terrible! Are you going to go see her? Where is she?" She held her mug with both hands and stared into the fire. "That poor woman."

I stretched out my legs to rest my feet on the coffee table. Despite the thick socks I wore, the heat from the fire felt good against my soles. "I visited with her. As soon as Tilly gave me the information, I went straight there. She lives in Monterey."

After shifting onto one hip, I pulled out my phone to find the photos we'd taken together. I handed the phone to Glenn.

She smiled and scrolled through the set. "Oh my god, she has your eyes. Look at that. Did she freak out when she realized who you were?"

I leaned in so I could look at the photos over her shoulder. Even in her sickness, Kelly's eyes sparkled. We'd talked for an hour before her coughing became too bad to continue. After that, I'd sat and visited with her son, Miller, while Kelly had dozed in her recliner.

"That's her son," I said, pointing to a photo of her with Miller. "He's the one who found Tilly through her brother Wes."

Glenn nudged her shoulder against mine. "He's cute. Is he

married? We could set him up with that young associate from Matt's office."

"He's gay. And I'm pretty sure the Marians are treating him like their new annual project the way they did with Noah a couple of years ago. No one stays single long with that crew."

I thought of the Marians with affection. I missed their craziness almost as much as I missed my Tilly.

I sighed again. "Kelly does this thing with her eyebrow that's just like Tilly. And she has the same aversion to cucumber."

Glenn smiled at me affectionately. "Plenty of people dislike cucumber."

"Well, anyway. It was weird. Surreal. And I have no idea how to tell the kids."

She leaned her head onto my shoulder. "They're grown adults, Harry. They'll understand. This was out of your control."

I shifted her head off me so I could turn and face her. "But it wasn't! I got her pregnant and then abandoned her. You remember her family, her asshole of a father. God, Glenn. She was sent to a home all alone. What was it like to be sent away, not be able to even tell me, and to live her entire life without someone giving her the love she deserves?"

By the time I finished, I was barely able to choke out the words. My breathing sped up, and the tears came hot and fast.

"Fuck! I just left her. She was pregnant and alone and I just left her!" I stood up and began pacing, hiding my face in my hands as I silently thanked God for my decision to discuss this with my sister instead of my daughter. I didn't want my kids and grandkids to see me this way. I was a complete mess.

Until learning about Tilly's and my child, I hadn't cried since my wife, Faith's, death seven years before. After a few minutes of trying to catch my breath, I wiped the back of my sleeve across my face and turned to the fire. Glenn's voice was so full of understanding, I almost started crying again.

"If you're this upset at abandoning her, why are you doing it again?"

And there it was. The same conclusion I'd come to days before but hadn't had the guts to face. I was still so full of bitterness and resentment toward her for keeping this secret even though I understood deep in my gut that she'd tried to do the right thing for me. She'd tried to preserve my future. Because of her decision, I'd gone on to become a Princeton graduate, an officer in the army, a Harvard law grad, a successful attorney, a local politician, and eventually a US senator. I'd met and fallen in love with a wonderful, deserving woman who'd made an ideal, loving companion through so many challenging years. Because of Tilly's sacrifice, I'd fathered a United States president who had done amazing things for our country during his two terms in office.

But I couldn't help but think of the alternative life I would have had if she'd told me about the pregnancy. I'd like to think I would have dropped out of school to come home and take care of her, but what money would we have lived on? My parents wouldn't have supported us any more than hers would have. We would have been broke, but at least we would have had each other.

I thought about the early days of parenthood and had to admit that it would have been hard on Tilly. At least Faith and I had been able to afford childcare. Hell, I'd made enough money as an attorney for Faith to stay home with the kids. What a different life that was from the one I would have had with Tilly.

And thinking about that life didn't matter. It wasn't the way things had turned out.

"How can I make her happy now?" I asked without turning to look at my sister. "There's so much water under this bridge, I feel like we'd both drown if we tried to stitch together a relationship after this."

Glenn stood up to wrap her arms around me from behind for a hug. "Then build a boat. You spent your entire career finding solutions to problems, building better systems for brighter futures. Why not do that now, with her?"

I turned around and hugged her tightly. "You always were smarter than I was," I muttered into the top of her hair.

"Damned straight," she said proudly. "Now beat it. I'll give your regrets to the family."

I was in Napa several hours later.

3

TILLY

Getting drunk wasn't helping. I'd already tried it three nights in a row, and now I was just plain old and hungover. And bitchy.

"What the hell is this?" I asked, holding up my coffee mug at the breakfast table in the vineyard restaurant.

Simone narrowed her eyes at me and then pointedly looked away. Maybe I shouldn't have asked if swollen ankles were as painful as they looked.

"Coffee?" Blue suggested, glancing at a few of his brothers around the table before looking back at me. "Isn't it?"

"Pah," I grumbled, shoving it in his face. "Can't be. It's not working."

"Mimosa it is, then," he said brightly, standing up and reaching for my mug.

"No, wait." I sighed and stood, sending him what I hoped passed as an appreciative smile. "Maybe what I need is some fresh air first. You know, meander down to the lake for a good old primal scream or something."

As I passed Simone, I leaned in and kissed the top of her head. "I love you, baby girl. You make me proud," I murmured, soft enough to not be overheard by anyone else and misinterpreted as me losing my edge. I didn't have very many fucks, and she'd just taken my last one. We'd all be in trouble if someone else needed one.

As I exited the building, I heard mumbled tones of concern as they all gossiped about what was going on with me. Granny told them to mind their own damned business and pass her more bacon. I chuckled as I let the door close behind me.

The wool pantsuit I wore was barely enough to keep me warm in the brisk morning chill, so I pulled my pink pashmina around my shoulders like a blanket. It was a clear day. The painfully bright blue sky confirmed we were, indeed, still in California. I sent up a prayer of gratitude the fires that had been so prevalent a couple of months ago had been contained and eventually extinguished. Tristan worked hard to keep the vineyard safe from fire risk, but we all knew it was a big fear of theirs. Hopefully someone would continue to look out for them.

Not that it was any kind of Christian god. I'd stopped believing in that asshole decades ago. But just in case, I squeezed my eyes closed and sent another prayer up for my daughter Kelly's comfort and health as well as my grandson Miller's peace of mind. It was one of a thousand such prayers I'd made since learning of her disease. Hell, it was one of millions I'd said since the early morning hours of her birth.

Keep her safe. Give her a good life. Please forgive me. Please watch over Harry and give him a good life too. Let them feel loved. Make them happy. Choose them over me, always. Please forgive me...

I cleared my throat and pulled the scarf even tighter around my shoulders before setting off on the path to the lake. My plan had worked, which was the kicker of this whole thing.

While I'd had a perfectly nice life with plenty of friends and family, scads of money, and more adventures than I'd ever dreamed of, I'd never had the one thing I'd really ever wanted.

Harold Cannon.

I'd watched his career from afar. Every public story about him brought me an exhausting mix of elation and grief. He was having his big life, but he was spending it with someone else. Someone wonderful and perfect for him. Someone kind and maternal in ways I never would be. Faith Cannon was everything I wasn't. The quintessential politician's wife. Well educated and beautiful. Peaceful and scandal-free.

I let out a snort, scaring a little bird out of a nearby shrub.

I was none of those things. After giving the baby up and taking the measly hush money my parents had offered me, I'd busted my ass assembling airplane components in a hot, stuffy factory in Sacramento for two years until I'd been noticed on the factory floor by the visiting daughter of the airplane company's CEO.

Who'd been with me at the Anne C. Raptor Maternity Home.

Maureen had been my closest friend and confidante during those months, even though we'd been discouraged from becoming close to anyone since confidentiality had been such a large part of our stay there. We hadn't been allowed to even exchange last names or addresses to stay in touch with each other.

But there she'd been at the factory that day, dressed in the adorable minidress of the times and touring around with her father.

And there I'd been, dressed in dirty dungarees and an old button-down work shirt I'd bought at thrift.

Yet, Maureen had looked at me like I was the brightest star she'd seen in two years, three months, and five days.

She'd immediately taken me off the factory floor and straight to her father's office where I'd been treated like a queen. It had been the first time in years I hadn't felt like a disgrace.

I'd found out later that Maureen had returned home after her childbirth with such a bad case of the baby blues, she'd tried to kill herself twice. Her parents had panicked, offering her absolutely anything she wanted if she'd just stay alive and be their healthy, happy daughter again.

So when she'd claimed me as the sister she'd always wanted, that's what I'd become. I'd had no idea she was the daughter of an incredibly wealthy family. From that day on, my life had completely changed to the point she'd start singing Tony Bennett's "Rags to Riches" sometimes.

The Dempsey family had pulled strings somehow to arrange for me to attend Stanford University with Maureen. In some ways, I'd felt like Mo's pet, but in others, I'd felt like I'd won a jackpot. If I couldn't have Harry and our baby, at least I could have a future beyond making airplane parts. I'd committed to my business degree like my entire life was at stake. Because it had been.

I'd worked hard to make the Dempseys proud, and I'd snuck in as many secretive babysitting hours as I could without Maureen finding out I was working for a paycheck. Thankfully, I'd had two professors with small children at home who'd needed help from time to time, and I'd been able to earn enough pocket money to keep from relying on Mo's parents for more than my school fees.

After graduation, Mo had thrown herself into the junior newspaper writer job she'd gotten in San Francisco while Mr. Dempsey had begged me to come work for him at the headquarters of his company in the city. We'd pretended to be hippies and, at the same time, reveled in our new status as career women. We hadn't needed men or babies or any of those cultural shackles. We'd had friends and jobs and a tiny basement apartment we'd insisted on paying for with our own, hard-earned dollars. We'd made friends with everyone: the gay men who'd owned the house we lived in and threw sex parties every third Saturday of the month, the oddball musicians who'd started up a band next door and played all hours of the day and night, and the little old ladies around the corner who'd sold homemade bread on their front stoop on Sunday mornings and homegrown pot on Friday afternoons.

Several years later, my teenaged nephew Thomas had tracked me down to tell me my father had died and my brother Walter wasn't taking it well. As soon as I'd finished dealing with one death, two more took its place.

Edith and Edward Dempsey died in a house fire while visiting friends in San Diego. It had been so tragic and awful, I'd thought Mo would never recover. It had taken us weeks before learning they'd split their enormous fortune between the two of us, leaving me a loving letter of gratitude I still couldn't read fifty years later without having a breakdown.

I finally reached my favorite lakeside bench and took a seat. As I shifted the scarf around my shoulders, I noticed the sun glinting off the gold charm bracelet I'd worn all these years. I ran a finger over the bracelet. Mo had given it to me the day of my graduation from Stanford. It'd had only one charm on it at the time. The gold lion to represent strength. Then Edith had given me the little house charm to tell me I always had a home with them. Over the years, I'd added to it and been gifted meaningful charms for it from friends and family until it jangled heavily with a life well lived, but that original pair of charms still had my heart. Strength and home.

There was no telling how long I sat there, remembering. I was so lost in thought, I didn't hear footsteps approach.

"Do you still have mine?"

Harry's voice washed over me with such a heady combination of relief and disbelief that I squeezed my eyes shut to fight off sudden tears. My fingers automatically found the interlocking hearts charm made of my favorite deep blue sapphires.

"Please tell me you're really here," I whispered without turning around. "Because if I've finally aged into hallucinations, I'm walking into this lake and never coming out."

His soft chuckle was so familiar, it made my heart ache with longing.

His hands landed on my shoulders, and his lips brushed my ear. "When I gave that to you, I told you our hearts were linked together —always have been, always would be."

I turned my head away, steeling myself for the disappointment and loneliness I'd tried to protect myself against for my entire life.

"Apparently not," I said in as steady a voice as I could manage.

He pulled away, confirming my deepest fear: that he would let me ruin us.

But then he walked around the front of the bench and lowered himself to his knees in the grass in front of me, placing his hands on the top of my thighs and sliding them up to circle my waist.

I looked down at him in shock. "You're an ad for knee and hip replacement surgery."

He barked out a laugh. "One hundred percent original parts as you well know." His face turned serious. "Matilda, I can't say I'm sorry for reacting the way I did. I was hurt. So very hurt." He shook his head. "I felt like everything we'd been building since finding each other again had been built on a lie."

I nodded, my throat thick with panic and expectation of the worst. My hands clenched together in a death grip on my lap. He must have noticed because he pulled his arms back and took my hands in his.

"I understand why you did it," he said in a rough voice. "All of it, including not telling me. It's a heavy burden to carry, and you've been carrying it alone for so long."

My tears betrayed me, but I ignored the insolent little fuckers.

Harry sighed before meeting my eyes again. "I would say I forgive you, but it's not really something that needs forgiveness. You did the best you could at the time. You were also still practically a child when you had to make those hard decisions. I'm more upset you didn't tell me when we came back together in Las Vegas."

"I told you—" I began.

"I know. You came to Vegas specifically to tell me, but then we got carried away. I get it. I was there, remember?" He cracked a smile. "It kind of explains all the drinking we ended up doing that night though."

"I was scared out of my mind and more nervous than I'd ever been," I admitted before pausing. "But I don't really regret it. Hell, I prayed that little Vegas wedding chapel marriage was real."

His eyes softened into the natural affectionate look he always had when he looked at me. It was better than any golden charm on my wrist. "Me too."

That surprised me. "Really?"

He narrowed his eyes at me. "Woman, I've wanted you since the dawn of time." A sparkle of knowing appeared in his eyes. "And I mean to have you."

4

HAROLD

She was so vulnerable in that moment, my heart wanted to break all over again. Instead, I reached in my pocket and pulled out the charm I'd picked out.

I held out my open palm to her with the little charm in the middle.

Tilly glanced down at it in confusion. "Handcuffs? What are you trying to tell me, pervert?"

Life with Matilda Marian was never boring.

"No. Look more closely. Do you need your glasses?"

She shot me a look. "Take it back."

I pulled back in surprise. "The charm?"

"The ageist comment. The charm stays with me." She reached for it and held it close enough to study. I saw the exact moment she realized what it was. "Are these—?"

"Wedding rings," I said gently, reaching for the box in my other pocket. I opened it, revealing the perfect antique wedding set it had taken me forever to find.

Tilly glanced up and did a comical double take at the sight of the rings. Realization was finally hitting her.

I chuckled, feeling bubbles of nerves and happiness in my gut.

"Matilda, I don't want to waste another moment without you. Please marry me and let me make up for all of the time we've lost. It may not be much, but it will be full of love and adventure and laughter and peace. I want you with me. Forever."

She sniffed and looked away, a quintessential Tilly move I'd finally learned how to translate. The feigned nonchalance covered internal terror.

I squeezed her hand. "I'm not going away. You don't have to say yes, and I'm still not going away. I'm never leaving you again. That's a promise, and it's one I want to make in front of all of our friends and family, darling. Please say yes."

She looked up to the sky, blinking back tears.

"I'm too old to get married," she croaked.

"You're not."

"I'm stubborn and set in my ways," she countered.

I bit back a laugh. "Tell me something I don't know."

She glanced at me out of the corner of her eye. "I fart."

"Oh, shit. Well, in that case..." I closed the ring box and moved like I was going to put it back in my pocket, but she reached out and grabbed my wrist.

"Not so fast. You fart too."

Now it was my time to sniff disdainfully. "Certainly not."

Tilly met my eyes. Hers were filled with a heartbreaking mix of uncertainty and hope. "I'm not leaving my home in San Francisco."

"Good, because Carl finally gave me permission to join him when he goes to that farmer's market around the corner from the house every Saturday morning," I said, referring to her butler. "And you already know I'm in love with the reading chair in the bay window."

"And you can't have a cat," she added.

"Damn. Crush a man's dreams," I said drily. She knew I didn't have an affinity for cats. They hated me. "Anything else?"

"I'm not wearing white at the wedding."

"Neither am I," I said solemnly. Tilly's hand shook in mine. She was terrified.

"Because I've had sex with lots of men. *Lots.*"

I glared at her. "Simmer down, Lolita. No need to remind me."

She looked around at the lake surrounded by the vineyard that had become the center of her family. "Well, I guess you picked a romantic enough spot for it."

I pressed my lips together to keep from grinning like a loon. "We could even have the ceremony here if you'd like," I suggested as calmly as I could. "Or someplace in the city like the Four Seasons..."

"Don't be an idiot. Of course we're doing it here."

Her eyes met mine.

"I love you more than I'll ever be able to say," I told her. "I don't want to spend any more time apart. Marry me, Tilly."

"Yes."

We leaned in at the same time and pressed our lips together. Whatever fancy perfume she wore enveloped me in its familiar soft hold. I ran my fingers into the back of her hair and held her lips to mine for a long time before pulling back just enough to whisper over and over that I loved her and I would take care of her forever.

"You're not alone anymore," I promised her softly. "You've carried this burden for so long, darling. It's time to set it down."

She hid her face in the crook of my neck and let go.

WHEN WE FINALLY PULLED OURSELVES together, we sat on that bench and talked for a long time. I couldn't help glance down from time to time at the glint of diamonds on her slender finger. I noticed her staring at it too, as if maybe it wasn't real. It would take time. She'd gone decades assuming she'd never wear a wedding ring.

We walked back to the lodge hand in hand with the hopes of ordering room service breakfast, but as soon as we entered the building, all the Marians looked up from where they congregated in front of the big fireplace.

Thomas stood and came over to check on Tilly. "Everything okay?" he asked, looking back and forth between the two of us with concern.

Tilly made a shooing motion with her left hand, deliberately waving the bright diamonds in a swath of sunlight so they lit up the surrounding area like a disco ball. "Oh, I guess," she said in her well-used dismissive tone.

Squeals and shrieks split the air as we were accosted from all sides with questions and exclamations and congratulations. I watched Tilly puff up under all of the attention and shine like the collection of rocks on her hand. She was beautiful and nuanced, with cut sharp edges and hidden facets. She was one of the treasures of my life, and I finally allowed myself to exhale.

It wasn't long before someone had pulled out mimosas to celebrate. Sam arranged for breakfast to be brought over from the restaurant, and Jude brought out his guitar to sing cheesy wedding-themed songs. At one point, Blue pulled me aside to have "the talk."

"Don't hurt her," he warned.

"I won't."

"She deserves all the love in the world," he added.

"Agreed."

"Shit," Blue muttered, glancing at his husband next to him. "What else goes in this speech?"

Tristan humored him with the crinkled forehead of deep thought. "Use protection?"

Blue elbowed him in the ribs. "Save that one for our kids."

"If only you'd been around in 1957 for that speech. We could have used it," I said absently, glancing around to make sure Tilly was still having a good time. I spied her giving a bouncy horsey ride to Wolfe on her lap while he held on to the front of her scarf like it was reins. He was her favorite little one, and everyone knew it.

Blue and Tristan stared at me while the pieces fell into place.

"No," Blue breathed. "No way."

I glanced back at them in surprise. "I thought you knew about it. Didn't you all meet Miller?"

"She told us it was from an anonymous one-night stand," Blue said in disbelief.

I winced. "Oh, right. Yeah, well, she told me that too until I saw a picture of Kelly and Miller. And I should have known better. She wasn't the one-night-stand type. We'd been in love since the age of sixteen. How I thought she could possibly turn to someone else that soon after I left for college was beyond me." I took a breath. "But then again, sometimes ignorance is bliss and we see what we want to see."

Blue's concerned expression was as sweet as it was expected. "How are you doing? Okay? It must have been quite a shock."

Tristan cut in. "That explains the breakup. I'm glad you two seem to have gotten past it."

I nodded and glanced at Tilly again. Her face was tilted back in laughter as Granny was clearly holding court nearby with her jokes. There was a strong tug in my chest at the sight. She was beautiful and full of life. I could only pray we had several good years together to enjoy each other.

Tilly turned her head and met my eyes with a soft smile.

"I'm more than okay," I told Blue. "I'm the luckiest man alive."

Granny noticed where Tilly was looking. "Christ on a cracker, stop giving him moony eyes. We have a bachelorette party to plan. And it's gonna be killer."

Everyone both groaned and tittered with excitement. I couldn't even begin to imagine what a bachelorette party done Marian style would look like.

But I knew Tilly would secretly adore every minute of it. It would make her happy.

And Matilda Marian deserved all the happiness in the world.

WAKING UP IN VEGAS

1

TILLY

(So, wait... didn't Aunt Tilly and Senator Cannon meet for the first time in Vegas during a crazy night described in *Delivering Dante*? Something about a mobster and a Beyoncé dance number? They ended up fake married? Yeah, it sounded insane, right? Here's the real version:)

WHAT REALLY HAPPENED:

How many times had I known where Harold Cannon was going to be making some kind of public appearance? The answer was a million. Yet, I'd never felt compelled to track him down before now. Why would I? I'd already made the decision decades ago that we weren't meant to be together.

But loneliness is a powerful motivator and a seductive mistress. Late one night after a few too many cocktails during poker night with the ladies, I let my fingers do the walking. Straight onto my keyboard and into a browser.

Senator Cannon would be making an appearance at a charity function at the Bellagio Hotel in Las Vegas in two days' time. And wouldn't you know it? I was due for a visit to Vegas. I'd won sixteen dollars (and an overly large used bra) that very night at poker, and it was burning a hole in my pocket.

When I sobered up the next morning, I knew it was a bad idea.

But did that stop me? No. Watching all of my grandnephews fall in love the past couple of years had only made me want Harry more, so when we arrived in Vegas, I had tunnel vision for the man. But he wasn't as easy to find as I'd expected, and I may have had one or five drinks while looking in the bars for him.

And then I may have had one or two more drinks while lying in my bed feeling sorry for myself about it.

So my judgment was a smidge off when I made the executive decision to take one more look around.

In my pajamas.

That was when I was apprehended by Secret Service agents. Apparently, I looked like a drunken crazy woman when I was, in fact, simply a...

Whatever. Anyway, I politely declined their efforts to remand me back to my room. Harold opened the door of his suite and began asking the agents why they were manhandling an old lady. When I turned to him to beat him about the head for his rude comment, he seemed to recognize me.

Only lord knows how because I was an old lady.

"Matilda?" he whispered.

It all hit me at once and my knees buckled. The Secret Service agents caught me and managed to help me back to my suite, which turned out to be only three doors down the same hallway.

Harry followed the agents in and made sure I was all right, shooing them out of the room and fetching me water from the suite's refrigerator.

I drank enough to sink a ship before feeling clearheaded enough to talk to him. But... I couldn't tell him about the pregnancy and giving our baby up. I simply couldn't. It was too horrible, too raw. And we were practically strangers. So many years had passed and... and I wanted him again. Telling him about the baby would have meant risking losing any chance of having him in my life again.

And he was the same sweet, caring man he'd been all those years ago. The affection in his eyes for me was just as heart-crushing as it had been when we were teenagers.

So I told him I'd missed him. I told him I was sorry. In my moments of weakness and desperation, I'd begged for another chance at a future together. He'd felt the same way. It was all so... perfect.

We kissed and touched and talked and talked and talked. We laughed until the wee hours of the morning and then had a bright idea.

We were in Vegas for god's sake. Why not get married?

Christ, what idiots we were. The Secret Service agents were easy to lose, and then it was just the two of us and our vows. And rings. And a night spent holding each other under the covers of the hotel bed.

But in the morning, reality hit me like a gut punch.

How could I even think for one moment that I could have a life with someone I'd lied to?

I bolted like a lead ball shot from a cannon and returned home to San Francisco as if none of it had ever happened.

Until the Secret Service showed up on my doorstep to inquire about my wedding to Senator Cannon. The wedding they desperately didn't want the media to find out about.

I needed to see Harry. Apologize. Explain. Maybe, finally, get up the guts to tell him about the baby.

Cue Dante, AJ, and the wild ride to Vegas in the party bus.

As soon as I found Harry in Vegas again, the paparazzi had found the both of us, discovered we'd married, and brought all of it into the light until we had to face the consequences together. I apologized for bolting. Then I apologized for marrying him.

The look on his face... Christ, it would haunt me forever. He was devastated.

"You don't want to be with me?" he asked.

Except that I did. And I couldn't lie to him.

"I... I do, but—"

His face relaxed with relief. "Thank god. Come here." And then he pulled me into his arms, and I knew the truth.

He was mine. And I was finally back home in his arms after all these years. Maybe we could just... start off slowly, date, and see where it went.

But holding a secret from someone you love is sometimes like boiling a toad. The heat turns up by degrees until before you know it, the pot boils over and all you're left with is a dead frog.

Two years after dating in blissful denial of the increasing heat, the pot finally boiled over when Miller Hobbs showed up sporting Harold Cannon's bright blue eyes.

After sixty-four years, it was time to tell Harold the truth.

ELEVATOR MUSIC

1

SAM

Of all the people I was *not* expecting to run into in an elevator at four in the morning, it was my husband.

"Griff, what the fuck?" I asked when the doors opened, revealing my curly-haired fox. He was half-asleep and wearing nothing but low-hanging flannel pajama pants (mine) and bunny rabbit slippers (definitely not mine).

"I woke up and you weren't there," he mumbled. "Lost you."

I stepped into the mirrored box and pressed the button for the seventh floor before pulling him into my arms and inhaling his sleepy scent.

"Never," I promised into the skin of his warm neck.

Griff nuzzled into me, leaning his head on my shoulder. "Couldn't sleep?"

The elevator shimmied a little which I'd learned was normal for this old hotel. Every time the Marians went skiing in Tahoe, they booked an entire floor of this resort. It wasn't fancy, but it was homey and family-owned which made it feel familiar and beloved. What we gave up in luxury we more than made up for in having rooms all together and the ability to keep our doors unlocked and gather in common areas like we owned the place. I adored the Marian traditions, and staying at the Regal Summit was one of them.

But that didn't mean I liked the fucking elevator from hell.

"Should have taken the stairs," I muttered into Griff's bare shoulder before nipping it. His dick brushed against my leg and began tenting his pants.

"Are you coming back from a Grindr hookup?" he asked. I could hear the smile in his voice, so I pulled back to give him a look.

"And what if I was?"

"I'd be impressed with your sex drive, quite frankly," Griff said with a low chuckle. "Thought I wore you out last night. Apparently not."

I squeezed his plump ass cheek through the well-worn flannel. "You're wearing my pj's."

"Still wearing your jizz too." The wink was quintessential Griffin Marian. I cupped his prickly cheeks and leaned in to kiss his lips.

The elevator shuddered again and something made a metallic screeching sound that froze both of us in place. We locked eyes just as our journey upward came to a sudden stop.

"Shit," Griff said with a sigh. "Guess it was only a matter of time. Where's your phone? We need to call Lenny at the front desk."

I stared at him. "I don't have my phone."

He blinked back at me. "Why not? Who goes on a Grindr hookup without their phone?"

I pinched his ass. "You know I didn't go on a fucking Grindr hookup, jackass. And if you must know, I went out to the car to get my wedding ring. I woke up in a panic, realizing I didn't have it on."

Griff tilted his head before I saw the lightbulb go off. "Shit. I took it off you and put it in the glove box when I made that joke about refusing to stay married to someone who doesn't recognize the chilling emotional impact of Lady Gaga singing 'Shallow' in that movie about my one true love."

I nodded. "Yes. I believe your exact words were, 'Bradley Coop—'" My words ended suddenly as Griff's hand closed around my throat.

"You don't deserve to say his name out loud," he warned. "Samantha Coxwell, you're treading on thin ice."

I grabbed his dick, which was still plenty plump. Arguing with me always made Griff horny. "It's Sam Marian, asshole. Until you serve me with actual divorce papers, I earned every bit of that last name and continue to do so every minute I spend putting up with your dramatics."

Griff's breathing picked up, and his eyes widened as I stroked his dick through the flannel. "The elevator is stuck."

I moved my hand from the front of his pajama pants to the waistband and down inside to grasp his sac as I leaned in to suck on one of his nipple barbells. "Yes it is."

He sucked in a breath. "And you're... *oh god*, and you're trying to make up for the fact your Grindr hookup never showed."

I laughed around the tight nub in my mouth. "No Grindr hookup, Foxy. Never anyone but you."

I moved my mouth lower, dropping wet kisses along his side until I lowered to my knees and pulled his pants down to his ankles.

"Oh fuck. Fuck, Sam. Please..."

Griff's hands threaded into my hair, and his head thunked against the mirrored wall.

I had him exactly where I wanted him.

2

———————

GRIFF

The image of Sam on his knees surrounded me in a never-ending repeat from all the elevator mirrors. For a split second I thought I was still asleep and dreaming, but then my head hit the mirror with a bang. I didn't even care. It was real. Sam was sucking me off in the Regal Summit elevator.

His tongue swirled around me, setting nerves on fucking fire and making my balls draw up. "Fuck, Sam. Suck it. *Go.* Just like that," I begged, nodding like an idiot as if he might be confused about any consent issues between us after all this time.

The slurping sounds were debauched and lewd which only made me lurch closer to shooting my load down his throat. Sam's hands were all over me. One was reaching up to fiddle with a nipple piercing while the other caressed and fondled my sac with a familiarity that only made me want him more. This man knew how to play me.

"Look at me," I grunted, pulling his head back a little with the grip I had in his hair. His eyes were glazed over, and his cheeks were flushed. He was stunning like that. Every ounce of love he had for me was clear in his expression. It made me crazy sometimes, thinking about how incredibly lucky I was.

Sam's sucking slowed down until I wanted to scream in frustration. A teasing smile took over his face, and the tip of his tongue toyed lazily around my shaft.

"Fuck you," I grumbled. "Suck it. Don't stop. Wanna come."

Both of Sam's hands reached up to pull hard at my nipples while his mouth moved over to nibble a line from my dick to my hip. I groaned and thunked my head back into the mirror again, releasing my hands from his hair and grabbing my own hair in frustration. "Why?"

"I love making you crazy," he said. His eyes were full of mischief. "Love seeing you get so frustrated, you can't stand still." Sam's hands moved around to my back and down to cup my ass and squeeze, pulling my cheeks apart. It only made me more desperate.

"Please, Sunshine," I whimpered. "The doors might open and—"

He took me all the way down his throat in one sudden move, yanking me into his face with the grip on my ass and not letting go.

"Ohh *fuck*," I cried, scrambling for a hold on something, anything. The feel of his hot, wet mouth surrounding my hard dick was too much, too fucking perfect. As soon as his tongue pulled me deeper into his throat and his fingertip brushed against the sensitive skin of my hole, I lost it. "Fuck, fuck." I gasped and shot into his throat, grabbing at his short hair and holding on for dear life.

When my head cleared from the orgasm, I noticed Sam chatting happily to someone on his phone.

The phone he claimed he didn't have.

I lifted an eyebrow at him. "WTF, Samson?"

He flapped a hand at me to hush and then followed it with a frown at my limp, wet dick hanging triumphantly spent between my legs. "Cover yourself," he hissed after placing a hand over the phone. "Lenny doesn't want to see that."

I yanked the pajama pants back up and shot him a look. "That's not what he told me last night in the hot tub," I muttered, crossing my arms in front of my bare chest and accidentally brushing my still-too-sensitive nipples. I winced and sucked in a breath.

Sam snorted, so I stepped forward and brushed my hand across the front of his pants for a little payback tease. After a muffled groan, Sam's eyes filled with mischief.

Suddenly, his smile blinded me as he turned back to the phone. "You know what, Lenny? Maybe give us a few minutes before you work your magic on the door. Griff here needs a few minutes to finish what he just started."

He clicked off the call and dropped the phone along with his pants onto the carpeted floor of the elevator before putting his hands on my shoulders.

"On your knees, Fox."

This time when the elevator shuddered and something made a screeching sound, it was for a very different reason.

LET IT SNOW

1

GIDEON

After escaping a restrictive, suffocating religious cult, some gay men go crazy and want to sleep with everyone. Some are too terrified to even kiss a man, their ingrown shame pulling at them still.

I was the former. Shortly after Ammon brought me to San Francisco, I went a little wild. Grindr was my candy store, and I gorged myself. There were no regrets either. It was... it was kind of like part of my healing process, as ridiculous as that may sound.

Fucking around with men made me finally feel free in a way I never had before. It was a giant middle finger to my father and his horrible beliefs.

But after two years of frantically trick-or-treating my way through the Bay Area, I finally slowed down to a crawl with an upset stomach from having indulged too much. It was fun, but it wasn't fulfilling. It was entertaining, but not intimate. I craved connection on a deeper level. It was like... suddenly I'd had my fun and was ready for more.

So I did something silly. I tried hiring a professional matchmaker. It was a disaster. Every time I fell for someone, they dumped me. Instead of a string of hookups, I had a string of failed relationships.

It turned out, I was terrible at both. No longer fulfilled by casual connections, and unable to form deeper ones.

As soon as the giant Marian clan found out I was looking for a boyfriend, they made it ten times worse. They took me on as a project and set me up with every gay monogamous-minded man in the Bay Area. It was further proof I was broken. Or unattractive. Or somehow not marriage material.

One night my brother Ammon sat me down and asked me what was wrong. After keeping these feelings to myself for so long, it actually felt good to let them out. I told him everything. How at first I'd wanted to spread my wings but now I wanted to be grounded. He thought for a few minutes before snapping his fingers.

"I know what you need. You need to hit the restart button and figure out what you want your life to be about with or without a partner. Take a vacation that's just about you. Something you've always wanted to do or somewhere you've always wanted to visit."

I nodded and played along, even though I was very sure of what I wanted my life to be about with or without a partner. I'd already begun the process of taking community college classes in preparation for applying to veterinary school. Simone had promised that her clinic would help pay for it as long as I planned to keep working there. It was an incredibly generous gift, and I wasn't going to mess it up. I'd also made several good friends since moving to San Francisco, and we got together to play board games and eat takeout every Friday night. Sometimes we met at a local bar to shoot darts or play pool too. I loved my life. I was confident in every single part of it.

Except this.

I wanted love. I wanted someone to binge-watch Netflix with and fight over pizza toppings with. I wanted someone to bring to Marian cookouts. More than that, I wanted someone to build my own family with, whether or not that included children.

But Ammon was right—I needed a break. I'd been working hard and taking classes for a while now, and time away from the city would help me recharge.

Jude's best friend, Ollie, had a small family cabin up near Tahoe that she'd mentioned several times. When I asked her if I could rent it for a week during my winter break, she rolled her eyes at me. "No. But you can borrow it. Don't be an idiot."

I grinned at her. Since I lived in the apartment over Jude and Derek's garage and Ollie was their nanny, we'd spent many hours bonding while playing with the kids in the front yard or swimming in the pool on the terrace.

She shifted neatly into Dad mode, quickly assessing whether the tires on my old truck were good enough for the snow and making sure I had emergency essentials in the back toolbox just in case. I called Simone to arrange time off work and practically vibrated with excitement for my first adult solo vacation. I was so excited, I decided to leave the Friday after work instead of waiting for Saturday morning sunshine.

When I finally arrived to the turnoff in the dark evening hours after taking way too many wrong turns, I marveled at how remote the cabin was. There had been several gravel driveways spaced along the rural road, but I hadn't seen an actual building in miles. I bumped carefully along the snowy tracks until the thick woods opened into a clearing and my headlights washed against the building. The cabin was like something out of a storybook. Small and square with a deep front porch and a red-painted door. Smoke curled out of the stone chimney, and another pickup truck sat still in the gravel parking area.

I pulled in next to it wondering if Ollie had arranged a caretaker to get things ready for me.

"Hello?" I said, pushing the unlocked door open. "Is someone here?"

An interior door opened and out walked a lumberjack from central casting. A million feet tall, sun burnished, and jacked with muscles. He had on worn jeans, a red plaid flannel shirt, and a thick dark beard that begged to be stroked. I couldn't wait to tease Ollie about her caretaker. Talk about a walking stereotype.

"Oh hi," I blurted stupidly. "I'm Gideon, Ollie's friend."

The man's forehead crinkled in confusion, and I thought for a crazy moment that maybe he didn't speak English. Maybe he was

Russian or Finnish or something. But then I realized that was crazy. I'd been watching too much porn.

"Who are you?" I asked when he didn't speak up.

"Hunter." His voice was deliciously deep and went straight to my lower belly.

"Is that your name or... maybe your occupation?"

Because, honestly, if his name was Hunter, I was calling Ollie right now and might laugh hard enough to piss myself.

He narrowed his eyes at me. "Name."

Great, now he was going to kill me.

"Oh, uh... okay. Well, nice to meet you, Hunter. I can take it from here. Thank you for..." I looked at the roaring fire in the fireplace and the groceries stacked on the counter. "The fire and everything. You didn't need to stock the fridge. I brought plenty of food with me."

The corner of his mouth turned up. "Did you now?"

I stayed by the front door since this was officially weird. The man didn't seem in any hurry to leave, and it was late. Then I noticed his boots were kicked off by the door and he only stood there in wool socks. Was that to keep from tracking in snow, or...?

"Did Ollie send you here?" Hunter asked. "For me?"

I was taken aback. "What do you mean for *you*? I'm here for *me*."

Okay, maybe that didn't make much sense. But, c'mon. He was the kind of attractive that made your tongue swell up with possibilities. Could he blame me for my stupid, confusing word-making?

"Hang on and let me call my sister. Clearly, there's been a misunderstanding." He reached into a pocket to pull out his phone. It took me a second to realize what he meant.

Just as I heard Ollie's loud voice pick up on the other end, I realized what he was saying.

Ollie was his sister. This was his family's cabin—*his* cabin. Which meant I'd barged in on his vacation, not the other way around.

"Shit," I muttered, turning to look back out the still-open front door to the dark, freezing night beyond.

There was no way I'd find my way back out of here before daybreak.

HUNTER

Well, he was adorable. I had to give Ollie credit for that, at least. The man was a thousand percent my type. Petite and blond. He looked like a good cross between someone I could boss around in bed but who wouldn't let me boss him around outside of it too much.

I glanced at him as I waited for my sister to answer the phone.

"Don't get mad," she said in a rush. "I get a hundred bucks if you two hit it off."

I almost choked on my tongue. "He paid you to sleep with me?"

Gideon sucked in a surprised breath and backed up toward the door. I held out a placating hand and shook my head to calm him.

"Of course not," Ollie snapped. "Don't be ridiculous."

"I'm the ridiculous one?" I asked.

"Well... I mean... yes, of course you are." She cleared her throat. "But you know how Jude's family is. Always placing bets on things and making up these silly challenges."

"Explain."

Just then, Chops came trotting in from doing whatever it was dogs did in the snowy woods. After a moment of being startled, Gideon grinned and squatted down to pet him, immediately starting the universal language of Labrador retriever baby talk. I stared at the two of them, and something in my chest did a little squeeze.

"... so that's what I did," Ollie finished.

I shook my head to clear it. "Do what now? I missed that."

"Forget it, asshole," she said. "He's Ammon's brother, so don't fuck it up. Charm him. Ask him out. Come out of your goddamned shell every once in a while and make new friends."

"He wasn't expecting me to be here," I said in a lower voice, hoping Gideon didn't feel like I was being rude by talking about him in third person while he was in the same room. I glanced at him again and realized belatedly that he looked very much like Ammon, who I'd met several times through Ollie.

"Yeah, well, I had to sort of, kind of, trick him. But believe me, you guys would be great together. You both want the same things."

Over Christmas a few weeks before, I'd had too much eggnog and had regrettably admitted to my sister that I wanted a serious boyfriend. I didn't mean for her to try and *send* me one.

"Um... so..." I was distracted by Chops knocking Gideon on his ass. Just as I was set to lurch forward and save him, I heard the most amazing giggle. "Um... gotta go."

I hung up to the sound of her sputtering.

"That's Chops," I told him, wandering over to make sure he was okay with the overly intimate canine attention. "Sorry for the aggressive love attack. Chocolate Labs are known for being overly generous with their affection."

Gideon's sparkling blue eyes looked up at me. His cheeks were flushed pink from the cold or the excitement. "I could use an aggressive love attack, quite frankly. It's no problem. Also, I'm, um... I'm an animal lover. I work in a vet's office. And, uh..." He took a breath and nodded as if making a decision. "I'm studying to become a veterinarian myself."

I could tell it cost him something to admit his hopes out loud to a stranger, so I reached out a hand to help pull him up. "That's exciting. I'll bet you'll make a wonderful vet someday."

He stood and shrugged, reaching back down to give Chops a few more head pats. "Lots of work to get there, but I've never minded hard work." He looked up at me. "What do you do? Besides looking like..." He gestured at me, waving his hand around in a circle. "That."

I laughed and tilted my head at him in mock confusion. "What do you mean?"

"Something tells me Ollie's brother doesn't chop wood for a living."

After stepping behind him to pull the door closed, I gestured for him to move closer to the fire to get warm. Chops followed him like a roadie.

"I'm a software developer, actually," I said, expecting the look of surprise he gave me. "I made a budget travel app for students when I was in college, and it took off. Since then, I—"

Gideon cut me off. "Wait! You're *Cubby*!"

I groaned. "If she doesn't stop telling people that's my name, I'm going to kill her."

He grinned at me, and damn if both cheeks didn't sport twin dimples. He was flipping adorable.

"She talks about you all the time. Ollie adores you." He sat down on the stone hearth with his back to the flames so he could face me.

"The feeling is mutual," I admitted grudgingly. "Even though she drives me crazy."

He flapped his hand. "She drives everyone crazy. It's what we love about her."

Chops nudged his nose under Gideon's other hand, forcing him to pay attention to the needy dog in the room. Gideon complied automatically. I watched his long, slender fingers scratch into my lucky dog's thick coat and wondered what those hands would feel like on me.

Gideon must have felt the change in the room, because suddenly he seemed a little nervous. "Um, so... I think... um, do you want me to leave? I'm not sure I can find my way out by morning, so maybe I could... sleep on the couch or...?"

"Oh. No. Not necessary. It's definitely too late for you to go, and actually, there's a second bedroom. I mean... you could stay here. It's your vacation, after all. I should be the one to go."

"No! Please don't go. I would feel awful if I put you out of your own cabin. Were you just taking a break from the city?"

I took a seat beside him, making sure to leave plenty of room so he didn't feel any threat from me. "I've been working around the clock for weeks to meet a new product launch deadline. The app finally launched week before last, so I came out here for a week to relax and enjoy some peace and quiet."

Gideon nodded, looking at me out of the corner of his eye. "This seems like the perfect place for it. That's what I was hoping for too."

The room went quiet for several moments. The only sounds were Chop's light snores and the pops of the logs in the fireplace.

I swallowed and turned to face him, suddenly nervous myself. "Would you like to stay? I mean, stay for the week? We could... we could have some peace and quiet together?"

Gideon turned to me, putting our lips kissably close. "Yeah," he breathed. "If... if you're sure?"

I looked from his lips to his eyes where the heat was undeniable, but for the first time in my entire life, my gut told me to wait instead of making a move. My cock downvoted the idea, but my brain overrode it.

I smiled instead and hopped up, willing my dick to stand down. "I'm really sure. I'd enjoy the company, and you'll give me an excuse to cook some good meals. I'll go grab your stuff so you can stay warm by the fire."

Gideon looked after me for a minute, seemingly dazed, before he snapped out of it and scurried after me. "I'll help."

When we got outside, the moonlight was fuzzy with heavy snowfall. The flakes disappeared in Gideon's light blond hair as we made a couple of trips inside with his bags and groceries. When we finally finished unloading and locked up the cabin door, I offered to make him some decaf or hot chocolate.

We spent the next several hours chatting over hot drinks and organizing our things in the kitchen area. Eventually, we moved to the sofa and continued talking in front of the fire. Gideon was funny and charming. He told me several funny stories from his job at the vet clinic and then told me a little bit about the way he'd grown up in Utah and how he'd come to live over Jude's garage.

I recounted the story of how I'd gotten the childhood nickname Cubby and how my sister had subsequently gotten the tiny scar over her eyebrow. After explaining that I'd bummed around Europe between high school and college, I told him the story of developing the app and how that had led to my founding the software company.

We exchanged stories about the hookup scene and failed dating attempts until both of us were laughing so hard, Chops woke up and grunted at us.

I didn't even realize how much time had passed until I noticed Gideon yawn for the second time and checked my phone.

"Christ, it's after three in the morning," I said in shock. Our eyes met, and I couldn't help grinning at him like a fool. "Guess we get along okay, huh?"

He grinned right back, dimples and all. "Guess so."

We stared at each other for a beat before he blinked and coughed. "Well, uh. Can you show me that room you mentioned?"

I nodded. "Shit, sorry. Of course. Yeah. Right over here next to mine. The bathroom is that door in between the two."

When we reached his door which was only three steps away, he looked up at me. "Thank you for tonight. Maybe it sounds silly, but I already feel more relaxed than I have for a while. Even if you change your mind and want me to go, it will have been a lovely vacation."

My hands itched to reach for him, but I balled them into fists.

"Gideon, I won't change my mind. I promise."

Just before I turned to head to my own room, he surprised me, lurching forward and wrapping his arms around my neck and dropping a quick peck on my cheek. By the time I realized what was happening and unballed my fists to hug him in return, he was gone.

The bedroom door clicked shut behind him, and Chops whined softly under his breath.

"I know, buddy. Me too," I murmured, reaching a hand up to touch my cheek where I still felt the warm press of his lips. "Me too."

3

GIDEON

I'd slept fitfully in the perfectly cozy bed. The flannel sheets and thick duvet made the perfect winter nest, but I hadn't stopped thinking about the lumberjack in the other room.

Hunter had surprised me with his easy manner and charming personality. He'd turned out not to be the gruff mountain man I'd expected. A software developer. Who would have guessed? Certainly not me. I shook my head and tried not to hear my mother's voice in my head lecturing me about judging not lest I be judged myself.

He was six and a half feet of muscular, masculine perfection. I'd been grateful for the baggy sweater that had covered my perma-rection all night because every time I looked over at him, all the blood in my body had whooshed south for winter. After I'd heard him brush his teeth and flush the toilet, I'd waited ten more minutes and taken my turn in the bathroom, hopping in a hot shower despite the late hour.

There'd been no other choice but to stroke off to relieve some of the pressure. I'd imagined myself climbing his naked body like a tree and then sliding back down just enough to impale myself on its thickest branch. Therefore, it had taken me approximately 2.5

seconds to blast cum all over the shower wall with a muffled grunt against my forearm.

I'd come to the woods and encountered a bear—the good kind of bear.

I sighed and threw the covers off before pulling one of the curtains open to see how light it was outside. As soon as I realized half the window was covered in snow because that much had fallen, I gasped and jumped back, nearly knocking myself out on the footboard of the bed.

"Ow, fuck," I whimpered, grabbing the back of my head to see if I was going to be found dead in my underwear by a sexy woodsman. That would have been just my luck.

The wooden door to my room slammed open and the bear invaded, followed by his trusty sidekick. "What's wrong?" Hunter's voice was scratchy from sleep.

I stared at him. He stood there in all of his hairy-chested glory. A wash-worn pair of flannel pajama bottoms hung dangerously low, revealing a thin strip of dark pubic hair above the frayed drawstring.

I gulped.

"Um," I began, trying for the life of me to think of actual words.

Hunter moved closer and reached for the hand on my head to see what I was feeling for. "Did you hit your head?" he murmured. "What happened? Bad dreams?"

Without thinking, I shook my head, accidentally causing his fingers to press hard against the bump. I winced.

"Shit, sorry," he said. "Crap. I'm making it worse." He stepped back and held his hands up like he was a victim in a bank robbery, and I couldn't help but laugh. Chops nosed the side of my leg with his dark snout.

"You're fine. My fault. Did you see how much it snowed last night? I looked out the window and was surprised. Then I, uh, flailed. Hence, the head injury. From flailing." I took a breath. "I'm a flailer."

I changed my mind about wishing I had actual words.

Hunter grinned and it was enough to make me want to dive into all that dark beard hair and do laps in it.

I reached out and combed my fingers through it. "This is just... perfection," I admitted dreamily without fully realizing what I was doing and saying. Or maybe I did know what I was doing and it was just so far out of my normal levels of bravery, it was hard to believe I was actually the one doing it.

The hair was thick and bristly but also softer than it looked. As I continued to stroke it, our eyes met and locked. I wasn't sure exactly when or how my beard stroking turned into beard pulling, but within moments, our lips were brushing against each other like a pathetic, overly slow attempt at lighting a match.

Suddenly, it caught fire.

The kiss turned feral and hard with tongue and teeth. I lunged at him and pushed him down on my bed so I could climb on top of him and keep kissing him forever and forever.

His hands immediately went to my ass and cupped it hard, pulling me closer until our erections pressed together. His thick cock was proportional to his giant self which meant mine wavered a little in its commitment to full-on sexy times.

But that lasted as long as it took Hunter to suck my bottom lip into his mouth and slide a hand down into the back of my boxer briefs.

"Oh god," I moaned, feeling my skin get tight everywhere he touched.

"Been wanting you all night," he said in a low voice between nips to my sensitive neck. "All fucking night. Couldn't sleep knowing you were so close."

I gasped when he latched onto my collarbone. "I jacked off in the shower thinking of you," I admitted. "Wanted to sneak in your room and climb all over you."

"Jesus. You should have." Hunter pulled back and met my eyes. "You sure you want this? I don't want you to feel—"

I put a finger over his lips. "I'm sure. Super sure. The most sure of all the sures."

He grinned, causing the hairs below to tickle my fingers. I scratched them into his beard again.

"You like that, huh?" he teased.

"It'll do," I said with a gentle tug and a grin.

Hunter continued to kiss me, moving quickly down my chest to my stomach. The sight of his huge tanned hands on my pale hips turned me on even more. It reminded me of the romance novels my mom used to hide in the laundry room where the savage takes the pure maiden.

Not that I was pure. Just pasty white like the English lasses on the covers of the books.

And maybe I'd had a Highlander fetish back then, so... that worked out fine. Kilt, plaid shirt, whatever. Same diff. They were both big, burly outdoor men who could throw me across a field (or bed) like a javelin.

I threaded my fingers into his dark hair, feeling how much thicker it was than mine. Lucky bastard. The man could be a model. I wondered if he was a model.

As soon as his mouth landed on my dick, all thoughts of lairds and models disappeared into the ether like Highland mist.

"Hngh!" I sucked in a breath and arched. His tongue was going to town on just the right spot, and I tried not to imagine how he'd perfected such an amazing move. My hands tightened in his hair. "Fuck, Hunter, f-fuck."

His large hand slid up my front until he was gently holding my neck. There was no way to know, but it was one of the hottest moves ever. That was all it took for me to scream my release.

Oh god.

He sucked and swallowed until I was shivering with sensitivity. When he released me from his mouth, he grinned up at me. A white speck of cum rested in his beard, and the sight of it would have made me come all over again if I'd been able.

I gestured to the spot on my own face. "You have a little something right here," I informed him with a cheeky grin.

Without looking away from me, he stuck out his tongue and licked it clean.

Holy hell.

"Yeah," I breathed. "Got it."

Hunter crawled up my body and kissed me with that salty mouth, rubbing his thick whiskers all over my face in the process. His hard cock pressed against my hip as he ground against me and reached a hand behind my head to hold me still for more kisses.

I wrapped my legs around him and held him tightly, wondering how in the world I'd wound up in someone's fantasy. It was like a real-life porn scene. Boy turns up at snowy cabin expecting to be alone, but instead, he finds sexy lumberjack waiting to debauch him in all the best ways. If I found a scene like that, I'd wear out the monitor on my laptop.

"You're sexy as hell, Gideon," Hunter said in a blowjob-roughened voice. He pulled back from the kiss and met my eyes. The heat in his expression nearly lit my face on fire, and my dick tried desperately to spring to life again. "I meant what I said last night about having a great time. I'm so glad you're here."

I reached up to brush a hank of dark hair off his forehead. "I thought you wanted alone time," I teased.

"I still do," he admitted, surprising me. Before my stomach could fully revolt, he continued.

"But now I want alone time with you. As much as I can get."

This time, my dick really did spring back to life, which surprised me since I felt like all the blood had suddenly rushed to my heart instead.

4

HUNTER

Gideon's dimpled grin was all the confirmation I needed that we were on the same page. Finally, I could relax knowing I hadn't ruined his week of solitude in the mountains.

I leaned down to kiss the smooth skin of his shoulder, and I relished in his shuddered reaction.

Gideon's fingers gripped my hair while his ankles crossed behind me with stark possession. I wanted to feast on his body all day and was beginning to realize there was nothing stopping me. I moved my lips down his biceps, but his hands in my hair gently tugged me to face him instead. His eyes were molten.

"Fuck me."

My heart slammed into my rib cage. "Really?"

Ugh. I sounded like an idiot.

His grin was sweet. "Yes, *really*. I mean, if you're into that..."

I clasped his face and touched my forehead to his. "Babe, I'm into that. I'm very, very into that."

He chuckled and arched his hips up, pressing the evidence of his readiness into my belly. I leaned down and kissed him again because I just couldn't help myself. His lips were full and soft, and I couldn't keep my mouth off them.

After making out for several more minutes, I rolled him over and trailed a line of kisses down the smooth, creamy skin of his back to the full globes of his ass. God, he tasted good. Like shower soap and warm, sleepy man. I knelt between his legs and kneaded his ass cheeks, separating them just enough to get a peek at his hole.

Gideon groaned and thrust his sexy butt up toward me, bringing that pink-brown hole even closer. He'd been so attracted to my beard, I wondered how he'd feel if I nuzzled it between his cheeks and tasted him. I leaned in and took a gentle bite of one cheek before kissing it. The sounds coming out of his throat urged me on.

"Please," he begged in a breathy voice. I wasn't sure what he was asking for. Did he want the rimming, or was he ready to be fucked? Honestly, it didn't matter. I wanted it all.

I nudged his cheeks apart with my chin, making sure to dig my thick, bristly beard into his sensitive skin along the way. Gideon cried out.

"Fuck, yes. Hunter, please. *Fuck*. More."

I teased his hole with the tip of my tongue, smiling as soon as his whimper escaped.

"You like that?" I teased.

"Uh-huh. More."

So I went to town, eating his ass like it was my favorite meal and I was starving. I licked, sucked, spit, and speared that hole until it was soft and wet and ready for my dick. By the time I remembered to get up and find a condom, Gideon was slurring his words and speaking nonsense.

"Stay here, babe," I said with a light smack to his ass.

"*Gnfh.*"

I smiled to myself as I wiped my face on the back of my hand and strode quickly to my duffle bag on the floor, returning with a tube of lube and strip of condoms thankfully left in a side pocket from a weekend away with my ex-boyfriend months ago.

After climbing back on the bed behind Gideon, I smoothed a palm over his ass and up his back. "You sure?"

"Fuck me," he mumbled into the pillow.

I laughed. "Are you still coherent enough for this?"

"Gnfh."

I leaned down and kissed his spine while tearing into the condom and rolling it on. The lube was cold, so I tried my best to warm it before slathering it over his hole. When Gideon's channel squeezed my fingers, I groaned.

"Fuck, that's going to feel amazing around my dick." I squeezed more lube onto myself and moved closer, positioning the tip of my cock at his entrance and watching every move like it was the best porn film I'd ever seen.

It may as well have been, since I knew I'd use it for jacking off material for the rest of my life. Gideon was the hottest man I'd ever been with. Willing and open, he was fun and sexy and responsive. I hadn't even been inside him yet, and I already wanted more.

His voice was a desperate whisper. "Please, Hunter. Want to feel you. Need you."

I ran a hand up his back again and around the front of his throat, clasping gently as I began to press in. He automatically tightened around me, making us both moan in pleasure.

"Let me in, baby," I urged softly, leaning in farther so I could kiss the side of his face. "Want to be inside you. Make you feel good." I continued murmuring into his ear until his body relaxed and let me nudge my way in with shallow thrusts. His body was so hot and tight, I had to squeeze my eyes closed and remember not to fuck into him like some kind of wild animal. Instead, I took it as slowly and steadily as I possibly could. When I finally felt my balls brush his, I let out a breath. "Oh fuck. Gid, Jesus, you feel incredible."

He reached back for one of my hands and pulled it under his chest to hold tight while I moved inside him. It was an intimate gesture and suddenly made my chest constrict. I had an odd sense of *this is not enough. I will not get enough of him. More, I want more.*

But I was here with him now, inside his body and wrapped around his back. My lips were on his ear, and my beard brushed the tender skin of his neck. I needed to enjoy what I had in this moment because in this moment, I had everything.

"You're so fucking beautiful," I murmured. "Feel so good, Gideon. So warm and tight. Want to make you come. Want to make you feel good." I pulled out and thrust back in again, flattening the angle of his hips and driving down in hopes of finding his spot.

"Oh, fuck," he whimpered. "*Yes.*"

I reached under him to stroke his dick since I felt close to coming. With a few quick, squeezing strokes, his body tightened and he cried out his release before warm cum coated my hand and his body squeezed me even tighter.

My teeth clamped down on his earlobe as I pushed in one last time and grunted, wishing stupidly I was fucking him raw instead of releasing into a condom.

When my body finally finished shuddering, I lay panting and sweating on top of Gideon's back. He felt amazing underneath me, and I imagined he'd feel even better curled up next to me while we slept.

"Let me get you cleaned up," I said, forcing myself to pull out and climb off him. "Stay there."

I quickly disposed of the condom and ran a washcloth under the water until it turned hot. When I returned, Gideon was on his back with his hands behind his head and his naked body laid out in glorious pale splendor.

"God, look at you," I said, moving up to wash off his stomach, dick, and between his legs. He gave me a sweet smile the entire time and seemed to luxuriate in being cared for.

I tossed the cloth away and climbed up beside him, pulling the flannel duvet over us and yanking him closer to me so I could spoon the shit out of him.

After a minute of snuggling back into me, he chuckled.

"What?" I asked, nuzzling into the side of his warm neck.

"I came to the woods and met a bear."

I nipped his skin between my teeth until he yelped and laughed harder. His laughter made me feel stupidly heroic.

After the laughter died down, I nudged him onto his back so I could make eye contact.

"I came to the woods and met someone I'm desperate to get to know better."

Gideon's eyes searched mine as if desperate to seek out the truth.

"I mean it, Gideon," I said, leaning down for a soft kiss. "I really like you, and I'm..."

He reached up to pull me down for another kiss before holding me close and brushing my nose with his.

"I really like you too," he whispered.

It was all we needed for now. A chance. Possibilities for the future.

And we had the entire week trapped in a snowy cabin together to figure it out.

BONUS SCENES

Remember when Silvio, Simone's wedding stylist, was arguing with Anton about teeth? That love connection, along with links to all the rest of Lucy's bonus and deleted scenes, can be found here:

bit.ly/GetBonusScenes

LETTER FROM LUCY

Dear Reader,

Thank you so much for reading *Made Marian Mixtape*, book nine in the Made Marian series. I wanted to revisit the Marian world and see how some of our favorites are doing as well as give some much-needed HEAs to some new faces.

If you're unfamiliar with the Made Marian series, check out the first book *Borrowing Blue* which is where the crazy tale of this even crazier family begins.

If you want a bit more of these fun shorts, sign up for my newsletter for a link to the bonus scene featuring **Silvio the wedding stylist** and a character inspired by my Facebook reader group suggestions! Sign up for the newsletter here:

bit.ly/LucyNewsletter

Be sure to follow me on Amazon to be notified of new releases, and look for me on Facebook for sneak peeks of upcoming stories.

Feel free to sign up for my newsletter, stop by www.LucyLennox.com or visit me on social media to stay in touch. We have a super fun reader group on Facebook that can be found here:

www.facebook.com/groups/lucyslair

To see fun inspiration photos for all of my stories, including *Made Marian Mixtape*, visit my Pinterest boards.

Happy reading!

Lucy

ABOUT LUCY LENNOX

Lucy Lennox is the creator of the bestselling Made Marian series, the Forever Wilde series, and co-creator of the Twist of Fate Series with Sloane Kennedy and the After Oscar series with Molly Maddox. Born and raised in the southeast, she is finally putting good use to that English Lit degree.

Lucy enjoys naps, pizza, and procrastinating. She is married to someone who is better at math than romance but who makes her laugh every single day and is the best dancer in the history of ever.

She stays up way too late each night reading M/M romance because that stuff is impossible to put down.

For more information and to stay updated about future releases, please sign up for Lucy's author newsletter on her website.

Connect with Lucy on social media:
www.LucyLennox.com
Lucy@LucyLennox.com

WANT MORE?

Join Lucy's Lair
Get Lucy's New Release Alerts
Like Lucy on Facebook
Follow Lucy on BookBub
Follow Lucy on Amazon
Follow Lucy on Instagram
Follow Lucy on Pinterest

Other books by Lucy:
Made Marian Series
Forever Wilde Series
Aster Valley Series
Twist of Fate Series with Sloane Kennedy
After Oscar Series with Molly Maddox
Licking Thicket Series with May Archer
Virgin Flyer
Say You'll Be Nine
Hostile Takeover

Visit Lucy's website at www.LucyLennox.com for a comprehensive list of titles, audio samples, freebies, suggested reading order, and more!

SUGGESTED READING ORDER

Determining reading order within a series isn't an exact science because some of these stories actually fall during the timeline of another story, or they can be placed in multiple spots because there's nothing in the story to indicate when, exactly, they happen.

There's also a difference between true chronological order and suggested reading order. For instance, "Waking Up In Vegas" takes place chronologically before "Poker Face," but it doesn't make sense if you actually read it first.

Because I started writing *Borrowing Blue* in 2016, I've always used it as the year the book takes place. The problem with that is that the passage of time in all the other stories brings us well past current day. To give you some benchmarks for the time in this world, *Borrowing Blue* starts in August of 2016, *Facing West* starts in September of 2019, and *King Me* starts in December 2021.

YEAR ONE 2016
    1) *Borrowing Blue* - Made Marian Book 1
    2) "Brad" from *Made Marian Shorts* - Made Marian Book 8
    3) *Taming Teddy* - Made Marian Book 2

4) *Jumping Jude - Made Marian Book 3*

YEAR TWO 2017

5) "Beck" from *Made Marian Shorts - Made Marian Book 8*

6) "Keller" from *Made Marian Shorts - Made Marian Book 8*

7) *Grounding Griffin - Made Marian Book 4*

8) "Love Shack" from *Made Marian Mixtape - Made Marian Book 9*

YEAR THREE 2018

9) *Moving Maverick - Made Marian Book 5*

YEAR FOUR 2019

10) *Delivering Dante - Made Marian Book 6*

11) *Facing West - Forever Wilde Book 1*

12) *A Very Marian Christmas - Made Marian Book 7*

YEAR FIVE 2020

13) *Felix and the Prince - Forever Wilde Book 2*

14) *Made Mine - Made Marian/Protectors (by Sloane Kennedy) Crossover*

15) *Wilde Fire - Forever Wilde Book 3*

16) "Wedding March" from *Made Marian Mixtape - Made Marian Book 9*

17) "Josh" from *Made Marian Shorts - Made Marian Book 8*

18) *Hudson's Luck - Forever Wilde Book 4*

19) *Flirt - Forever Wilde Short*

20) "Club Mix" from *Made Marian Mixtape - Made Marian Book 9*

YEAR SIX 2021

21) "Jude's Lullabye" from *Made Marian Mixtape - Made Marian Book 8*

22) *Hay - A Made Marian Short Standalone*

23) "Beach Music" from *Made Marian Mixtape - Made Marian Book 9*

24) "Birthday Song" from *Made Marian Mixtape - Made Marian Book 9*

25) "Hard Rock" from *Made Marian Mixtape - Made Marian Book 9*

26) *His Saint - Forever Wilde Book 5*

27) *Wilde Love - Forever Wilde Book 6*

28) *King Me - Forever Wilde Book 7*

YEAR SEVEN 2022

29) "Yakkity-Yak" from *Made Marian Mixtape - Made Marian Book 9*

30) "Tibetan Chants" from *Made Marian Mixtape - Made Marian Book 9*

31) "Poker Face" from *Made Marian Mixtape - Made Marian Book 9*

32) "Waking Up in Vegas" from *Made Marian Mixtape - Made Marian Book 9*

33) "Elevator Music" from *Made Marian Mixtape - Made Marian Book 9*

YEAR EIGHT 2023

34) "Let it Snow" from *Made Marian Mixtape - Made Marian Book 9*